P9-ARD-258

STAR WARS™
POE DAMERON
FREE FALL

Written by

ALEX SEGURA

LOS ANGELES • NEW YORK

For information address Disney • Lucasfilm Press,
1200 Grand Central Avenue, Glendale, California 91201.

Printed in the United States of America

First Edition, August 2020

1 3 5 7 9 10 8 6 4 2

FAC-021131-20178

ISBN 978-1-368-05166-8

Library of Congress Control Number on file

Reinforced binding

Design by Leigh Zieske

Visit the official *Star Wars* website at: www.starwars.com.

For my family, always.

With huge thanks to the entire *Star Wars* family, especially Michael Siglain and my amazing editor, Jen Heddle; my agent, Josh Getzler; my good pal Bryan Young; and the many people who helped make this book a reality. I'm in your debt forever.

PART I: GROUNDED

CHAPTER 1

"Waaahoooo!"

The scream erupted from Poe Dameron's lips as the A-wing veered upward with a long, painful shudder, the old ship barely dodging the trio of Civilian Defense Force vessels careening toward it.

"Not good, Poe, not good," he muttered to himself as he checked his ship's display. Four ships total. All armed. All probably angry. All in better shape than his mother's old bird. Not great odds.

"What else is new?" he asked, a smirk forming on his face.

This was supposed to be fun, he told himself—just a quick jaunt to blow off some steam. But he'd gone farther—higher—than he'd intended, and by the time he noticed, he was in someone else's crosshairs.

A crackle of sound signaled a message from his pursuers. Poe ignored it. The man's gruff voice cut through anyway.

"Poe, this is your last warning, son," said Griffus Pinter, one of his father's closest friends and a mainstay of the Yavin system's Defense Force. Poe could visualize the older man's expression, the scraggly gray beard quivering slightly with each rage-fueled word. "I don't want to have to shoot you down."

Poe hesitated for a second, his hand hovering over the ship's controls. Even at sixteen, Poe was mature enough to know a turning point when he reached one. He could give up, surrender—and maybe skate by. Get another slap on the wrist. He'd face his father's wrath again, sure, but even those cold shoulders were finite. It would be another incident in a long line of rebellious incidents for Poe since, well, since eight years prior.

Since the darkest day of his young life.

The A-wing turned downward, as if heading toward the moon, the sudden move putting a strain on the old ship—as evidenced by sounds Poe had never heard it make. Griffus sounded equally aghast. The expletives jumping through the comm were almost musical—a collection of words Poe could've hardly imagined in his most creative moments.

It had started as a lark. A lark fueled by anger, if Poe was being honest with himself. The argument with his father had hit the same notes as many earlier ones. The slightest suggestion of Poe becoming a pilot—of leaving Yavin 4 and following in the footsteps of his mother, Shara Bey—was met with an immediate rejection. A spark of emotion Poe only saw in his father in moments like that one. The rest of the time, Kes Dameron was sullen, isolated, and distant. This time, harsh words were exchanged. Poe was reminded of his inexperience and youth. Tears. Yelling. Shut doors and a growing canyon between the two Dameron men.

Slipping into the A-wing had been a quick escape. A place to hide and think. The smell and feel of his mother's ship served as a last sanctuary of her memory. A final place where Poe could commune with a woman who should still be around. Should still be at home when he'd storm in late, waiting with a hot cup of Tarine tea in her work-worn hands, a comforting smile on her face.

"Do we need to talk, Poe?" she'd ask in those imaginary moments, in those scenes that still felt all too real. Hurt all too much.

Before he knew it, though, he had been flipping switches and taking the ship out. In that moment, Poe's mind had drifted back—to the same cockpit, the same A-wing, eight years before—to his mother, her hand over his, guiding him. They used to take it out from time to time. She wanted Poe to learn, she'd tell Poe's father, Kes, when he protested. Who better to teach him? The ship had flipped into a barrel roll, their heads bumping into each other as she laughed—that clear, strong laugh.

Confident and warm—like everything his mother did. Poe knew, even then, Shara Bey was a hero. Maybe he didn't know she was a hero to the Rebellion, to the forces that would come together to create the New Republic, but she was a hero to him. A light he was always drawn to, a source he drew strength from.

And she was gone.

His mind was yanked back to the present, Griffus's static-fueled screaming replaced by a clearer voice. Menacing. Unfamiliar.

The sentence was brief, but its message was very, very clear.

"Open fire."

The first two were warning shots. Poe, despite his inexperience when it came to space battles, knew enough. "You tell them what you're doing, every step," his mother had said. "If you want the conflict to deescalate, you have to give them every chance to do it for you."

But that third shot came in strong, knocking the A-wing for a loop. The ship began to spin, and the controls flickered.

"Uh, think we got him—"

"No, dammit, no," another voice said. "Change course, immediately. We have to retrieve—"

Then the feed went dead. An eerie silence permeated the A-wing's tight quarters, replacing the clatter. Poe's skin grew cold as he tried to regain some kind of equilibrium.

The Defense Force officer's voice had been nervous. Someone had overreached. Fired with the wrong intent. The hiss of air—a compartment breached, something gone awry—filled Poe's ears as his head slammed back, a loud thunk following a split second after. The spins couldn't be counted anymore—it was a constant rotation as the ship veered downward, the control display a muted gray.

Poe tried to keep his eyes open. Tried to focus on what he could do. The ship wasn't dead—couldn't be. It was his mother's ship. Had been her faithful partner for more rebel missions than Poe could imagine. Shara Bey of the Rebellion. Hero of the Battle of Endor. Friend to Princess Leia Organa and Jedi Knight Luke Skywalker.

Mother.

As the pressure increased, as the ship fell apart around him, Poe's mind drifted to the farm. His eyes rolled back in their sockets, his mind overwhelmed with the vertigo as the shaky A-wing gained speed, propelling into the Yavin moon's atmosphere. He was going home.

"I'm sorry, Dad," Poe said, his voice a whisper. "Mom."

CHAPTER 2

Kes Dameron opened the front door to the small house he'd built himself. He looked out into the Yavin 4 night, over the hectares of farmland he tended daily, and strained his eyes in an effort to catch a glimpse of something. Anything. A flicker of light, a shadowy figure. A sign that he hadn't made another terrible mistake.

He'd heard the A-wing power up. He hadn't been surprised. Over the past eight years, since Shara died, they'd been having some version of this discussion. Poe would mention a desire to fly—to be like her, to join the New Republic, to see the stars. It would vary. Sometimes it would be an offhand remark about Shara; other times it would be an innocent question about the past.

"What was Han Solo like, Dad?"

"Can we talk about the Battle of Endor?"

"Did Mom really help take down a Death Star?"

Each time, in different ways, Kes would rebuff his son. Even after eight years, he couldn't bring himself to talk about Shara. The mementos were gone, boxed up and stored in a shed Kes didn't dare get close to, on the edge of the swatch of farmland they'd once owned together. He couldn't bring himself to think of how her smile would shine through the darkest moments, or how her hand on his face could calm him. It hurt too much. It hurt to see her, or parts of her, living and breathing and moving in Poe. The thirst for adventure. The charm. He was Shara's boy. But Shara was gone. As much as he loved his son, it still stung to see his wife in their boy's eyes.

Kes knew he'd been distant. With the boy, with his old friends—with people who knew them as Kes and Shara. The messages ignored. The long stretches spent on the farm, not venturing out to town or to the docks. The tropical climate of Yavin 4 had appealed to them when they'd first bought this land, began to tend it together as a family. Now what appealed to Kes was how small the settlement was. He knew pretty much everyone on the moon, and knew their routines—which made it easier to avoid them and go about his business on his own terms.

Most friends took the hint. Stopped checking in after a few years. If he saw them in town, their exchanges would be brief—pleasant enough, but no staying power. Kes preferred to be alone, anyway. He had enough trouble with that. But L'ulo L'ampar remained.

The Duros pilot was a friend. His green skin and winning smile were able to brighten any situation. He was loyal and honest, and if Kes was being true to himself—he didn't want to lose the man from his and Poe's life. L'ulo had flown in the Rebellion with Shara before and after the Battle of Endor. Had pushed her to retire after the Empire's epic loss. Had even settled on Yavin 4 as part of the system's Civilian Defense Force, though he traveled frequently. He was more like family than a friend, and when he came to visit, Kes tried his best to make those moments special. Poe, even as a recalcitrant teenager, adored L'ulo, seeing him as a lost talisman, a link to the mother he was forgetting as more time passed. To Kes, L'ulo was a link to a life he no longer lived or was interested in. A life of danger and intrigue—and, in his clearer moments, one of love. But that love had paid a price eight years back, and he would never be able to risk himself in that way again. So when L'ulo appeared, they would celebrate. He'd allow his friend to regale Poe with stories of battles with the Empire, to share flying tips and tricks, and to wash them in Shara's glow for a bit longer.

Poe.

Where had Kes gone wrong? Had he been so selfish with his own grief—putting shields up, erasing the past—that he didn't stop to consider his son might need to connect with someone? To laugh, grieve, or think about his mother? Kes knew this to be true, but he couldn't control what he'd done. Poe was the best of them, but Kes only saw the best of Shara when he looked at his boy—now closer to a man than a child. He saw the fearlessness. He saw Poe's wide-eyed wonder and hunger for adventure. He saw, starkly, the limits of Yavin 4. He knew that in time Poe would leave—with or without Kes's blessing.

Kes stepped out into his front yard, kicking some of the clumpy dirt off the long walkway that led to the small house. He could've made it easier on Poe, supported him and just hoped that the values he and Shara instilled in him—caution, confidence in his abilities, faith in the Force—would carry him through. But Kes wasn't that type. Not anymore. He'd lost too much already. He couldn't lose Poe, too. If that meant building a wall between him and Shara's memory, if it meant preventing Poe from hopping into space until Kes thought he was ready, so be it.

Kes shook his head slightly. He heard the noise, but it took him a moment to track it.

Footsteps.

He turned toward the far end of his property. Two figures. Armed. He reached for the sidearm that hadn't been there in years, not since his days as a Pathfinder for the Rebellion. He thought about darting back into the house, grabbing the blaster rifle he kept locked behind his bed—but he knew he didn't have time. Kes wasn't as fast as he used to be, ex-Pathfinder or not, and the men approaching him were coming at a good clip. He'd be dead before he got to the door.

The man on the left waved. Kes waited. A sign of peace, he thought, but he'd been tricked by better men before. His hand felt like it was cramping as his fingers again stretched to find the gun that was not by his side. *What do these men want?*

When they came within range, the man on the left spoke in a loud, low voice.

"Kes Dameron?"

Their features were finally visible in the light that reflected off Yavin. Defense Force personnel. The man on the left, Robhar Dern, was known to Kes. He'd worked with Shara. The man on the right wasn't. Whoever they were, it was bad news. The Defense Force didn't come to your house to say hello, or to check in and ask about the kids.

Poe.

Kes felt like his skin had gone ice-cold.

"Kes, sorry to bother you," Dern said, taking Kes's hand in a firm shake. He looked winded. They'd tried to get there quickly. That didn't bode well.

"No bother," Kes said. "What brings you boys here so late?"

"Guz Austin, sir," the new one said, his eyes hungry and young. "We wanted to thank—"

"Why are you here?" Kes asked, more forcefully this time, his eyes on Dern.

Dern squirmed a bit, his face contorting into an awkward grimace.

"Kes, we're gonna need you to come down to the station with us, all right?" Dern said.

Kes didn't need to hear anything else. His heart sank, a widening void filling him from the inside out.

CHAPTER 3

"Wake up," someone said. "Get up, kid. Time to move."

Every other word, Poe felt a jolt of pain at his side. Gentle but focused. He knew what it was. The butt of a blaster rifle. It wasn't the first time Poe had been there. But it was the first time he'd felt this bad—or this surprised to have made it. *I'm alive,* he thought. He should be jumping up and down with glee. But all he felt was pain and—shame? He didn't want to open his eyes. He didn't want to be alive. Not feeling like this—his entire body aching, his mouth dry, his face cold and wet with his own tears. Those frantic moments in space, in his mother's ship, were gone. His memory of his landing was fuzzy—visions of the A-wing crashing in water, Defense Force specialists circling the incoming vessel to soften its fall—but he remembered enough to know his mother's ship had been destroyed. That wasn't what he should be thinking about, though, he mused. He should be happy he'd made it out with two legs, two arms, and his head intact. But the ache he felt wasn't physical—it was for his mother's ship, the ship he'd learned to fly in with her. Like Shara Bey, it was gone. Like Shara Bey, it had been shot down from the sky, right outside his very window.

He felt a hand on his collar, pulling him into a standing position. Instinct, not desire, made him stand up. His legs were wobbly, his back stung, and a quick hand over his face told him he had more bruises and scrapes than he'd like. A scan of the inside of his mouth revealed that he still had his teeth. There was always a bright side, Poe thought.

He opened his eyes. The Civilian Defense Force officer seemed a bit relieved at any sign that Poe was alive.

"You with us, Dameron?" the woman said, her expression stern but caring. "The medics said you were okay—just some scrapes and bumps, but nothing too serious, which, honestly, is all kinds of miraculous."

"The . . . the ship," Poe said, his voice sounding like metal scraping on rock. "Where is it . . . ? Who are you?"

"Elia Litte, Civilian Defense. Let me get this straight—are you seriously asking about the ship?" the officer said. "Kid, are you out of your mind? That ship isn't anything anymore. Just spare parts and slag. Who cares about the ship? You're alive."

"I care, okay?" Poe said, his voice rising and his eyes welling up. "I want it back. It's mine."

Litte took a step back, shaking her head.

"You gotta get your priorities in order, buddy," she said, pushing a button on the cell door. It hissed open and she stepped out. "Lucky for you, you've got a free pass out of here. Must be nice to have connections."

Litte motioned for him to follow. Poe hesitated at first, but even his innate defiance told him this opportunity wouldn't crop up again. She led him down a long hallway lined with other cells that housed the night's collection of drunks, petty criminals, and unseemly characters. Yavin 4 wasn't a large colony. It was a sparse assortment of settlements that tended to cluster around the moon's ports and temples, a transient place. The settlers had not been there for a very long time—a little over a decade. Before being converted into a rebel base, Yavin 4 had no intelligent life to speak of; the civilization that had built its temples had long since disappeared. After the destruction of the Empire's first Death Star, the rebels abandoned the moon as a base and, after a brief occupation by the Empire and in the wake of the destruction of the second Death Star, settlers began pouring into Yavin 4, many of them retired rebel fighters looking for a bit of peace and quiet after the war. Yavin 4's permanent residents were paired with traders, skilled laborers, harvesters who dove into the gas giant's atmosphere to collect gems, and people looking for a place to refuel and recharge before reaching their actual destination. Prospectors who spent time on Yavin's other moons came to Yavin 4 to cut loose—to drink their earnings away and enjoy themselves. That was all well and good for them, for people who could hop on their ships and head off-world at a moment's notice. But to Poe, that meant one thing—Yavin 4 was a boring, dead-end place with no chance of getting any livelier.

"You're clear to go, Dameron," Litte said, shaking Poe from his reverie.

It took him a moment to figure out what was going on. They were in some kind of cramped vestibule, a long narrow desk separating them from what many of the other tenants taking up space behind Poe would consider freedom. But once Poe saw *him*, he knew what had happened. Knew how he'd managed to get out of containment with such ease.

"Of course," Poe said under his breath.

She grabbed his arm and pushed him forward.

"Kid, you should be on your knees thanking that man over there," Litte said. "I wish I had a father half as loyal as he's been to you. Mine would've given up on me the second or third time I pulled a stunt like this. Hear you made it to seven or eight, according to your record."

Poe shook off the officer's grip and limped past the desk, past Kes Dameron, and out into the Yavin 4 night.

"You could have died, Poe," Kes said, finally, as he caught up with Poe outside the station.

His father looked more hurt than angry. The confusion and pain on his face showed Poe more emotion in a few moments than his father had expressed in what felt like months.

"Well, I'm fine," Poe said, not meeting his father's gaze but slowing down just enough for Kes to reach him. The truth was, he wasn't fine—at least not physically. The crash had been miraculous in that Poe had survived. But he was still trying to get a sense of the orchestra of aches and pains his body was experiencing. He felt wrecked.

His father placed his hands on Poe's shoulders.

"You're not fine," Kes said, shaking his head. "You almost died. You lucked out. That won't last forever, you hear me? This is exactly—"

"Exactly what?" Poe spat. "What you warned me about the million times you stopped me from flying? Before I could even fit in a cockpit? When you warned me about things before I even knew what you were talking about, because you couldn't bear the thought of me doing anything but sitting on this dead-end moon, watching our grass grow?"

Kes grimaced, as if swallowing words he knew he'd regret.

"Poe, do you even realize what it took? For me to get you out again?" Kes said, his eyes widening. "The favors I had to call in? The people I had to plead to? This isn't the first time, and they were ready to just leave you on ice. If it hadn't been for your—"

"My mother?" Poe said, his voice rising, angry. "Can you say it, Dad? Can you say her name now? Sure seems like she didn't even exist the last time we argued."

Kes stepped back. Poe could see his father's jaw clenching. He instantly felt regret. *Some* regret. The words were his truth—his anger. But he knew his father didn't deserve their full wrath. Not now. Not ever. The anger was followed by shame.

"I'm—I'm sorry, Dad," Poe said, turning around. "I just—I can't right now."

"Can't what, Poe?" Kes asked, stepping toward his son. But before he could react, Poe was in a full sprint. Poe looked back for a moment and saw his father struggling to react, to give chase. But Kes didn't move. As Poe sped farther into the Yavin night, he looked back again to see Kes Dameron, just a small speck growing smaller and smaller in the distance.

CHAPTER 4

As he expected, L'ulo L'ampar found Poe Dameron running toward the docks. Toward escape.

L'ulo pulled his landspeeder up on Poe's right as the younger man turned to face him. Poe's expression was one of anger mixed with fear and shame. His stance was stiff—like he was running through pain. He didn't move toward L'ulo's vehicle. In fact, L'ulo half expected him to bolt.

But their bond was strong, L'ulo told himself. The boy would listen to reason.

He didn't need to hear from Kes to know what had happened. His colleagues at the Yavin 4 Defense Force station had alerted him to Poe's joyride, and the subsequent crash. L'ulo allowed himself a moment of regret and nostalgia for Shara's aging A-wing, but that was quickly overcome with the relief he felt over Poe. Surely Kes had reminded his son how close he'd come to death, but L'ulo also figured Kes's voice had become a bit of white noise to the boy, and perhaps a different tack would help.

"Poe," L'ulo said, his voice clear and focused. "What's going on?"

Poe shook his head, as if realizing what side L'ulo was on already.

"Not you, too, L'ulo," Poe said, the words sounding more like a question than a statement. "I can't take it from you, too."

"It's not like that, kid. You know me," L'ulo said, keeping his tone calm. "Let's just talk."

"I don't want to talk. Maybe I don't want to hash it out anymore, L'ulo, all right?" Poe said.

He was getting more agitated, his eyes wide, his tunic sticking to his chest with sweat. The boy had survived a near-death experience and probably just had an epic argument with his father, whom L'ulo knew Poe loved but also resented in equal degrees. The fact was, Poe Dameron was tearing himself up inside, and L'ulo wasn't sure what to do about it.

"Talk to me, kid," L'ulo said, motioning for Poe to approach the vehicle. Hesitatingly, he did. L'ulo gently slapped Poe's face—a sign of affection. "I'm not some Yavin farmer, you know? I've seen a lot of stuff out there." He motioned to the night sky with his chin. "With your mom. With the Rebellion. This place isn't for me, either. But—"

Poe backed up.

"No, no buts, L'ulo," Poe said. "I'm done debating it, with you, Dad, this place—"

He moved around, arms out, as if to say, *Look around you.*

"There's nothing for me here, okay? I don't want to be a farmer. I don't want to live with Dad, or tend to the land, or spend my days in quiet introspection, you know?" Poe said, gripping the edge of the landspeeder, his knuckles whitening from the strain. "I want to see what's out there. I want to do something. Something that matters. I want to fly and explore, like—"

"Like Shara," L'ulo said. "I know, kid. I know."

Poe looked down at his feet. He spun around and kicked dirt, seemingly unsure what else to do with his body.

"Why doesn't *he* get that, L'ulo?" Poe asked. "Why can't he just let me go?"

"Can you blame him? You're all he has."

"And he's all I have," Poe said, turning to face his friend. "But what does Dad expect? That I'll just be here, sitting with him, forever?"

"Doubt he's thought it through to that degree," L'ulo said. "But he wants to protect you."

"He doesn't want me to die like Mom did," Poe said. "In space. Alone."

"Right."

"But I won't," Poe said, his voice quavering as if he didn't really believe himself. "I can fly. She taught me. You helped. You know I can do it. I'm good."

L'ulo nodded. The kid was right. He had talent. Not much polish, but from what little L'ulo had seen, he knew Poe had the markings of a great pilot. All the elements were there. The confidence. The willpower. The fearless nature. The ability to absorb complicated technical ideas and transform them into action. Poe had it all. He just wanted a chance.

Would Shara Bey have given it to him?

L'ulo shut off the landspeeder and stepped out.

He sensed the answer to the question ringing in his head, but he didn't want to hear it. His instinct was to keep Poe safe—to keep him on Yavin 4. That was what Kes wanted.

The real answer was a complicated one, he realized as he walked toward the boy he loved like a son.

"Your mother ever talk about Endor, Poe?" L'ulo asked, sitting down and motioning for the boy to sidle up next to him. "That last firefight?"

"With the Death Star?" Poe asked, taking a seat. "No, not really. Not that I remember."

L'ulo remembered—their attack on the second Death Star, the friends they lost, their sinking hopes, and the sudden rush of victory. The euphoric celebration on Endor that followed felt like it had happened moments before and eons before at the same time. There'd been no limit to what they could do then. They'd toppled a supposedly invincible giant.

"On Endor, after the battle, after we'd won," L'ulo said, picking his words with care, knowing the impact they'd have, "your mother looked so radiant. So alive. Your father, too. Tired, but also relieved and happy and eager to see what was next. We knew the work wasn't done. The Empire wasn't fully dead. But the beast had been beheaded, and it was only a question of watching the body die.

"I knew—I mean, we all knew—that eventually she and your father would settle down," L'ulo continued. "We knew they'd want to raise you somewhere and not have to see you only while on leave, or worse, never again."

Poe seemed mesmerized, his expression hanging on every word.

"Our job involved huge risk, Poe," L'ulo said. "There was always the chance we wouldn't come back. That there'd be dust where our ship had been a few seconds before. Your mom and dad knew that."

"So, they didn't want that anymore? To live in fear?" Poe asked, almost pleaded. "Is that what you're telling me?"

L'ulo raised a hand to calm him. *Let me finish*, it said to Poe.

"They wanted to be there for you. That outweighed everything else—their desire for adventure, their duty, their own lives," L'ulo said. "But when I asked your mother, in a brief, quiet moment amidst all that chaos and celebration, 'What will it feel like to not be out there anymore, Shara? To not be flying through the stars on a new adventure each day?' she turned and looked at me as if I was insane."

"What—what did she say?"

"She told me, 'I'll always be out there, L'ulo. I'll always be out among the stars—flying,'" L'ulo said, his words rolling off his tongue methodically. He understood Poe was in a fragile state. That anything he said could be misconstrued, could do more damage than good. But he also felt a responsibility to Shara, and what she might have done in his shoes, on this night. "But she also realized the risk that brought, and she knew the price she might pay if she ignored what she'd worked so hard to build—her family, her life—to chase after adventure and thrills."

"Don't play both sides for me, L'ulo," Poe said, shaking his head. "That's not your style. Aside from my dad, you knew my mom best. Quit parsing your words. Give me the truth."

"I don't know what—"

"You do know," Poe said, his eyes unblinking. He was not backing down, L'ulo realized. "You know exactly what my mom would do. So does Kes. She was a thrill seeker. A hero. She took risks and she fought hard. She's part of me. You see that, L'ulo. And that terrifies you, doesn't it?"

The nod L'ulo gave in response was almost reflexive, coming so quickly the older Duros couldn't have stopped it if he had wanted to. It was enough for Poe Dameron.

Poe stood up with a jolt. His hands shook. He backed away from L'ulo, almost stumbling over himself.

"Poe?"

"I—I have to go. I have to go," Poe muttered to himself. "I . . . I need to go."

With that, Poe Dameron turned around and ran.

L'ulo gave himself a moment or two before he stood up, dusted off his uniform, and made his way back to his landspeeder. He looked at his hands and saw the bruises and wear and tear of a Duros who'd lived a life of action and adventure, a man who wasn't bored and didn't walk through each day weighed down by regrets and hesitation. He wanted that for Poe. He knew it was selfish. Had his own ego, L'ulo thought, just sent the boy hurtling toward his demise? He heard his own words almost before he could think them, as if he was overhearing a strange conversation. But they rang true, and they would haunt him for a long, long time.

"What have I done?"

CHAPTER 5

The main settlement on Yavin 4 was often referred to as Wetyin's Colony, whose inhabitants were originally from the planet Setor. The settlers had moved to Yavin 4 and become farmers. Though the moon's population was sparse and mainly focused on agriculture, Yavin 4 was a nexus point—a hotbed for trade and transit. For every farmer and family, there were a dozen or so business-people making their way through the moon's active port area, which consisted of a long swath of docks and an even longer row of restaurants, cantinas, and more nefarious entertainment corners. It was the only flicker of excitement in town, as far as young people like Poe Dameron were concerned. To many spacefaring traders and dealers, it was one of many entertaining pit stops on the long road to their final destination.

Gully's was a cantina in that row—loud, raucous, and crowded, but also nondescript in comparison with its fellow watering holes. The kapok bar ran across the length of the place, a red-skinned and horned Devaronian named Fontis behind it. The smattering of tables that littered the space had mismatched chairs, if any, and were usually crowded with people telling tales of their latest deal or swindle, war stories and complaints, or nostalgic, drunken odes to better times. Though Yavin 4 had begun as a rebel base, even becoming a key scene in the epic struggle between the Rebel Alliance and the Empire—few of Gully's patrons could give a flurrg's hide over who was in charge. To these Outer Rim traders, who were more focused on staying afloat and making a profit, the politics were secondary.

But something was different that night. Fontis could feel it. It was busy, sure. That was a given. People needed to blow off some steam after long stints in the stars, or before signing up for another tour of duty. Fontis believed in providing his customers with an undeniable resource, something they'd never have their fill of. He'd run into many a rowdy customer over the years. He knew how to handle himself, and he wasn't scared of a scrap or a slow blade into an offending customer's midsection. But there was something else in the air, something hot—electric. Something more dangerous than the usual riffraff of unkempt traders and townies looking for a rush.

And Fontis knew where it was coming from.

He scanned the crowd, past the burly Dowutin bouncer, around the Nimbanel numbers guy—his scaly skin shimmering in the bar's dim light—who'd made Gully's his second home, and over the stout, surly Delphidian arms dealer who was well on his way to passing out at his small table, his pocket begging to be picked. Fontis's gaze settled on the bar's far corner, and a rickety table that hosted four people he'd never seen, and would never want to see again after the night was through.

Fontis had a good sense for these things—for trouble, really. While his entire business was built on casual customers and the transient nature of the port, he still had a bad feeling about these four. Years of running a dive like Gully's gave you a second sight that normal people didn't have. The ability to suss out trouble hours before it happened. But Fontis also had eyes, and what he saw screamed, *Watch out for these people.*

The first red flag was the group's leader, a fierce-looking Klatooinian with an eye patch who didn't seem to have the facial muscles to smile. His long brow and sagging jowls added to his dour expression. It seemed to Fontis the others in his group deferred to the Klatooinian, if with a bit of resignation. Close to him was a young human girl—couldn't be older than sixteen—her expression blank. She was tall, with dark wavy hair and swampy green eyes that made her seem older. Unlike the other members of the party, she seemed calm and collected in a way that belied her years. Her cool expression almost made Fontis think she was in charge, but that couldn't be. And in charge of what? These weren't your typical traders. They'd come to Gully's for a reason—a reason they probably shared with many of the darker elements that filtered through Yavin 4: they didn't want to be noticed. That was fine by Fontis, as long as they didn't bring trouble into his bar. *Wishful thinking*, the barkeep mused.

"I made my decision, I stand by it," the Klatooinian named Vigilch said, slapping his palm gently on the shoddy table. "He was taking from us. That sneaky little Ishi Tib—"

"That sneaky little Ishi Tib was our pilot," said the female Twi'lek seated across from Vigilch, her red lekku appendages moving slightly around her young face. Her name was Marinda Gan, and she was not happy to be stuck on Yavin 4. She'd been recruited by Vigilch to serve as muscle for their operation, not to sit in a bar and wonder what to do next. She could think of a million other places she'd prefer to be in the galaxy. All of them more exciting and appealing to a bounty hunter of her caliber. "And, as you're fond of reminding us, you're our leader—what now? How do you plan to get our ship off Yavin Four before they find us?"

"The longer our ship sits in dock, our goods tucked away, the greater the risk of it being discovered," said the gaunt-looking Pau'an named Gen Tri. Their voice was a slight hiss, their tone flat. They continued to speak as their long fingers rapped on the table. "Our friends back home won't be happy if that gets . . . lost in translation."

"We will not lose our . . . what we are tasked with retrieving," Vigilch snarled, turning to face Gen Tri. It was no secret they weren't fond of each other. But Vigilch was much more prone to showing it, the Pau'an's serene demeanor throwing him off with regularity. "I open the discussion to the group, then. Are there any suggestions? How do we find a pilot to get us off this miserable back-water moon?"

The young woman to Vigilch's right stirred, as if noticing something past the group, her young eyes locked on the bar's entrance. Her name was Zorii Wynn. As Fontis had surmised, she was a teenager. But she had seen much in her short life, and her comrades knew to trust her instincts.

Gen Tri, Marinda, and Vigilch followed Zorii's stare—and what they saw seemed underwhelming at first, until they heard Fontis's bellow at the sight of the young man stumbling into Gully's crowded entryway.

"Well, if it isn't the best damn pilot on Yavin Four, Mr. Poe Dameron himself!"

CHAPTER 6

New Republic Security Bureau officer Sela Trune walked briskly toward the main entranceway of the Yavin 4 Civilian Defense Force headquarters. She was not happy. All eyes were on her. She was certain word of her team's arrival had trickled down to the locals, and she didn't care. Now wasn't a time for municipal politics. It was a time for action.

"Can I help you?" the officer manning the front terminal asked, genuinely curious. Trune was used to this reaction. She was a few days over twenty-two and had risen up the NRSB ranks quickly, often finding herself in charge of people ten or more years her senior. She got over it fast. Others not so much.

"Officer Trune, NRSB," she said briskly. Trune savored how the officer's expression went from blank to anxious in less than a second. "I'm here to get debriefed on the spice runner situation."

"Spice runner . . . situation?"

"Did I stutter?" Trune said. "What's your name?"

The officer blanched, her already white skin going paler.

"Reservist Chant Osman, sir," she said, trying to rattle off the basic words but still stumbling over them. "My apologies."

"None needed, Reservist," Trune said, leaning over the desk, her palms on the faded wood. "Not if you can help me, that is. I've got a team of officers waiting outside, and we need to get to work immediately on something that concerns New Republic security. Doesn't that seem important to you?"

Osman nodded, eager to please.

"Wonderful," Trune said. "Now, who's in charge? And when can I speak to them?"

Lieutenant Davim Ak sipped his Sauweceran tea slowly, letting the warm liquid calm his fraught nerves. He couldn't delay this much longer, but how he longed for his own home, the windows sealed, and complete darkness. Running Yavin 4's Civilian Defense Force was enough on a normal day, but today was—what had Shara used to call it?—a "redball" kind of day. One thing after another. Each one bigger than the last.

"Almost over," he muttered to himself as the door to his office opened and a tall, confident figure strode in. He'd heard of the rising star that was Sela Trune, of course. The human woman's reputation preceded her. The New Republic Security Bureau handled the cases that bubbled under the surface—crime, bounty hunters, spice runners, and their ilk. The corruption that always threatened to weaken the greater good. The cracks that might turn into giant fissures and pull the nascent Republic down into the canyon that had consumed the previous one, leaving a monstrous, savage Empire in its place. Ak knew the drill. It was bad news that Trune was on Yavin 4. Even worse that she was hunting spice runners.

He'd heard the stories—about the young Trune's background and her swift climb to the upper echelons of the NRSB. Ak also knew Trune had made it her personal vendetta to shut down any and all spice runners, whether they be an overt threat to the New Republic or not. Ak also knew that the NRSB's tactics were not without flaws, and not pristine. Yes, Ak had gleaned much knowledge during his years presiding over Yavin 4's Defense Force, and all of it had helped him retain his role—despite the efforts of more powerful people to replace him.

He turned and greeted Trune with a knowing smile, which shook the usually stoic officer's demeanor for a moment.

"Sela Trune, what a pleasure," Ak said, bowing his head

slightly. "Welcome to Yavin Four. I see you've brought an impressive coterie of troops with you."

"My team is here, yes," Trune said, no sign of worry or confusion in her tone. She'd recovered fast and was taking the offensive. "I don't appreciate having to wait this long to see you. It was made clear by our advance communications team that this was of great importance."

Ak nodded. She was right, of course. The team's intent had been communicated directly. But Ak didn't exactly feel like making things easy. He was tired. The day had been long—first the hubbub with Shara's hotheaded son and now this. Spice runners on Yavin 4. Ak almost rolled his eyes. He was a few years from retirement, and part of the reason he'd clung so desperately to his post was his feeling that it would provide him with a smooth, mostly easy path toward his true goal in life: to settle down on a distant, tropical Outer Rim planet, away from the exceedingly neurotic and bureaucratic tentacles of the New Republic and safe from the fringe elements, like the smugglers and bounty hunters who cropped up everywhere, and live out the rest of his days in peace. A cold drink in his hand. The warm sun of a strange system hitting his face. It would be nice. Someday.

"Lieutenant?" Trune said, frustrated by Ak's slow response. "I'm here to get—"

"Oh, I know why you're here, Officer," Ak said, taking the seat behind his desk and leaning back. "As you've noted repeatedly, your intent was announced well in advance of your boots hitting the surface of our lovely Yavin moon. I get it. You're in a hurry. Aren't we all?"

Trune stiffened. This was not what she'd hoped for. A glimmer of joy jolted through Ak. He loved to make an upstart like Trune squirm.

But this game could only be played for so long, he realized. While it was fun to needle the higher-ups, at a certain point it became an actual offense, and Ak wasn't in the mood to have any datawork make its way to her personnel file. He tapped a finger on the desk and began to speak.

"We have received numerous reports of suspicious activity on Yavin Four—a group of at least four individuals docking at the main port who match descriptions of persons wanted in connection to the Spice Runners of Kijimi," Ak said, and waited for a response.

Trune's expression was enough. A look of desire—not lust, but a wanting, nonetheless—spread over her face. Trune was unable to hide it, and she didn't seem particularly inclined to. Ak knew the why of this, too.

The Spice Runners were a secretive, upstart organization that had managed to piece together an impressive—if still feisty and small—alliance of thieves, murderers, and scoundrels to capitalize on the chaos that had sprung from the collapse of the Empire, which had left the lucrative spice trade coming out of Kessel in a state of complete disarray. Without Imperial oversight, the battle for spice was a violent struggle among various factions, leaving busy processing terminals inoperational. That opened the door for the Spice Runners of Kijimi, with their pirate vessels focused on striking any spice-loaded ships trying to move their product into the rest of the galaxy. The Spice Runners of Kijimi were definitely of particular interest to the New Republic. Like many other gangs and crews, the Spice Runners were working their own, new relationships with the mine operators, choosing business over mindless violence in an effort to assert themselves as a power in the realm of running spice. Unlike other criminal syndicates, though, the Spice Runners confederacy was growing fast—and building a reputation for being cunning and relentless in their quest. But Ak knew that as far as Sela Trune was concerned, the Spice Runners of Kijimi were more than just a criminal target. For her it was personal.

"Kijimi," she said, her voice almost a whisper. "Do we have names? Last locations?"

"Yes, it's all in the file," Ak said, producing a small datapad and sliding it over to Trune, who grabbed it hungrily. "I believe the Klatooinian, Vigilch, is in charge here. Quite a nasty character, that one."

"What's your intel say?" Trune asked. "Where could they be hiding out?"

"Our agents have sighted them not far from their ship," Ak said, drawing out his words, relishing the moment a bit more than he probably should have. "There are a number of unsavory locales where people of their ilk can set up shop and go undetected, but with your overly qualified team, I'm sure it won't be long before—"

The door opened. It was another Security Bureau officer, one of Trune's men. Youthful, excited, and desperate to talk.

"Apologies for the interruption," the officer said as Trune turned around, the displeasure on her face looming large.

"What is it?" Trune snapped.

"We . . . we have a problem—" the officer started.

Trune cut him off. "What is it? Spit it out."

"Reports from the dock," the officer said. "They've found a body."

CHAPTER 7

"I'm in trouble," Poe said, sliding into a seat at the bar. "Big trouble."

Fontis waved a hand at Poe dismissively.

"You keep playing this game, Poe, but you know the score," the barkeep said. "You're a sprout. I don't serve sprouts."

Poe slammed a hand on the bar—more a joke than a show of anger.

"C'mon, Fontis, cut me a break," Poe said. "I've had a rough day."

"Looks like it, kid. And, hey, I will be happy to take your scraps of money in a few years," Fontis said with a devious smile. "I'm quite fond of allowing people to drown their sorrows, as you well know. But I also need to avoid having my place shut down because an unruly teenager wants to get a buzz going, you see? It's just not worth the cost of a drink, assuming you have any credits in those rumpled pants."

Poe smiled. He wasn't sure he considered Fontis a friend, but he enjoyed the Devaronian's dry humor and shadowy demeanor. Gully's felt like a doorway to another world to Poe, a sign of what was out there, beyond the Yavin system. A galaxy of scoundrels and double crosses and space travel that seemed within Poe's reach.

"Can I at least stick around?" Poe asked. "Too hot for me to go home just yet."

"What else is new?" Fontis said, pouring Poe a glass of Jawa juice. "Here you go. The worst this'll do is make you want to dance, which I think is worth risking my license."

Poe thanked the barkeep, tossing a few credits onto the counter before turning around to scan the bar. It was another loud, unruly night at Gully's, and Poe wouldn't have had it any other way. He didn't want to dwell on what'd happened earlier. He'd pore over his conversations with his father and L'ulo later, probably after another argument with Kes Dameron, on his way to another sleepless night in his room on the farm. Another night resigned to his exile, dreaming of the expanse above Yavin 4 and the secrets and adventures it held.

The tavern was loud, the music—a festive Laki Lembeng number—boomed through the place, making it feel like the entire venue was swaying softly. Most of the customers seemed oblivious, enraptured by their own table-centric squabbles or well on their way to obliterating their memories of the night. Poe found himself jealous of that option.

He'd love to go back a bit and just wipe the day clean, start over. As much as his father angered him, he loved the man and really wanted there to be some kind of understanding between them. Why couldn't his father just let him go? Let him find his own path? Poe was young. Adventure was in his blood. How could his father—who'd married a Rebellion pilot and been a Pathfinder during the war himself—expect any less? But time had a way of hardening men, of making them more set in their ways and frightened of the possibilities of life. Even as a young man, Poe saw this in his father, in L'ulo, and in many people he came across on humid, dark nights like this—when Poe would come to Gully's and spend his time flirting and dancing and laughing, the one pure escape he had that didn't involve a ship and a course that would get him out of the Yavin system for a long time.

He saw her out of the corner of his eye—a lithe figure swaying to the music, which was now playing a Calamari waterballad. She was about Poe's age, he guessed, her long, wavy brown hair and sharp features giving her an almost feline quality, like a patient predator able to perch on a tree for days, waiting for its prey to finally make a move. Her young friend—or comrade—was a Twi'lek. Poe had seen them often near the port, a species used to space travel and the business of the Outer Rim. She seemed less confident in her movements but was clearly enjoying the chance to blow off some steam. They made for an alluring pair, and Poe was mesmerized.

"Who is that?" Poe asked, more of himself than of anyone in particular.

Fontis sidled up across from the bar, his eyes also on the pair.

"Never seen them before," Fontis said. "Which means only one thing."

"What's that?" Poe asked.

"Trouble."

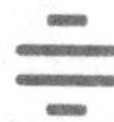

A rush of bravery coursed through Poe as the song ended and a pulsing, newer, fast tune began to filter through the tavern. The two dancers seemed hesitant, so entranced by their slithering movements that they were unwilling to change their pace. Poe watched them both carefully, his attention locked on the human woman—her smile confident and knowing, her eyes seeming much older than her years. Next thing he knew, he was in front of her. He hadn't put much thought into what he'd say, but by the time that dawned on him, a few seconds had passed—and she was looking at him with a quizzical expression.

"Hey," Poe said with a slight jerk of his chin. "Seems like you two were having fun out here."

The young woman arched an eyebrow before responding.

"We *were*," she said, emphasizing the last word. "But now you're here."

"Well, don't stop having fun on my account," Poe said with a shrug. "Just thought I'd say hello."

"You've done that," she continued, her voice confident and distant. "Mr. . . . ?"

"Poe. I'm Poe Dameron," he said, extending his hand. She took it briefly. "I'm a local."

She nodded, a slight smile on her face. Her Twi'lek friend had wandered back to their table, where she joined two others who were looking on, watching Poe banter with their friend. Their expressions were a mix of worry, anger, and . . . fear?

"A townie. How quaint," she said. "I'm Zorii Wynn."

Poe bowed quickly.

"A pleasure to meet you, Zorii," he said. "Welcome to our tiny fringe moon. I'd be happy to show you and your friends around, if you're staying long."

"We're not," Zorii said, shaking her head. "In fact, we're in the process of figuring out how to . . . continue our journey."

Journey? Poe thought. They had a ship. They were going somewhere. His mind buzzed with possibility. Surely he was jumping ahead of himself, but he let it happen. The idea of stepping onto a ship and leaving all this behind had never been stronger in him. He realized he had no desire to reenter the repetitive loop of his life. The arguments. The escapes. The eventual returns home. The resentment. It was time to go, whether it was on this ship or the next one.

"So, tell me, Poe Dameron of Yavin Four," she said, bringing him back to the present. "Why should I care who you are?"

"Because I'm going to be the best pilot the galaxy's ever seen," Poe said. "Bank on it."

"I've heard that before," Zorii said with a shrug. "So what?"

"I can fly anything," Poe said, his tone growing defensive. "Trust me."

Zorii's smile melted into a curious, intrigued expression—like a reptile squinting its eyes.

"Anything?"

The temperature seemed to drop around Poe as he took a seat at the table with Zorii's group, her hand on his shoulder.

"This is Poe Dameron," she said after she'd introduced her comrades to him. "And he is a pilot."

"A pilot? He's just a boy," the Klatooinian Zorii had identified as Vigilch said with a grunt. "A pilot of what? A landspeeder?"

The group laughed—the Twi'lek Poe now knew as Marinda Gan heartily, the Pau'an named Gen Tri softly. Zorii remained quiet, her hand still on Poe's shoulder.

"I don't see you rattling off any options that might help us get off Yavin Four," Zorii said. "Unless I missed that while I was recruiting our ticket out of here?"

They want me to fly their ship, Poe realized. He swallowed hard. Was he ready for that? He'd soon find out.

Gen Tri turned to look at Poe more closely, their dark eyes probing Poe in a way that made him shiver with discomfort. It wasn't their appearance—Poe had seen every type of species cruise through the Yavin 4 ports. It was something else. They made him uneasy in a way he'd not yet figured out.

"We do need a pilot," Gen Tri said, their voice

hollow-sounding and whispery. "But are you ready to do what's needed?"

"If you need a pilot, I'm your man," Poe said, not missing a beat. "Point me to your ship and I'll get you where you need to go."

Marinda Gan laughed dryly.

"That's all well and good, Poe Dameron, but do you want to go where we're going?" she asked. "That's the big question."

"Well, I mean, I can just drop the coordinates and plot a course. It's not that compli—"

Zorii's hand gripped Poe's shoulder.

"It's not getting there that's the problem, Poe," she said. "It's what we're doing. We're not traders or members of the mining consortium. Our travels are a bit more . . . adventurous."

Poe waited a beat before responding.

"Adventure's what I'm after," Poe said, the words reaching his mouth fully formed, as if coming directly from his heart instead of his brain. "I'm not afraid of that. I'm done with Yavin Four."

Zorii's grip loosened, and she took the empty seat to Poe's right. Their eyes met.

"I'm not going to dance around what we are," Zorii said. "Because you seem smart, and even if you do get scared and tell anyone, we'll be gone before it can mean anything."

Poe nodded. Vigilch raised a hand, as if to try to stop Zorii from continuing. She ignored him.

"We're smugglers," she said flatly. "And our pilot is dead. If you can get us off this moon, you will begin a life of adventure and uncertainty unlike anything you've imagined. This place will be a blurry memory before too long."

Smugglers?

Poe leaned back in his chair. He hadn't considered the possibility. But the information revealed the fork in the road in front of him. The pounding in his chest grew louder, drumming through his veins into his ears and head. Was this what he wanted? Like he had said, he wanted adventure—a chance to fly free and leave Yavin 4 behind. But was throwing his lot in with smugglers the best way to get there? To achieve what he'd dreamt of? A chance at a life not mired in the ordinary and mundane?

He'd met his fair share of unsavory characters before—bounty hunters, arms dealers, and other smugglers. They'd wander through Gully's from time to time. But those were fleeting encounters—and Poe could always keep his distance. This was very different. If he threw his lot in with this group, he wouldn't just be in the same room as a band of criminals—he would be a criminal, too. What would Shara Bey think of that?

This would not be the kind of thing Poe could backtrack from. Joining forces with a group of smugglers would mean he'd never see Yavin 4, L'ulo, or his father again. But it was the only opening that pointed toward the freedom Poe hungered for. Maybe he could make it a temporary stay? Find his way off the moon, then strike out on his own. The rationalization calmed Poe a bit. He still felt a pang of sadness at the idea of leaving, but it was soon replaced by a determination and desire he'd only grazed over in the past few months.

"I'm in," Poe said with a quick nod. "Take me to the ship and we'll be out of here faster than the *Millennium Falcon*."

Poe's face grew hot as his boast was met not with cheers from his new comrades—but another round of laughter.

CHAPTER 8

Gully's was quite different a few hours later, as Kes Dameron and L'ulo L'ampar entered. The bar still reeked of stale ale and smoke, still pulsed with the same melodious drone, but the crowd had thinned, and the energy of the place—if there was such a thing—had calcified. The few remaining customers were sluggish and distant, feeling the effects of their beverages or the weight of their bad decisions. Kes made a beeline for the bar.

"Where is he?" Kes said as he leaned over the bar, his face centimeters from the Devaronian bartender's. "Where's Poe?"

Fontis raised his hands in mock defense, a slight smile on his face.

"Kes Dameron, now, now, you can't just come in here full of bluster like this," he said, baring his sharp teeth.

Before Fontis could continue, Kes grabbed him by his tunic and started to drag him over the bar. The slithery bartender's voice rose in pitch the closer he got to being off his feet.

"Wait, wait, what are you doing?" Fontis said. As Kes got closer to pulling Fontis over, L'ulo closed in, his hands on Kes's shoulders.

"Put him down, Kes," L'ulo said, his voice relaxed but not without presence. "This isn't the way to get answers."

Kes paused a second before complying. Fontis dusted himself off and looked up at the two men.

"Well, that's no way to start a friendly conversation, don't you think?"

"Cut to it, Fontis," L'ulo said. "Where is he?"

After his encounter with Poe, L'ulo had felt aimless—like a cloud of guilt was hanging over him. Yes, he'd been honest with the boy. Poe Dameron deserved as much, he'd thought in the moment. Why not give him a little nudge to set things in motion? Isn't that what Shara Bey would have wanted? But as he watched the boy—man—he loved like a son run into the dank, dark Yavin 4 night, he knew he'd overstepped, and that guilt propelled him in the other direction: to Kes Dameron's farm, hat in hand.

They'd scoured the relatively small Yavin 4 settlement—focusing on the docks and surrounding areas. It was only a matter of time before they honed in on Gully's. L'ulo felt in his gut that Poe had ended up there.

"You need to keep a better handle on your spawn,

Kes," Fontis hissed. "If you did, you and your Duros police friend wouldn't need to come here and disrupt my business."

"Answer the question," Kes said, spittle flying out of his mouth. "Where is my son?"

Fontis raised his fists to defend himself. Though he'd seen his fair share of barroom scraps, he wouldn't stand a chance against a former Pathfinder like Kes, and he knew it. Like much of what Fontis did, it was all for show.

"He's gone, all right? I don't know where he went," Fontis said. "Now leave. You're not welcome here anymore."

Before Kes or L'ulo could respond, the saloon's main door hissed open. A young, tall woman with short blond hair stepped in. Her uniform immediately gave her away: New Republic Security Bureau. But why was the NRSB there, on Yavin 4? Kes wondered. He wouldn't have to wait long to find out.

"Kes Dameron?" the woman asked. She stepped toward them, not waiting for Kes to respond. "Sela Trune, NRSB. I was sent to Yavin Four on a special, highly confidential mission. A mission that—unfortunately—your son has gotten entangled in."

"What are you talking about?" L'ulo said, stepping between Kes and Trune. "What's happening?"

"Ever heard of the Spice Runners of Kijimi?" Trune asked.

L'ulo felt a jolt run through him. Sela Trune hadn't been blowing smoke. Not if it involved the Spice Runners. Though L'ulo was a member of Yavin 4's Civilian Defense Force, he still did his best to stay apprised of what was going on in the greater galaxy. The Spice Runners of Kijimi were one of a handful of upstart organizations scratching and clawing their way toward recognition—and it wasn't because they were warm and cuddly. No, the Spice Runners were cunning, calculating, and when needed, bloodthirsty—willing to solve their problems with an efficient blaster shot to the head, as opposed to a genteel conversation over tea.

"What about them?" L'ulo asked.

"They're here, on Yavin Four," Trune said, her speech rushed. She had somewhere else to be. "They pulled off a massive heist on Kellgar Seven, on the fringes of the Outer Rim. The kind of score that can set you up for life. But they ran into some trouble."

"Trouble?" Kes asked. He shook his head. He wasn't sure what this had to do with Poe—or him. "What are you talking about?"

"Trouble as in, their pilot was skimming from the top—sending bits and pieces of their big mother lode to his real employers—and the main competitors to the Spice

Runners," Trune said, pacing around the empty bar. Funny how the arrival of NRSB could clear a room full of people wallowing in the gray areas of criminal life. "The pilot—an Ishi Tib named Beke Mon'z—is dead. They figured him out. Or think they did."

"He was working for you," L'ulo said. A statement, not a question.

Trune responded with a dry smile.

"You're smart. I like that," she said. "Yes. He was feeding us intel. Helping me get a better picture of who the Spice Runners are. But he was sloppy. My only hope is they think he was just a greedy mercenary instead of a double agent. Either way, they're desperate for a pilot. And I think they zeroed in on your kid, who, from what I hear, isn't bad up there."

"Poe? Where is he?" Kes said, forgetting Fontis and L'ulo were even there, turning to face this new player. "Where's my son?"

"That's what I'm getting at. Your son is long gone, Dameron," Trune said matter-of-factly. "And he's in a hell of a lot of trouble."

CHAPTER 9

Poe's eyes widened as the group approached the ship. The Yavin 4 docks were a hotbed of controlled chaos—ships landing, ships being unloaded, workers moving goods, pilots and crew wandering to find food or room and board. The Defense Force presence on the docks was minimal—the area was just too hard to patrol, and on a small moon like this one, staffing was already stretched thin. Zorii Wynn motioned toward the vessel.

"This is the *Ragged Claw*," she said with some pride.

The *Claw* was an XS stock light freighter, a Corellian starship that could be used for a variety of things—warfare, smuggling, transport. Poe was familiar with the model, which had been around for generations. It was a small ship, as such things went—but it was also inconspicuous. The kind of ship you wouldn't look twice at, it was so common—and outdated.

They walked around the *Claw*'s yellow-plated saucer and boarded, trying to keep a casual air about them. Poe thought he heard Vigilch grumble something to Marinda Gan but couldn't be certain. He'd been a blend of nerves and excitement since their conversation at the bar, and he was still not sure if this was really happening. Was he really leaving Yavin 4? With a band of smugglers he'd just met? It was exhilarating and terrifying all at once. He turned to look at Zorii. Their eyes met and she offered him a brief, welcoming smile. She had some idea what he was going through, he thought. Or rather—he hoped.

"You familiar with this kind of ship, boy?" Vigilch said, leading him into the *Claw*'s cramped cockpit.

Poe nodded confidently.

"Count on it," he said. "Are the laser cannons up to snuff? How's the hyperdrive?"

Vigilch scoffed. "Have you ever piloted something out of this system?"

"Vigilch, do you have another pilot in your sheath?" Marinda Gan asked, her words dripping with disdain. "Or do you think we'll be safer here, hunted and with a bounty on our heads, than on our way back home?"

Vigilch shrugged.

Poe slid into the pilot's seat, facing the ship's narrow viewport, which jutted from the ship like a sharp nose. Poe hadn't lied to Vigilch. He knew about the freighter class—had studied it, like he'd studied many ships while pining away for a shot like this. He knew about the *Ragged*

Claw's armored hull, the kind of sublight engines it had. But could he fly it?

"Only one way to find out," he said under his breath.

"What?" Zorii asked as she took the copilot's seat. "Talking to yourself already?"

"No, just getting situated," Poe said, leaning forward and flicking through some of the prelaunch protocols. "Getting acquainted with the ship and all."

"You've never flown one of these, have you?" Zorii asked, a sharp smirk on her face. Her eyes seemed to be smiling, too—looking through Poe as if he was made of glass. He felt vulnerable. Like she was reading his mind—which he knew was impossible, but still. It made for a chilling sensation.

"Not exactly," he said, keeping his voice low so only she could hear. "But I can figure it out."

Zorii turned away and looked through the ship's small cockpit window.

"You'd better figure it out fast, Poe," she said, not keeping her voice down. "We've got company."

She was right. Five armed NRSB officers were making their way through the docking area—trying to look nonchalant and failing miserably, their buttoned-up demeanor and wandering eyes giving them away even before their starched uniforms could. The standard dock people parted like bunkbugs scurrying for cover. They could sense trouble, too, and were not looking to stick around to see what came next.

Poe felt a hand on his shoulder. Vigilch.

"Get us out of here now, boy," the Klatooinian said. "Or your tenure with the Spice Runners of Kijimi will be a short one."

Poe tried to speak but found himself unable to produce a sound.

Spice Runners?

His head felt light. For a moment, his vision went dark. No. That was not what he'd signed up for—was it?

The Spice Runners of Kijimi.

Poe had heard enough, listened in on his fair share of hushed conversations, to know the name—and what it meant. This was bad. He'd gone from consorting with a group of shady thieves to signing up with something much worse. What was he willing to sacrifice for his shot at adventure? Would it be worth it? He was going to find out one way or another. He was in too deep.

"Are you listening, boy?" Vigilch spat, his voice rising in anger and volume. "Now. Get us out of here."

Poe swallowed hard and mentally walked through the

steps to launch. He knew what to do, of that he had no doubt. He just hadn't, well, done it before. Flying an A-wing was one thing—especially one he'd sat in and tinkered with since as far back as he could remember. The *Ragged Claw* was different—he was in someone else's house and being asked to make dinner without really knowing where all the ingredients were. He knew he could cook, though. So it was time to turn on the heat.

Then the shooting started.

The blaster fire was sudden. It took Poe a second to realize what was going on. But the Spice Runners didn't have his delay and immediately took their positions. Vigilch's grip tightened on Poe's shoulder.

"Now, boy, now," he seethed.

Poe took a quick breath. He flipped the switch that engaged the ship's thrusters, feeling the hum of the *Ragged Claw*'s deceptively powerful engines. Marinda Gan, Gen Tri, and Vigilch swayed as the ship lurched forward, still rattling from the barrage of blaster fire coming at them from the five officers on the ground.

"We're being fired on!" Marinda yelled over the rising sound of the ship's engine.

Before she could continue, the ship lurched forward again—this time with more purpose, and it wasn't stopping.

"What are you doing?" Zorii asked, scanning the controls from the copilot's terminal. "We're moving too fast for port traffic. We're going to hit something."

"Just trust me," Poe said as the ship careened past the firing NRSB officers, seeming to shrug off their blaster fire, and wove around a few smaller ships in mid-transit. "Trust me."

"What is going on?" Vigilch said as he toppled backward into the other two crew members.

Poe ignored their leader. He had to focus. Had to push past everything—his fears, the blaster fire outside, his new allies. He wove the ship—which was pushing speeds not meant for ground-level travel—around the docking area, scraping and bumping the freighter toward open air in less than a minute.

"They're behind us," Zorii said, her voice alarmed but not alarmist. "Three NRSB orbital jumpers."

"Good," Poe said.

"Good?" Zorii asked incredulously. "They're on to us, Poe. I don't know how familiar you are with this ship, but it's not exactly the star of the fleet. Speed is not our strong suit."

"Orbital jumpers don't have hyperdrives—once we get clear, we're golden," Poe said, pulling up on the ship's throttle. The ship's artificial gravity pushed him farther into his seat as the ship veered toward orbit around Yavin 4.

"Zorii, handle the weapons while our pilot tries to get us out of here," Vigilch barked.

Poe clenched his jaw. He wanted to focus on what was in front of him—piloting the ship off Yavin 4—but he couldn't help thinking about the bigger picture. For better or worse, he was on the wrong side.

"On it," Zorii said, swiveling her seat to scan the weapons terminal. "Laser cannons are locked. Just let me know when we should create an intergalactic incident."

"Fire," Vigilch said. "Get us out of here, Dameron. Or else."

Poe nodded to himself. He felt his entire demeanor change. Felt himself push past his doubt and keep going, because the only other option was untenable. His movements gained strength and confidence. It was as if his entire being was making a decision—to leave Yavin 4, to repudiate what came before and carve a new path for himself, and deal with the consequences later. Either that or he'd be in a jam not even his father's connections could get him out of.

They were in orbit, speeding along with Yavin 4's swampy atmosphere in the ship's rear scopes. Poe caught sight of the jumpers, firing indiscriminately. He knew their laser cannons would sting like any bigger ship's, but he also knew—just based on the short time he'd been flying the *Claw*—that the freighter was deceptively nimble. He wove through another barrage of fire, pulling the ship up—as if heading directly back to Yavin 4's surface—only to wheel around.

"What in blazes—"

Vigilch's curses crashed with similar obscenities and cries of surprise from the rest of the crew, not tethered to a terminal. Poe ignored them. He leveled the ship's navigation and positioned it where he wanted it—right behind the jumpers.

"Fire, Zorii," Vigilch said.

"Shoot to harm, not to kill," Poe interjected. "There are good people on those ships."

"You have a lot to learn about being a Spice Runner, Poe Dameron," Zorii said.

Poe watched as the *Ragged Claw* blindsided the two ships, laser fire blanketing the unsuspecting NRSB vessels. Zorii was true to his request, sending firepower in or around the essential areas—just enough to disable them, not enough to destroy them—making sure to spare whoever was piloting the ships. He made a mental note. He might be able to trust the woman named Zorii Wynn. He'd need a few allies.

But Poe didn't get time to ponder his new status quo. Marinda Gan was behind him, her arm outstretched—pointing at a larger, more present problem.

"Is that—is that what I think it is?"

Poe told himself it couldn't be true, but nonetheless a long shadow had fallen over the group and their small battered ship.

The *Hammerhead*-class cruiser seemed to almost pivot at the sight of the *Ragged Claw*, as if the giant vessel was sentient and able to flinch. The long cruiser could easily outgun the *Claw*, and Poe and his new crewmates knew it. The message sliced through the static of space, crackling to life on Poe's terminal.

"This is the New Republic Security Bureau. You are harboring people wanted for questioning in regards to a crime committed on the surface of Yavin Four." The voice sounded haggard and spent. "You are to disable your ship's defenses immediately and prepare to be boarded and searched. If you do not reply shortly, we will begin occupation protocols."

"The more things change," Gen Tri muttered, their ethereal voice jarring Poe out of his own anxiety spiral. "It seems the so-called New Republic is sounding much like the Empire it dethroned, no?"

Poe ignored the comment. They had more important

things to deal with. They were in deep trouble, and no matter how quickly he tried to work out a solution, he knew it was pointless. They were out of luck.

"Any ideas?" Zorii asked. "We're still in a pretty dense gravity shadow—we couldn't jump to lightspeed if we wanted to, unless we override the system."

Poe could hear Vigilch scampering behind them, the nervous pacing doing little to stave off their impending capture. Then his eyes widened. *Could it work?* Poe wondered. It would have to.

Poe turned to Zorii.

"Can you open a comm channel with that ship?" Poe said. "I have an idea."

"If you want Poe Dameron to live, you will let us pass," Zorii said, her tone gruff and defiant. The rest of the crew huddled around her seat as Poe looked on. "This point is not negotiable. Continue your aggression and we will be forced to eliminate the boy, and will do it without hesitation."

Static and silence followed. The moments stretched on for what seemed like days but couldn't have been more than a minute. Poe could hear his own breath.

"This isn't going to work," Vigilch muttered, stepping back from the control panel and pacing around the ship's small cockpit again. He couldn't get a few steps without bumping into something or someone. "We'll have to shoot first. That's our only chance of escape."

"We're outgunned, severely," Marinda Gan said, turning her head quickly to face their leader. Her look was loaded with contempt. "Is it worth getting the first shot off if you're just going to be overwhelmed after? Why don't you let the girl do . . . what she's meant to do?"

Gen Tri shot Marinda an uncharacteristically sharp glance. She didn't respond. Vigilch shook his head as if to say, *Fine, we'll see how this plays*.

"Where can we retrieve Dameron?" the NRSB officer said, each word slow and pained as it came through the speaker. "How do we know you'll keep him alive?"

Zorii didn't hesitate, her response prepped and polished.

"We'll drop him somewhere in the Sawaya system," she said, her words coming across casually, as if she was asking for an extra portion at dinner. "You have our word."

"The Sawaya system?" The NRSB officer sounded incredulous. "There are almost a dozen inhabitable planets. It could take—"

Zorii didn't back down. The ruse was all they had.

"That is our final offer," she said, the casual air gone, her voice clear and tinged with menace. "We are prepared to die if these terms are not accepted."

Poe watched her closely, his heart in his throat. Who was this girl—this woman—who could so casually toss aside all their lives, who knew how to outmaneuver a seasoned New Republic officer, who remained cool and collected while her crew of miscreants and criminals hemmed and hawed? Poe thought he was fairly tough for his age—having dealt with his share of tragedy and knowing his own parents had fought valiantly for the New Republic. Where did this Zorii Wynn come from?

The response from the opposing ship was brief, but it took all their willpower to not whoop and holler with victory as the words filtered through.

"You may proceed."

Poe flicked the comm off hastily before anyone on the other end could somehow sense the smile forming on his face. He slowly steered the *Claw* out of orbit and away from Yavin 4. He turned to face Zorii.

"That was something else," he said, his body humming with excitement. "You saved our butts."

"*You* did, actually," she said, her smile slight, as if things like this happened every day for her. Perhaps they did, Poe mused. "Tricking them into thinking you'd been kidnapped—that was sharp. And you performed some fancy footwork getting us off the surface. Looks like you are a good pilot, after all."

"Could use a copilot," Poe said, nodding toward her seat. "You seem to fit the bill. Maybe you can show me some of those spice runner tricks in exchange?"

"Something tells me you're no stranger to being a scoundrel, Poe Dameron," she said, her smile widening for a split second, an unexpected warmth in her eyes. "But it's a deal."

CHAPTER 10

The dense swamp planet Sorgan was the only inhabitable rock in an otherwise forgettable system nestled deep in the Outer Rim. Known for little more than being a marker on the way to something more notable, Sorgan was underdeveloped—a mostly agrarian culture with minimal planetary governance and an even smaller native population—making it a perfect pit stop for the Spice Runners of Kijimi. At least that was what Poe assumed.

"Here we are," Poe announced to his new teammates as the *Ragged Claw* dropped out of hyperspace. "Home, sweet temporary home."

Poe didn't turn around, but he felt Vigilch looming over him. Their leader had seemed restless during the journey. Was he put off by *how* they had managed to get off Yavin 4? That he hadn't had a direct hand in solving the problem? Poe had no idea. He was still unsure where he stood with all of them. He hadn't even known they were spice runners until he'd boarded the ship and committed himself to escaping Yavin 4. Zorii had misled him about who they were. Poe wasn't just high-flying with some shady smugglers, but teaming up with an actual criminal network. It left a bitter taste in his mouth, and he had no one to talk to about it. His "teammates" were barely that.

Gen Tri was mostly silent and mysterious, and when they spoke, it was to either Zorii or Vigilch. Marinda Gan was friendlier—the Twi'lek seemed lively and excited to be on the way to the next thing. But that boisterousness masked something darker that Poe couldn't fully see, like a fyrnock lurking in the shadows, waiting to strike. And then there was Zorii. Like Marinda, she and Poe were close in age, but Zorii talked and moved like a woman twice as old. Mature, confident, world-weary. What had Zorii Wynn experienced? Where did she stand? The questions had danced around his head for the entire trip as he tried to navigate the ship and maintain his own external cool. There was only one way to find out the truth, he figured, and he had little choice in the matter anyway.

"Temporary?" Vigilch barked as Poe brought the ship down on Sorgan's clouded surface. The *Claw* jostled noticeably, Vigilch straining to maintain his posture before continuing. "What makes you think that, pup?"

Poe ignored the insult and made sure the ship was settled before he spun his seat around.

"I mean, Sorgan? This place is more boring than Yavin Four. I don't think anyone—even a space cartographer—can find this rock on a map," he said. "We're just making time before we hit up Kijimi, right?"

He could have sworn he heard Gen Tri cackle, but the sound resembled a snarl mixed with a sneeze. They didn't meet Poe's eyes.

Vigilch shrugged and moved out of the cockpit, evidently feeling the conversation had resolved itself. Poe turned his seat around and rapped his fingers near Zorii's copilot station. She looked up, uninterested in the exchange with Vigilch.

"So, what about it?" Poe asked.

"What?"

"What about Kijimi?"

"What about it, Poe?" Zorii asked, impatient. Her mood could veer from warm and friendly to frigid and disinterested in moments, it seemed.

"You're the Spice Runners of Kijimi, right?" Poe said. "So why don't we just head there? Isn't that where we set up shop? Forgive me, I'm new to this smugg—*spice running* thing."

Zorii furrowed her brow, her expression a blend of surprise and disdain.

"Kijimi isn't for just anyone, hotshot." The final word left Zorii's mouth with some added heat. "You wouldn't last a second there if you weren't under Spice Runners protection."

"Well, I mean, aren't I?"

"Not yet. Don't kid yourself," Zorii said, a slight tilt to her head. The rest of the crew was beginning to disembark, leaving them alone on the ship. "You got us here, great. We appreciate that. You showed some real smarts out there. But what do you think we do, Poe? Just fly around having wild, fancy-free adventures?"

Poe didn't respond. He wasn't sure what he thought. He had just wanted to experience not being on Yavin 4. Not answering to his father or hearing L'ulo regale him with stories about his parents that he could never experience himself. He wanted something different and new. And now he was trapped. He had no means to survive on his own, and nowhere to go. He was or soon would be a fugitive in the eyes of Yavin 4 and the New Republic. Poe had to think fast if he wanted to find a way out of this mess, but the plans weren't coming together. All he could dwell on was what he'd left behind—and the damage his hasty exit had caused. What was his dad thinking? That Poe had been kidnapped? By whom? Who had Poe just entrusted his life to?

"This isn't the space circus, Poe," Zorii said, shaking

her head and letting out a quick, clipped laugh. "This is something else. Something real and important that you have to feel in your blood. You have to not only want to be here, you have to sacrifice everything to be here. This is your life now. Nothing else matters because nothing else came before, okay? If you want to be one of us, one of us has to be all you are—or ever will be."

Poe's throat tightened. His fingers froze over the *Ragged Claw*'s controls. His eyes, locked on Zorii's, went dry. Poe's head spun as he tried to remain focused—on the ship, on Zorii, on what was next. But what was next? He couldn't shake the feeling he'd made a terrible mistake, and he couldn't avoid the question that pulsed through his mind like a siren's call:

What have you done, Poe Dameron?

PART II: RENEGADE

CHAPTER 11

"How are you feeling?"

Zorii Wynn's words cut through the silence of the camp, the solid black that coated the Outer Rim planet Quintil's cloudy sky, giving her young voice an ethereal, distant quality.

They'd come to the frigid rock under mysterious circumstances. Vigilch, who was snoring in his sleepsack on the edge of their rudimentary camp, had shared little of their mission with Zorii and Poe—which Poe assumed was by design. He was the new kid, he realized, and Zorii—for all her experience and passion—was at the bottom of the crew's hierarchy. Poe had piloted the *Ragged Claw* onto the planet as covertly as possible, unsure as to why they were being so secretive—especially when the planet they were approaching seemed lifeless. But upon landing, Vigilch had been clear with Poe and the rest of the team: They would set out on their mission in the morning. Be ready. No questions.

"Feeling?" Poe asked. "What do you mean?"

He heard Zorii's dry chuckle but couldn't see

her—though he knew she was nearby, if not next to him. They'd set up their camp in the dark, the only light coming from the white, snow-coated ground. A light that was long gone, the last flickers of Quintil's sun a distant memory.

"Not everything is doublespeak, Poe," she said, keeping her voice to a low whisper. "Even in our business. I mean, how are you doing?"

"I'm good, I'm great," Poe said, reflexively.

The truth was very different. It had been a few weeks since he'd piloted the *Claw* off Yavin 4 and left his life behind. If he was being honest with himself, he was still reeling from the move—one born of impetus and emotion but fraught with real, concrete consequences Poe was not yet ready to accept.

His early days with the Spice Runners had added details to the little Poe had known about the group before their encounter on Yavin 4. Though he wasn't an expert, he'd learned a fair share about them, and from where they'd sprung. The collapse of the Empire had created a seismic shake-up in the galactic criminal underworld. The battle for Kessel spice had become chaotic, with various gangs vying for a hold on the market. Processing terminals like Obah Diah and Formos that had once boasted Imperial Mining Guild protection were now easy targets—and forced to fend for themselves. Enter the Spice Runners of Kijimi.

They specialized in striking and seizing transport ships that managed to emerge from the chaos of the spice trade. Over time, the band of spice runners worked out their own, independent partnership with the mine operators, becoming an exclusive pipeline for Kessel spice that reached all the way to Kijimi, and was still growing.

A dry laugh pulled Poe back to the moment.

"You're a liar," Zorii said. Poe heard a rustling sound. She was rolling over, turning her back to him.

"Why do you do this?" Poe asked, unsure where the words came from. "Why'd you join the Spice Runners?"

Poe was only sure that he felt a longing, a need to connect with someone other than himself. The Yavin 4 settlement was relatively small and consisted mostly of professionals, traders, and New Republic officials—in short, not a lot of people Poe's age. It had become normal to Poe to not have anyone his age to talk to, so much so that he didn't really think on it much until now, as he got to know Zorii. That longing came into focus as he sat alone in the freezing darkness of a strange world he'd never heard of until a few hours before.

"I asked you first," she said, her voice muffled by her sleepsack.

"Didn't realize we were having a formal debate," Poe said, a spark of defiance in his voice. "Why don't you tell me, then? How am I feeling?"

Zorii rolled back over. He couldn't see her but knew her eyes were on him.

"That's easy. You miss your family," she said. It wasn't a question. She was right. "You don't trust anyone. You're questioning whether you did the right thing. You're homesick, too."

"It was time for me to go," Poe said, his defenses still up. "I needed a change."

"Those two things can exist at the same time," Zorii said. "You can love your family and still want to be far from them."

"Yeah?" he asked. "Sounds like you're talking from personal experience."

Zorii waited a moment before responding, her words coming out methodically.

"My life . . . is complicated," she said. "But yes, I love my family. My mother. I just don't see them often. It's been a long time. That's okay."

"What are they like?"

"Difficult," Zorii said, her tone flat. "My mother in particular. They have big expectations. I have a lot to live up to. It's . . . hard. I try not to think about it all the time. What about you? What are your parents like?"

"My parents were . . . well, my mom is gone," Poe said, straining to find the right words.

"Oh," Zorii said. "I'm sorry. . . . I didn't mean—"

"No, it's fine," Poe said. "It's been a while."

"That can't help much," Zorii said, her words pensive and lingering. "She's your mother."

"They're good people. They fought for the rebellion," Poe said. "My dad, he's tough. Very set in his ways. He cares for me, but . . . almost too much. Does that make sense?"

"It does," she said. "Perfectly."

"I had to leave Yavin. I had to try something else," Poe said. He felt lighter—as if an anchor had been lifted from his chest. "But I know he's hurt. He'd strangle me if he saw me."

Zorii laughed—a free, musical sound that seemed at odds with the stoic, steely exterior Poe had come to know. He liked the sound.

"I know what that's like," she said.

"Yeah?"

"Yes," she said. "And it's nice to know I'm not . . . well, I'm not alone here."

"Yeah," Poe said. "I don't know if I could keep going without someone to talk to."

"Good," Zorii said. "Now you're stuck with me."

"There are worse fates in the galaxy, I guess."

"I dunno," she said with a quick laugh.

After a few moments of silence, she spoke again.

"Look—don't worry so much, Poe," she said. He imagined her wide eyes locked on his and felt a warm comfort wash over him. "Get some sleep. It sounds like tomorrow will be a busy day. You'll be fine."

"Is that a promise?"

"Yes," she said, the humor in her voice gone. "I promise."

Poe wasn't sure why he reached his hand out into the darkness. He didn't know Zorii Wynn. But he didn't know anyone in his life, not anymore. And of the people he'd come into contact with since leaving Yavin 4's orbit, she'd been the only member of their ragtag group to show any speck of concern for his well-being. Part of it was their lot—they were both inexperienced and new to the Spice Runners organization, so it made sense for them to be working together, handling the grunt work, comparing notes. But Poe felt like there was something else there. A kinship he couldn't yet wrap his head around but still managed to take comfort in. Poe Dameron needed a friend, and Zorii Wynn was the closest thing to that.

He felt a soft hand grip his, their fingers interlacing naturally. Her palm was warm, which was nice on his cold fingers. It seemed natural and intimate, but still new and exciting. A crackle of nervous energy shot up his arm. He leaned his head back and looked up into the black sky.

For the first time since he'd boarded the *Ragged Claw*, he felt at peace.

It would be quite a while before he felt that way again.

"No more questions," Vigilch barked. "That's all you need to know. Now find that wreckage so we can get off this planet."

The gruff Klatooinian stormed off toward the *Claw*, leaving Poe and Zorii to exchange glances. Poe could feel Gen Tri and Marinda Gan watching them from a few meters away. It was barely morning—the Quintilian sun just peeking through the dense clouds that coated the entirety of the ice planet—but they'd been up for some time. Vigilch had roused them each with a rough shove, shouting orders and quickly shutting down the makeshift camp they'd created upon landing. The life of a spice runner was anything but luxurious, Poe had soon realized.

"Why do we need to find this ship?" Poe asked as he followed Zorii toward the edge of their encampment. "I mean, would it kill the guy to give us a little more info here?"

"He gave us what we need to know," Zorii said, not looking at Poe as she walked briskly toward a densely forested area. "Are you ready?"

"Do I have a choice?"

"Not really," she said, a light smile on her face as she turned to look at him.

"Then I'm ready."

Poe wasn't sure if the plan—or orders—Vigilch had shared with them was actually simple or just exceedingly sparse. It was clear to Poe that their leader was hesitant to give too many details to the runts of the group—either out of fear they'd betray him and the organization or because they just weren't ready to know the plan. Poe hoped it was the latter, but from what little he knew of Vigilch, he had to accept that it was also a bit of the former.

Zorii looked down at a small datapad in her hand and nodded to herself.

"Vigilch said the ship is about a kilometer and a half away," she said. "If these sensors are right, we should cut through this patch of forest and we'll be there."

"But then what?" Poe asked. "We find the ship and pat it gently and say 'Good job'? Where are the others going?"

"You ask too many questions."

"My sincere apologies," Poe said. "It's not like—oh, I don't know—our lives depend on it? This isn't exactly Coruscant or some other Core World. If we get lost, we'll probably end up frozen, and not nearly as tasty as bantha milk ice cream."

Zorii didn't respond, instead moving a few paces ahead of Poe, forcing him to pick up his speed.

"Doesn't it bother you that Vigilch won't even tell us why we're here?"

"He's in charge," Zorii said, her eyes on her datapad. "His orders come from the top. From Zeva."

Zeva—their mysterious, all-knowing leader. The name had come up infrequently during Poe's brief time with the Spice Runners, and when it did, it faded quickly—as if saying the name and lingering over it would prove unlucky or dangerous. It had the desired effect, Poe thought. He grew anxious at every mention.

The trees around them thickened, the dense, wooded forest feeling more claustrophobic the farther they wandered in. The visibility was getting worse, the trees obscuring what little bit of sunlight had cracked through the skies. Whatever sliver of serenity he'd felt the night before—after his chat with Zorii—was gone, overwhelmed by a wave of anxiety and fear he couldn't put his finger on. Vigilch had handed them the datapad and ordered them to find a wayward Spice Runners ship—one they'd been looking for discreetly for months. But then what? Who was on the ship? What were they walking into?

"There," Zorii said, making a sharp left turn. "It's closer than we thought."

The small branches jutting out from the crowded forest scratched and poked at Poe's face and body as he ran to keep up with Zorii, who'd darted off toward a small clearing in the distance. Beyond the opening of the trees, Poe saw a large, metallic pile of . . . wreckage?

They both hit the brakes as they reached the edge of the forest, before stepping into the clearing. Poe turned to Zorii. Her expression was wide-eyed and, if Poe was being honest with himself, fearful.

"What?" Poe asked. "What is it?"

She didn't respond. Poe followed her eyes. The pile of metal and debris that rose into the sky had probably once been a ship, Poe thought, but it would never fly again. The damage was so severe—the pieces so disparate and mangled—he couldn't even guess what kind of class the small cruiser had been. But from Zorii's expression, he could tell this was not what she—or Vigilch—had been expecting.

"Oh, no," she said.

"What happened here?" Poe asked.

Zorii started tapping on her datapad, each one landing harder as her frustration and fear increased.

"Comms are down," she said. "Someone is running interference."

"I'd say that's not great," Poe said.

The blaster shot skated past him, a few centimeters from his face. He jumped back with an embarrassing squeal of fear.

"That is also not great," Poe said.

Zorii drew a blaster, her arm across Poe's chest, motioning for him to step back into the forest. She turned to look at him for a second.

"Where's your blaster?"

"My blaster?"

"You don't have a blaster."

"I do not have a blaster."

She rummaged through her sack and tossed him a small weapon. He held it gingerly, his other hand rubbing the phantom wound on the right side of his face. *So close.*

“Please tell me you know how to use one,” Zorii said as she crouched down, looking past the clearing and toward the wreckage—where the shot had originated.

“I know how to use one.”

Zorii shook her head. She looked back at Poe and motioned toward her hand and blaster.

“You point it, you shoot it,” she said. “Then you do it again. Keep it down if you’re not going to use it. Fire at will if you are. It’s set to stun, so don’t worry too much.”

Poe nodded.

Another wave of fire. Zorii and Poe backed farther into the forest as the blaster shots hit the trees. Whoever was shooting didn’t have a clear line on them. For now.

“They seem upset,” Poe said.

“Not sure it’s a ‘they,’ ” Zorii said. She crept closer to the clearing and sent off a few quick shots—hitting the wreckage around the area where the initial fire had come from.

Zorii stood up. Poe reached for her arm, but she shook it off.

“What are you doing?” Poe asked. “Are you insane?”

She stepped into the clearing, her blaster raised. She spoke in a loud, commanding voice that sent a strange chill through Poe’s entire being.

"If you've hurt him," she said, "you will pay the ultimate price. Show yourself now and we will be merciful."

Her words were followed by a low creaking sound and the appearance of a shadowy, unstable figure—blaster raised in the universal sign of surrender.

Zorii motioned for Poe to follow without looking back. She stepped toward the shape cautiously, blaster drawn and locked on the target. Poe scurried after her, his stance a passable imitation of her own.

As they approached, the figure stepped out of the shadows. A tall, older man—his face worn and beaten but his air regal and commanding. He looked like he'd seen better days, Poe thought. There was a long gash on his forehead that could use a medpac, and his tailored clothes were torn and smeared with dirt and dust. A muted but relieved smile broke out on his face.

"My dear Zorii," the man said. "What a marvelous surprise."

Poe watched as Zorii ran to the older man and embraced him. He hadn't known Zorii Wynn very long—but from that brief period he'd describe her as stoic and distant, with flashes of warmth and a temper. He couldn't say he'd ever seen her truly happy. Not until now. Poe walked toward them, a confused smile on his face.

"How is Babu, Tomasso?" Zorii said. "I miss our charming droidsmith."

"Skilled as ever," Tomasso said. "He asked me to send you his very best."

Zorii responded with a warm smile.

Poe was shaken to his core. Not only was Zorii happy, she was mooning over this Babu character. He tried to ignore what he was feeling—*jealousy?*—but wasn't having much luck.

"Is that how you guys say hi? By shooting?" Poe asked. "Seems off."

The older man stepped back from Zorii and turned his attention to Poe, a quizzical look on his face.

"This is Dameron?" he said. "The pilot that got you out of the Yavin system?"

"That's me, Poe Dameron," Poe said. "I'm right here."

The man nodded but didn't extend a hand. He was tall, his face worn and jagged-looking, coated with a coarse white beard though there were only wisps of hair on his head. Zorii spoke, filling what had almost immediately become an awkward pause.

"Poe, this is Tomasso," she said. "He's one of the

highest ranking members of the Spice Runners of Kijimi. Second only to our leader, Zeva."

She leaned into the man, resting her head on his shoulder. Poe felt another pang of jealousy. Not because he thought there was any romantic connection between the two but because Zorii's affections toward Tomasso seemed so natural and genuine.

"Nice to meet you," Poe said with a nod. "Glad we found you in one piece. Though, I gotta say, I didn't expect to find a top spice runner just hanging out in a pile of scrap metal, all alone."

Tomasso sighed.

"Your humor comes from fear," he said. "We'll fix that."

He turned to Zorii, placing his hands gently on her shoulders.

"Tell me you have a ship," he said. "And that we can get off this tundra immediately."

"The *Claw* is about a kilometer and a half away, through those woods. Vigilch—and Gen Tri and Marinda—are there," she said, pointing toward their camp. "We'll take you. Can you walk?"

"Somewhat," Tomasso said with a wince. "Though, the last few hours have been—problematic. I am happy to see you, though."

Poe scanned the older man's features. Despite the unexpected discovery of his allies, the spice runner seemed concerned, his expression stricken.

"What's wrong?" Poe asked him.

Tomasso looked at Poe, an eyebrow raised slightly.

"You're perceptive," he said before turning to Zorii. "Let me ask, my dear—are you able to contact Vigilch and the team?"

Zorii shook her head.

"Then I fear," Tomasso said, "it might be too late for all of us."

CHAPTER 12

Running was out of the question, Poe realized as they cut through the clearing and into the woods. Tomasso wasn't in tip-top shape, and Poe doubted the older man could keep up with them even at peak form. But as he was reeling from whatever he'd just been through, the best they could hope for was a meaningful jog. Zorii and Poe stood on either side of Tomasso and took turns looking over their shoulders to see what—or who—was on their trail.

"It's the Zualjinn Syndicate, isn't it?" Zorii asked as they paused at a fallen tree, taking turns climbing over it. "That's the only thing that makes sense."

"You are correct, Zorii," Tomasso said. He didn't seem out of breath, to Poe's surprise. Perhaps there was more to the aging criminal than he'd first thought. "Things got a bit out of hand."

"Who?" Poe asked.

"The Zualjinn are spice runners, too—but not as, well, friendly as our crew," Zorii said, picking up her pace as they made it to the other side of the fallen tree. "They really like shooting over talking."

"I was here on a bit of a diplomatic mission," Tomasso said, taking the lead.

"Oh?" Poe asked. "Pooling our resources and all that?"

"Not exactly," Tomasso said, stopping for a moment. He looked around, then shook his head. Nothing. Whoever was chasing them hadn't made their presence known. "It was a more complicated endeavor."

"Were you successful?" Zorii asked.

"Very much so," Tomasso said. "Too successful, I'd wager."

"You did such a great job that the Zualjinn destroyed your ship and left you for dead?" Poe asked.

"They did seem rather upset I eliminated their high commander, yes," Tomasso said, his tone casual and dismissive. "I guess their expectations were more—conciliatory in nature."

Tomasso's words froze every muscle in Poe's body for a split second. Before he could say anything else, the elder spice runner was motioning for them to continue.

Zorii noticed Poe's blank expression as they continued their brisk walk through the forest. She gripped his arm tightly. When he didn't react to that, she grabbed his face and turned it toward her.

"Poe, look at me," she said. "Are you all right?"

"I—I think so," Poe said. He wasn't all right, though.

He knew that. But there was no time to process it. Not yet.

"Then act like it," she said, letting go and darting ahead.

Tomasso looked at Poe, as if noticing the young pilot for the first time.

"She's a complicated woman," he said. "And this is a complicated world you've entered, my friend. Best to keep that in mind."

Poe nodded. He wasn't sure what kind of response the older pirate wanted. But he was spared from having to give one. As they neared the end of the stretch of trees and what should have been their camp, they were startled by the violent sound of blasters—forcing them to approach with greater caution. When they entered the clearing, they were met not by their allies, waiting for them to board the *Claw* and escape—but by a bloody firefight.

Poe couldn't make out what was going on—not the full picture. But he did see enough to know their side was losing. The Zualjinn—or the people Poe presumed were the Zualjinn—were tall, spindly figures covered in dark, tattered rags and tunics, their faces hidden by faded silver helmets. And there were a lot of them—at least a dozen—each armed with a blaster rifle and firing at will.

Huddled next to the *Claw* were Vigilch, Gen Tri, and Marinda Gan—returning fire as best they could but clearly outnumbered and stalling for time. Poe started to run toward his teammates but was stopped by Tomasso—his arm blocking the way.

"They haven't noticed us yet," Tomasso said, looking from Poe to Zorii. "That gives us an advantage. A slight one."

Zorii nodded, her blaster ready.

"The forest winds around the clearing," she said, motioning toward the expansive stretch of trees and woods.

"We go around and blindside them," Poe said, picking up on her suggestion.

"And we pick them off," Tomasso said with a nod. "Zorii—you take their left flank with young Poe. I will approach from the other side."

Zorii started to move almost immediately, leaving Poe a half step behind as Tomasso went in the other direction. Poe's body ached. He was scratched and bruised from the rough terrain, and the weight of what they were spiraling into seemed to be settling on his shoulders, slowing his movements and thoughts. But he had to keep up. Zorii wasn't going to wait, and there was no other way off this frigid planet.

The sound of blaster fire echoed through the dense forest as they retraced their steps, then veered right, away from the path that would have led them back to where they'd found Tomasso. Zorii's movements were quick and focused, as if she'd run through the snow-caked terrain a thousand times instead of just one. Poe did his best to match Zorii's pace. They stopped about a meter from the rear side of the *Claw*, the battle still raging.

"You knew we were coming for him," Poe said.

"What?"

"Tomasso," Poe said. "You knew that's why we were here."

Zorii didn't answer. She turned her attention to the Zualjinn spice runners closing in on the *Claw*.

"We're never going to outblast them," she said.

Poe started to respond, but Zorii cut him off.

"Drop it, Poe," she said. "Yes, it's true—I knew that's why we were here. But now isn't the time to complain about not being looped in. We need to save our ship—and our crew. We need a distraction."

Poe picked up his blaster and pointed it at Zorii with a smile.

"I think I've got one."

"Hey, hey, guys?" Poe's voice sliced through the sounds of blaster fire and battle.

The handful of Zualjinn Syndicate members turned to

face the two figures stepping out of the forest—one with a blaster pointed at the head of the other.

"You will not believe what I found running around in those woods back there," Poe said, motioning his head toward Zorii, who sported a defiant expression. Poe's blaster rested calmly on the side of her head, his other arm wrapped around her neck.

"Identify yourself, stranger," one of the Zualjinn said.

The various etchings and engravings on his helmet made it different from the blank headgear the others wore. *The leader*, Poe thought.

"Poe—what are you doing?" Vigilch screamed across the clearing, the spice runner's voice booming over the whipping wind. "Have you gone mad?"

"Just playin' the averages, pal, sorry," Poe said with a shrug. "This spice runner thing isn't for me." A voice in the back of his head observed that he was in fact telling the truth with those last words, but he ignored it. "And hey, I think our friends here in the winter gear might be able to get me on a ship back home. Right, guys? I mean, I know where Tomasso is. That's who you're after?"

Zorii struggled in Poe's grasp, his arm tightening and pulling her closer. He brought his mouth close to her ear for a moment.

"The elbow to my stomach was a bit too real," Poe said.

"Just playing my part," Zorii said through gritted teeth as she tried to pull herself from Poe's grasp.

The lead Zualjinn stepped toward Poe, blaster rifle trained on them.

"Your man, Tomasso, betrayed our trust," he said. "The Zualjinn Syndicate will not be fooled twice."

He motioned toward Poe and Zorii with his free arm and the Zualjinn soldiers shifted their attention from the cornered Spice Runners to Poe. Poe, pulling Zorii with him, took a few cautious steps back.

"I get it, I get it, you've been burned before," Poe said. "But I'm your path to getting your hands on Tomasso and evening the odds, all right? I need a way out of this whole spice runner thing, and—"

"Enough," the lead Zualjinn said, his voice firm. The Zualjinn Syndicate was not known as a diplomatic organization, Zorii had told Poe. They tended to shoot first, then shoot again.

The leader stepped closer to Poe and Zorii. Out of the corner of Poe's eye, he saw motion near the *Claw*'s boarding ramp. *Just a few more moments*, he thought.

The Zualjinn leader stepped closer to Poe, their faces centimeters apart. Poe could see past the syndicate member's helmet to his scarred humanoid face—red eyes glowing in the darkness.

"You think this is some kind of game, boy?" he said. "You can just have a laugh and save the day?"

Poe felt the blaster rifle press into his midsection. Zorii wasn't squirming anymore. She'd stepped away from Poe now that their ruse had been revealed. Their eyes met briefly and her expression screamed, *What now?*

The other Zualjinn soldiers were making their way toward Poe and Zorii, weapons drawn. Poe saw a small contingent of three or four still stationed near Vigilch, Marinda Gan, and Gen Tri. He didn't hear any blasting—so they were either dead or disabled. Poe hoped for the latter.

The thought of his new comrades dying suddenly stuck with Poe and tapped into a greater, darker feeling—a sense that he was in way over his head—and the thrill of hopping aboard a strange ship to explore the galaxy was being replaced by a much more dangerous reality.

"Answer me," the leader spat, poking Poe with his weapon again, spittle flying out of his helmet. "Or will I have to teach you how to truly fear us?"

Poe waited another beat. Surely Tomasso had reached the *Claw* by now, he thought.

"He didn't make it," Zorii said, a whispered defeat only Poe could here.

"I don't think you need to teach me," Poe said, trying to step away. His back slammed into another Zualjinn gunman, who grunted in response. Poe raised his hands. "All right, all right, you got me—don't I get some kind of pass for creativity?"

The Zualjinn leader raised the handle of his rifle to swing at Poe—but before he could complete the action, a commotion behind him drew his attention. He spun around. Poe and Zorii turned, as well. Something was happening on the *Claw*. A shock of hope shot through Poe—then faded as quickly as it had appeared. As he watched—a Zualjinn soldier stepped down from the *Claw* dragging an unwilling figure with him. The defiant figure was bloodied and beaten. It took Poe a moment to look past the bruising and recognize the man who'd been on the wrong side of the Zualjinn.

"Tomasso," Zorii said. "No . . ."

The Zualjinn leader turned around to face Zorii and Poe. Even with the helmet covering most of his face, Poe was certain the syndicate member was smiling.

"A valiant effort, but a failed one," he said before waving an arm toward the bulk of his men. "Gather them up. We got what we came for."

The order was followed by a series of loud, rage-fueled cheers.

Poe looked at Zorii.

"That can't be good."

CHAPTER 13

"That was a foolish ruse, Dameron," Vigilch said, his voice seething with anger. "You're not invincible, boy. Now look at us."

Vigilch swung his large tan arm across the small holding cell. The whole team was packed into the fetid, small space—with only one seat in the far corner, which had been reserved for the ailing Tomasso. The Zualjinn had not been gentle with the high-ranking spice runner, and Poe imagined whatever final fate they had in mind for them would be even worse.

"You really think they would've been much kinder to us if I hadn't tried something?" Poe said. He was tired. Weary. He'd taken a risk, sure—but he wasn't sure he'd had much choice. "It didn't look like you three were doing much else aside from getting shot at."

"Your impudence doesn't become you," Gen Tri said, their voice hollow. They stood next to Tomasso, who was hunched in the small chair, hands clutching his midsection. "Remember that you are but a novice in our ways. This is not some colonial game."

Poe ignored Gen Tri's jab and walked toward the opposite side of the small room, his back to the rest of the group. They'd been in the cell—which seemed more like a half-finished structure or cave, in terms of technology and amenities—for a few hours at least. Though it certainly felt like longer. They were all bruised or injured in some way. A few Zualjinn guards stood sentry outside of the room's single doorway. After multiple attempts to communicate with the guards, Poe learned they weren't keen on talking.

"He did the right thing," Zorii said. "You all know that."

Poe turned around. Zorii was standing behind him, facing the group. Her fists were clenched and she looked like a cornered, feral tooka cat. To Poe's surprise, the group seemed taken aback. Why were they so passive with her? Wasn't Zorii as low on the Spice Runners ladder as Poe?

"You were outnumbered, and it was only a matter of time before the Zualjinn took us all prisoner," she continued. "Was Poe's plan perfect? Of course not. But did it buy us some time? Yes. You should be praising him. Instead, you're taking out the anger you feel over being captured on him, when you should really turn it on yourselves. He's been a spice runner for less than a month. What's your excuse?"

Marinda Gan broke the awkward silence, her posture defiant.

"This all means nothing if we die on this planet," she said. "They have our weapons. They have our ship. We're locked up. What now? Do you have another great idea, little Poe?"

Poe had tried to be patient, to be aware of his role with the Spice Runners—in short, undefined and of little importance—but he'd had enough. If he was going to die there, on a frozen planet on the fringes of the galaxy, surrounded by strangers—*criminals!*—with little chance of escape, he was going to defend himself at least.

He opened his mouth to speak but fell silent. Tomasso's hand was raised slightly, not so much a call for attention as an alert to the group.

"Let's discuss this later," Tomasso said, his voice sounding haggard and frail. "Now is not the time."

"Then when?" Marinda Gan said, defiant. "Do you think we'll even be getting out of here alive? You're insane, old man."

Tomasso closed his eyes, as if he was fighting off a painful headache. Zorii clutched Poe's hand in hers as the old pirate spoke.

"Oh, I think we'll be out of here soon," Tomasso said, a soft smile appearing on his face. "Imminently, even."

Before Poe could think to look at Zorii, the entire room shook as a massive explosion rocked the building.

Poe tried to open his eyes. He was dizzy. Every part of his body felt heavy, as if weighed down by shackles.

When he did manage to get his eyes open, they stung from dust and debris. He could see Zorii looking down on him, her own eyes awash with worry.

"Poe, get up—you have to try to move," she said. He felt someone behind him, firm hands sliding under his arms and lifting him.

"This is our chance. We have to go."

It was Vigilch. He started to remember. The Zualjinn. The cell. An explosion. But there were more people in the space—or what used to be the space—three Kyuzo in particular he hadn't seen before. The shortest of the three stepped forward.

"We've carved out a path to your ship, but we don't have much time," she said, looking at Tomasso, who seemed refreshed somehow.

"Thank you, Zatticha," Tomasso said as the Kyuzo spun around and made their way out of the destroyed holding cell. "Zorii, can he walk?"

"I—I think . . ." she started.

"I'm fine," Poe said, wincing as he stepped forward, trying his best to hide it. Vigilch, Marinda Gan, and Gen Tri exited next, with Zorii, Tomasso, and Poe not far behind.

As he hobbled out of the wreckage, Poe saw a number of fallen Zualjinn—some unconscious, others much worse off, their orange blood standing out against the pristine Quintil snow. It took him a second to realize what he was seeing at first, but it soon sent him into a dizzy spell he had to strain to fight off.

"Are you all right?" Zorii asked, trying to keep Poe steady. "We have to go. We don't have much time."

"Yeah, I'm fine—don't worry," Poe lied. The look on Zorii's face told him she could see through his bravado. "Let's go."

She wrapped an arm around Poe's shoulders and led him into the snow-coated expanse.

"I've got you, Poe Dameron."

CHAPTER 14

"We've got company, folks," Poe said, scanning the *Ragged Claw*'s display at his station. He squinted, trying to focus despite the throbbing pain in his forehead. "And they don't seem happy."

"Three ships—Zualjinn," Marinda Gan said at her terminal behind Poe and Zorii. "Coming in hot."

The Twi'lek mercenary's eyes were locked on Vigilch, who despite being below Tomasso in the Spice Runners of Kijimi hierarchy, was still the captain of the ship—at least in her view.

The Zualjinn ships were small and fast—they'd quickly overcome whatever lead the *Claw* had gained through the element of surprise.

"If they catch us, we're in real trouble," Zorii said as she tapped a few buttons on her terminal. "Can we jump yet?"

"Doesn't matter," Marinda said, her voice booming across the bridge. "Prelim scans show we've got a tracker on us. They'll follow us all over the galaxy as long as this thing's working."

Poe shook his head.

"Tracker?" Poe asked, turning to Zorii. "How'd that happen?"

"It's basic protocol when you capture a ship you think might make a hasty exit—like we're doing here," Zorii said, not looking up from her terminal. "They probably placed it while we were held prisoner."

"So we can't jump?" Poe asked, his mind racing through the few options the *Claw* had left. He felt wrecked—his body still recovering from the explosion that got them free of the Zualjinn. His reflexes felt sluggish. He had to get it together, or risk hurting their chances of survival. "We're stuck here?"

"We could, sure, but they'll be right behind us," Zorii said. "It'd only delay the inevitable. We either turn around and fight, or we come up with something else—very fast."

Poe felt Tomasso's hand on his shoulder as the aging spice runner looked past him. The man's slow, steady breathing seemed out of place in such a tense moment, but Poe found a bit of solace in it.

"We will not have the benefit of our Kyuzo comrades if we're captured again," Tomasso said. "It was sheer luck they were nearby when I sent out my distress call. Even luckier they owed me a favor. But I think there's a solution here."

"I'm all ears," Poe said, his eyebrows popping up in anticipation. "Because it doesn't feel like we have much time."

Tomasso turned to Marinda. Unlike the fiery Twi'lek, the old pirate gave off an air of ease and serenity that felt almost jarring under the circumstances.

"Any word on the tracker?"

"Still trying to pin it down," Marinda Gan said, shaking her head. "It's going to be a moment."

"They're firing on us," Gen Tri said. They hovered behind Vigilch and didn't have a set terminal. Poe wasn't really sure how they were getting the information—but the ship's sudden lurch forward confirmed it. Poe braced himself as the ship spun out.

"Gonna level out in a second," Poe said, trying his best to pull the ship out of its tailspin. "Hyperdrive's still intact, but shields are acting moody. All suggestions welcome, folks."

"Return fire," Vigilch said, slamming his fist on his seat. It was both an act of defiant rage and frustration. Everyone was coming up short.

Poe watched as Zorii tapped a few keys on her display, starting a futile return volley. Her expression was blank, but Poe could sense a growing resignation among the crew.

"Tomasso, what's the plan here? You said you had a

solution?" Poe asked. His words came out fast and sharp. Time was running out. "What've you got?"

"Are you familiar with hyperspace skipping, Poe Dameron?" Tomasso asked.

Poe almost said yes, scared of seeming ignorant in front of Tomasso. But now wasn't the time to protect his ego.

"No, but if it's something I can learn in the next ten seconds, I'm open to it," Poe said, turning to his terminal briefly to veer around an unexpected wave of debris. "What can I do?"

"Zorii?" Tomasso asked, looking toward the other terminal. "You probably know the specifics better than I do."

"It's risky," Zorii said, her voice grim. "But it can buy us some time until Marinda can pinpoint that tracker. Basically, we hyperspace jump along a series of preset coordinates. They're supposed to seem random to the ships on our tail, but they're not. We're dragging the Zualjinn along with us, to dangerous places we know—"

"And they don't—so they get jammed up and we can keep running," Poe said with a nod. "That's how we shake them off. Got it."

"That's the idea," Tomasso said. "At the very least, it buys us some time to track down and dismantle this cursed device."

"Can you do it, Poe?" Zorii asked, looking at him

directly, the ship shaking around them. "It won't work without a good pilot. It's going to be even harder for you—since you don't know what's waiting for us at these locations."

"I've got this, don't worry about me," Poe said, the shrug of his shoulder confident and flip. But he knew very well he didn't have a handle on it. Not yet. But that was something he'd have to work out on his own. "Let's go."

"How hard did you get hit on the head, pup?" Vigilch said, stepping toward the front of the ship and interrupting Poe. "This is not a time for stupid bravado."

"Leave him be, Vigilch," Tomasso said, stepping toward Poe, subtly telling the Klatooinian to back off with a simple movement. "It's Poe's moment. We haven't much time."

"I'm sending you the locations through the navicomputer," Zorii said, glancing at Poe. "That's your road map—wish I had more info I could give you. Have you done anything like this before?"

"Not, well—not directly, no," Poe stammered. He felt the entire crew's eyes on him. "But I'll do my best."

"Even with the coordinates Zorii is sending to you, Poe, this is not a simple matter of punching them in and moving on to the next location," Tomasso said, keeping his voice calm. "As you've surely guessed by now. We need you to not only get us to each jump, but get us *through* them—surviving whatever unexpected hurdles appear, in the hopes that our pursuers are not as . . . adept as you are."

"Get me the path and I'll get us through it," Poe said, trying to sound confident. He wasn't sure if he succeeded.

The ship shook again—reeling from another flurry of fire. Poe gripped the sides of his terminal to stay in place. He felt a wave of dizziness wash over him, residual damage from their escape. He winced, trying to push himself past the sensation and focus on the job in front of him. He spun his seat around and looked at Vigilch and Tomasso, who were still recovering their footing.

"Okay, I've got the coordinates. If we're gonna do something, we need to do it now," Poe said. "Marinda, any update on that tracker?"

"I've located it, but that's only half the battle," she said. "We need to dismantle it. The Zualjinn are known for their impenetrable tech."

"Gen Tri, help Marinda with the tracker—we're dead no matter how many jumps we take if that thing is still screaming our location to the Zualjinn," Vigilch said through gritted teeth. "We need more time. More time."

"I'll buy you some time, but not a lot," Poe said. Whatever hesitation had been in his voice moments before was gone—replaced with a steely determination he hadn't been sure existed within him. "We good to go, folks?"

Tomasso nodded. That was all Poe needed. He turned back to his terminal. Before he started the ship's first jump, he glanced at Zorii. She was looking back—as if she'd been waiting for him to turn toward her.

"You can do this," she said, no hint of sarcasm or humor in her voice. Zorii Wynn was dead serious. "We're with you. I'm with you."

Poe nodded. He took a few quick breaths. The intel Zorii had sent his way was clear, but very basic—a few locations, few details about where they were going, exactly. What was clear were the risks attached to skipping through hyperspace. A bad jump could leave the *Ragged Claw* in the middle of an asteroid storm or someone else's firefight, even if they knew where they were heading. It would certainly put undue strain on the old ship, raising the potential for the cruiser to literally fall apart mid-jump. But Poe didn't have any alternatives. They had to keep jumping until that tracker was gone.

"Here we go," Poe said.

SHUNT.

The *Ragged Claw* stalled painfully as it came out of hyperspace, the entire ship spinning uncontrollably—a loud, scratching creak emanating from the core of the vessel. Poe scrambled to get a sense of where they were. The power and lights flickered.

"Asteroids, incoming—it's like a wall, not sure how we can—" Zorii said, a frantic undercurrent to her words. "I'm working as fast as I—"

"They're still on us," Marinda Gan said. "Incoming."

"No progress on the tracker," Gen Tri said, their voice sounding like a distant echo. "We haven't had enough time to tinker with the device. It's—"

Poe didn't wait for more.

SHUNT.

The ship was stalling, Poe realized—stopping, starting, groaning with each command. The display was dark, too, everyone desperately tapping their terminals to figure out where the systems stood—and what was in store.

"Any sign of the Zualjinn?" Poe said, yelling across the screeching and thumping sounds that were part of the vessel's new, anguished vocabulary. "If we don't have the tracker settled, I think we can get a few more jumps out of this bucket of—"

The display screen crackled to life, and what Poe saw wasn't open space—there was no black background flecked with the white of distant planets and stars. No, they were speeding into something red and gaping. And very much alive.

"We're . . . we're somewhere along the Davezra Way, I know that much," Zorii said, trying her best to get information out of the ship's uncooperative computers. "But . . . I'm having trouble finding a landmark."

"Not where," Gen Tri said. They almost floated toward Zorii's terminal. "But what."

"Explain yourself, Gen Tri," Vigilch said, also on his feet. "There's no time for smoke and mirrors here. I need—"

Then it roared, baring a gigantic set of sharp, blood-coated teeth to accompany its nightmarish visage.

"What is *that*?" Poe asked, his own mouth agape. "What *is* that?"

He swerved the *Claw* out of the path of the creature's mouth, and the change in perspective showed him they were close to the surface of a planetoid, buildings and structures littering the landscape as the mammoth, slithering, scaly creature pivoted to keep pace with the ship. The monster—long, large, and terrifying—possessed a graceful quality, almost as if it was swimming underwater rather than flying through space after their damaged ship.

"A garsath," Vigilch spat, apparently familiar with the

monster. "They're massive. Bloodthirsty. It's indestructible—we have to—"

"It's right behind us," Zorii noted, shaking her head. "And I don't think we lost the Zualjinn—"

"I see them," Poe said. The three ships seemed no worse for wear, even after the jumps—two on their left and another lagging behind on the right. Poe shifted the *Claw*, aiming toward the rampaging creature.

"How's that tracker coming along, Marinda? Really hoping you'll say 'It's off, Poe, don't worry,'" Poe said, sounding urgent and a bit desperate. "Not that many jumps left on this path, in case you needed added motivation."

"We've made some progress," Marinda Gan said, tapping at her terminal angrily. "But not enough. We're only getting past the initial firewall."

"Not ideal, not ideal," Poe said, shifting the *Claw*'s course drastically. The ship shook as it veered right. "I'll see what I can do."

"We're heading . . . toward the beast?" Zorii asked.

Poe didn't answer. The ship chugged forward, straining at the uptick in speed. He heard his crewmates talking around him—some yelling, some questioning—but pushed the sounds away. All he could register was the garsath's wide, hungry mouth—waiting for the *Claw* to reach it.

As the ship reached the creature, Poe pulled up—hard.

The *Claw* shrieked—the bottom of the vessel scraping against the monster's face. Then there was a loud crash as the pursuing Zualjinn ship exploded, sending the garsath spinning backward.

SHUNT.

Darkness. Screaming. A wave of fire from an unknown ship. The smell of rust and blood.

"Tracker," Poe said, the word sounding more like a cough. He was seeing double for a moment. "Report?"

Poe looked back and saw Marinda Gan writhing on the floor, Gen Tri standing over her. The ship was an array of moving shapes and flickering lights.

"We're almost there," they said with some hesitation. It didn't inspire much confidence in Poe. "But we need—"

"More time, more time, yup, I get it," Poe said, nodding to himself as he tried to pull the ship back under his control, the multiple jumps taking a massive toll on its instrumentation. "We got one more jump on this path and then we're out of luck. Any idea where those ships are?"

"One ship gone, probably providing a choking hazard for the garsath," Zorii said dryly. "But there are still two right behind us—and they don't seem as affected by the jumps as we've been."

"Meaning they can fly and shoot," Poe said incredulously. "Great."

"Can we take another attack, Zorii?" Vigilch spat. "Where do we stand?"

"We risk losing vital systems if we take another hit or two," Zorii said grimly. "Our only hope is to—"

"On it," Poe said. He braced himself. They were running out of options.

SHUNT.

"—think we cracked the track—"

"One of the Zualjinn ships just exploded—"

"I can't breathe. . . . I can't . . ."

"Poe? Poe? We need to get—"

Poe tried to shake off the cacophony of sounds, tried to focus on his display. They were out of options. The path had been spent. All the programmed locations hit. The ship was barely holding together. He couldn't tell which crew members were still upright, much less alive.

"Report? Report?" Poe said, screaming the last word. "Where's that damn tracker?"

"We're almost there—it's almost disabled. Just . . . a few more moments . . ."

It was Marinda Gan, sounding shaky and tired. Poe didn't dare turn around.

"The last Zualjinn ship is coming in fast, it seems unaffected," Zorii said. "They're targeting us."

Poe could feel her eyes on him. They both knew the score. If they took another jump, it'd be a complete gamble. If the tracker wasn't disabled now or soon, the Zualjinn would be on them, and the *Claw* might not be able to jump—or move—again.

Poe picked the jump location, figuring if he was going to risk everything, he might as well gamble big. As the ship lurched into the skip, he thought he heard Marinda Gan scream something.

"All in," Poe whispered to himself.

SHUNT.

Poe's eyes fluttered open. He sat up, the pressure pushing him back into his seat. The ship was moving. Fast. He felt his forehead. Blood. He looked around. Zorii was climbing back into her seat, her movements slow, stiff, and confused. Vigilch was on the floor, clutching his stomach. Tomasso was near the back of the bridge, helping Gen Tri to their feet. He couldn't figure out where Marinda Gan had gone.

The terminal readings were off the charts. The ship was shaking, its shields were gone, and they had no firepower. He knew that the dizziness he was feeling couldn't make the world around him move the way it was. They were in complete free fall.

But falling where?

The only sound was the high-pitched drone of the ship as it tumbled toward the surface. Poe reached for the controls and tried to pull the ship up. It was working—but not fast enough. In a few moments, they'd be crashing directly into the ground of some unknown wasteland.

"We're not going to make it," Gen Tri said, their words hanging over Poe like some kind of toxic cloud. Poe's throat tightened as they continued to speak. "It's been truly an—"

"Hit the brakes on the eulogies, Gen Tri," Poe said, tapping the ship's thrusters—getting more of a response than he expected. While logic would suggest he not accelerate into their demise, Poe had angled the ship enough that a little push was just what he needed. "Zorii, can you blast the ground? Create a streak—a runway of some kind?"

"What does that even mean?" Vigilch said, groaning slightly as he got to his feet.

Zorii ignored their leader. She understood what Poe meant. Now all they needed was for it to work. The gravity pull got heavier—pushing everything back as the *Claw* propelled toward the lush surface of the planet. The green ground fell apart as the ship got closer—firepower from the *Claw*'s blasters creating a path of destruction that, if

Poe's idea was right, would soften the impact on the bottom of the ship. If that was how it all played, he thought.

"Thruster power dwindling," Zorii said. "Hope you got the angle you wanted, because we don't have much juice left."

Poe nodded. He allowed himself a split second to appreciate that Zorii, at least, understood what he was trying to do. She looked at Poe and gave him a brief nod, as if to say, *We tried*. Poe cracked a small smile, but that was all he could spare. The *Claw* was at an odd angle, and even with the added push of the thrusters, it still seemed like it was on a deadly collision course with the rock and dirt of the planet. He pulled up again, trying to use whatever power the ship had over itself to their advantage.

"Brace for impact," Tomasso said, standing next to Gen Tri, his voice emotionless and remote. "Hold on to what—"

The ship crashed, slamming into the ground at an odd angle—sending everyone in different directions. Poe shot from his seat, hurtling toward the ship's back wall. The last thing he remembered was the sight of Zorii's hand, reaching out to him—trying to keep him close. But then the screams and sounds went quiet, the shaking stopped, and Poe's vision went black.

Poe was the first one to wake up.

He got to his feet slowly. His right arm ached and his mouth tasted coppery and dry. The *Ragged Claw* barely resembled a ship—the bridge was a mess of exposed wires, smoke, electrical sparks, and metal plating. Tomasso and Vigilch were slumped together at odd angles in a far corner. Poe could also see Gen Tri hunched over the nearest terminal, Marinda Gan at their feet. But he ran to Zorii first.

She was crumpled on the floor about a meter from her station, her face covered in dust and dirt, a deep cut down her right arm. But she was breathing. Poe crouched down and patted her cheek gently. She didn't respond. He gripped her shoulders and leaned in.

"Zorii? You there, Zorii?" Poe said, his tone growing more desperate the more time passed without a response. "C'mon, Zorii—"

Her eyes opened—surprise and fear jolting her awake. She clutched Poe's armed and looked around, then reached for her temples.

"Poe . . . what . . . what happened?"

"We made it. The tracker was disabled," Tomasso said

across the bridge, cautiously limping toward a terminal for balance. "We're alive."

"We're not only alive . . ." Marinda Gan said as she scanned a readout from her station. "We're on Sorgan. Poe's last jump brought us here. . . . Quite the risk there, flyboy."

"Any sign of the Zualjinn?" Gen Tri asked. "If we brought them here . . ."

"Nothing," Marinda Gan said. "If we're lucky, they were destroyed. Either way, they didn't follow us here. They couldn't."

Poe looked back and caught the others doing their own versions of Tomasso's climb—slowly regaining their footing, scanning the ship to figure out just how they were still alive.

"Good to see you awake," Poe said, softly patting Zorii's cheek. She shook him off and got to her feet.

"Thanks to you," she said, her gaze steely and focused. "You made a crazy idea work. You are quite the pilot, Poe Dameron."

"Just tried to keep a level head and give us some time to dismantle that tracker," Poe said with a nod. "Though, I'm not sure I ever want to jump like that again . . . if I can help it."

A firm hand landed on his shoulder and pulled him back. Then he was being spun around and brought face to face with Vigilch, who sported a very un-Vigilch grin underneath the cuts and bruises on his face. The burly Klatooinian lifted Poe up, his throaty, haunting laugh echoing through the *Ragged Claw*'s shattered bridge.

"Well done, Poe Dameron," Vigilch said. "Welcome to the Spice Runners of Kijimi."

CHAPTER 15

"Are you sure you spoke to Tomasso about this?"

Poe turned to Zorii and gave her a quick, noncommittal shrug.

"That gives me zero assurances," she said sharply. But Poe could sense the smile on her face, even if he couldn't see it in the pitch-black Sorgan night.

Zorii followed Poe onto the *Ragged Claw*, trying to keep their footfalls light as they boarded the ship. The rest of the team had called it a night, leaving Poe and Zorii up and chatting—as things often went on Sorgan. It'd been a busy few days—spent mostly on tedious, often repetitive tasks: gathering provisions, scouting their next assignment, and training, all while recovering mentally and physically from their frantic hyperspace-jumping escape. They'd just finished up repairs on the *Claw*, and everything about the vessel felt unsteady and unfinished.

"Technically, he just said that, yes, the *Claw* needed a test run—to ensure it was back up to speed," Poe said, sliding into his pilot's seat and flicking a few switches. "So, that feels like tacit approval."

" 'Tacit approval'?" Zorii said, standing behind him, leaning on the back of his seat. He could feel her warm breath on his neck. "Are you a diplomat or a spice runner, Poe?"

"I'm a complex individual," Poe said, glancing back. "Now, hop in."

Poe stood and stepped away from the pilot's seat quickly, motioning with his arm for Zorii to take his place.

"You can't be serious?" Zorii said. "Now? I thought this was—a test flight? Like, practice. I'd watch you and . . ."

"The best way to learn is to do," Poe said, motioning again for Zorii to sit. "That's what my mom always told me."

Zorii took the seat cautiously, keeping her hands on her legs, as if touching the console might send the ship throttling into orbit.

Poe leaned forward, his hand hovering over the terminal.

"You ready?"

"No," she said, her voice dry. "This is very different than just talking about it."

"Zorii, you're extremely sharp. I'd say the sharpest, even," Poe said, their eyes meeting. "We've done all the talking we can. Now, we do."

Zorii nodded and faced the controls. Poe could see

her take a second to assess the situ forward—with confidence and calculat opening sequence of buttons. The ship Her hands jumped a bit at the first sound, imperceptible, and she moved on to the n focus and precision that brought a smile to

The *Claw* shuddered before it began a wob

Poe watched, making minor suggestions eve as Zorii took the ship into orbit. The vast expan dominated the ship's viewscreen, adding to the ee in stark contrast to the frantic bustle and chaos o few times they'd been on the ship together—with th low Spice Runners of Kijimi.

"We could go anywhere," Poe said, resting his han the back of Zorii's seat.

"Is that what you want?"

Zorii's response pulled him back to the present. H leaned over and tapped a button Zorii had overlooked—trying to soften the blow of her mistake by making it seem trivial, his movement slow and slight. It didn't work.

"Damn, can't believe I missed that," she muttered.

"It's fine," Poe said. "You're doing great."

He watched her. Hands on the directional controls, eyes focused on what was in front of her. She was nervous, he could tell, but also locked into the task at hand

nwilling to fail. Zorii Wynn was mysterious in many but her drive and intensity were no secret.

Your mom taught you . . . how to fly?" Zorii said after w moments of silence.

"Yeah, she'd take me up in her A-wing when I was a l," Poe said, trying to keep it light—but already finding himself transported to the past, feeling the warmth of is mother around him, the familiarity of her voice and mell. "Just the basics, you know—a few tricks. She loved o teach. Loved the idea that she'd be able to see me . . ."

His voice trailed off. The words wouldn't come anymore. He swallowed hard and was about to continue. But before he could speak he felt Zorii's hand gripping his.

She let go as abruptly, retaking the ship's controls and moving the *Claw* through an unexpected wave of debris. The execution was solid, if a bit stiff, and Poe was impressed.

"Well done there," Poe said. " I didn't even have to buckle up."

She allowed herself to look back and give Poe a brief but genuine smile.

"Don't want to lose points for being asleep on the job," she said.

Poe let out a short laugh and felt his body loosen up. The muscles seemed to relax for the first time in weeks. He'd needed this. A few minutes of . . . fun. Sometimes

he'd forget that he and Zorii weren't hardened criminals—they were teenagers.

"Where would you want to go?"

"Hm?" Poe responded, too caught up in his own head to register what Zorii was asking.

"You said, 'We could go anywhere,' " Zorii said. "So where would you want to go, Poe Dameron?"

"I—well, I didn't mean—"

"It's fine," Zorii said with a chuckle. "I'm not going to snitch on you to Vigilch or Tomasso. We all have our dreams. Though I am worried . . ."

"Worried?" Poe asked. "About what?"

Zorii tapped at a few of the ship's directional controls before responding, letting Poe simmer for a moment.

"That you'd try to leave without me," she said, not looking back to catch his expression.

Poe started to respond but was interrupted by a warning chime from the *Claw*. Zorii checked the display, then turned to Poe.

"Incoming transmission," she said.

"From where?" Poe asked.

"The surface," she said, checking the readout. "We've been caught."

Poe sighed.

"I guess it wasn't going to last forever," Poe said.

"These moments rarely do," she said.

Zorii flipped a switch, allowing the transmission to play over the ship's speakers. The voice boomed through, the tone resigned but also unsurprised.

"Bring the ship back immediately and I'll forget to mention this to not only your crewmates, but to my own leader," Tomasso said. Poe wasn't sure if he was imagining a slight tinge of humor in the old pirate's voice. "Consider your joyride over."

Before Poe or Zorii could respond, the line went dead.

They looked at each other for a moment, their eyes wide and mouths forced shut—a combination of anxiety and surprise—before bursting into a wave of joyous, uncontrolled laughter.

CHAPTER 16

"What the hell are these things?"

Poe could barely hear Marinda Gan's scream as he tried to dodge another barrage of fire. The ships—small drone-like vehicles that looked more like giant bugs than modes of transport—were everywhere, firing at the *Ragged Claw* from every angle. Poe had managed to minimize some of the damage, but the *Claw* was already hurting, and they were still far from their destination.

It had been about a month since Poe joined the Spice Runners—and much had changed. In the short-term, the group had gotten a new mission from the highest rungs of the Spice Runners of Kijimi's command structure: to locate a female Zabrak mercenary named Ledesmar, who'd absconded with a fleet's worth of ships from the Pyke Syndicate, a fading but still formidable galactic criminal organization. But that wasn't Poe's immediate concern. They'd only scraped together a few days of rest after the Zualjinn affair before they'd had to focus on the next job. The crew was tired, edgy, and under heavy fire.

"It's Moraysian tech," Zorii said, raising her voice to

be heard over the chaos on the ship. Moraysi was a mining system on the edge of the Outer Rim, populated by a race of tan, stout humanoids who were known for their ship-building and inventiveness—but also an ability to actualize their schematics. Thinkers and workers, an honorable, hardworking people, they'd found themselves overrun by groups like the Pykes for the past few generations—forced to use their abilities to arm and equip thieves, bounty hunters, criminal syndicates, and spice runners.

"That cruiser comes equipped with dozens of these—drones?" Zorii continued. "They're automated but can adapt—"

Before Zorii could finish her sentence, the *Claw* was rocked by another volley of laser fire. Vigilch slammed into the main console, a low moan emanating from him as he stood up. He placed a hand on Poe's shoulder to steady himself.

The Pykes had once controlled almost all of the galaxy's raw spice, a staggering accomplishment. But after the Clone Wars and the Galactic Civil War, their influence had sputtered—opening the door for smaller, more vicious groups to try to claim territory. These new fringe groups posed a threat not only to the fading Pyke Syndicate but to the Spice Runners of Kijimi, as well. That meant taking out

Ledesmar—who'd been enslaved by the Pykes and somehow managed to escape with many of the organization's deepest secrets and prime equipment—would be a boon for the Spice Runners.

"Boy, can you handle this?" Vigilch asked, his concern genuine. "Can you get us through these ships?"

"Viggy, don't worry, I got this," Poe said, nodding confidently but very much aware that the sheen of sweat on his forehead sent a different message. He turned to Zorii, who sat in her usual copilot's spot. "Try to scatter the fire. Shoot where you think they're going to be instead of where they are, all right?"

"On it," she said.

Ledesmar's strategy was simple—take the weapons and confidential information she'd siphoned off her captors and strike out on her own. In their current state, the Pyke Syndicate couldn't risk another rising star sucking more of their air. For the Spice Runners, it was less complicated: new competitors had to be dealt with swiftly.

But intel was also valuable, and Ledesmar reportedly had plenty of that. Tomasso, the man who'd served as the main point of contact between Vigilch's crew and the mysterious, shadowy leader behind the Spice Runners, Zeva, had made that abundantly clear. Take her out if they had to, he'd warned, but Zeva would greatly prefer Ledesmar be brought back alive—along with whatever valuable information she held close.

It was that knowledge—collected over years of enslavement—that had helped Ledesmar escape and find her way to the Moraysian fleet of ships, which looked slapdash and beat-up on the outside but boasted power and speed that belied their gnarly exteriors. The command ship loomed large—a clear and present target. But as they had moved closer to the cruiser, the swarm hit, and Poe finally understood what Tomasso had said when he warned, "The fleet can be deceptive. Be ready for anything, Poe Dameron."

Tomasso's absence hung over the group, even though Poe knew the aging pirate preferred to leave the field missions to Vigilch's command. Tomasso had become almost ubiquitous on their small slice of Sorgan, settling in with the crew after the incident with the Zualjinn. He wasn't always there—often disappearing for hours without word—but his influence was ever present. From certain angles, Tomasso looked like he might topple over and die at any second. Other times, Poe felt a great strength radiating from the man. It made sense that he'd be deceptive even in repose—a thief, con artist, and pirate his entire life, a creature built on changing colors. A man wearing an armor of lies.

Vigilch, usually quick to assume the role of leader, deferred to the older man immediately. The lanky, shadowy Gen Tri would often sit with him for hours—their voices hushed and hurried. If anyone got close, they'd go silent and part ways. Tomasso steered clear of Marinda Gan for no clear reason Poe could discern. The young Twi'lek was boisterous and loud, true, but she was part of the team, Poe thought, and he couldn't figure out why the older man would isolate her.

While they were on Sorgan, as the runts of the team, Zorii and Poe got most of the thankless tasks—oiling blasters, charging packs, cooking meals, standing watch—while the rest of the group focused on combat training and strategizing. The time spent doing mindless, repetitive chores gave Poe the opportunity to think—about what he'd done, abandoning Yavin 4 and his family, but mostly about what lay ahead. The adventures he'd have with these people he was starting to consider friends. It was that mirage-like vision that kept him going, a sense of freedom and escape he couldn't explain or quantify but brought him great joy. That reminded him, in some way, of his mother. He wanted to explore. To be free and see what was out there on his own terms. To take chances and to be the person making the call when those things came up. He loved his father and L'ulo. He loved Yavin 4, despite how he'd come to resent it. But it was time to do something else, whether Kes Dameron wanted him to or not. His parents had fought back the Galactic Empire. They'd been essential pieces in a rebellion that toppled an iron claw that gripped the entire known galaxy. It was time for Poe to figure out what *his* role would be. But was it really there, among criminals? Did the adventure and thrill erase the harsh truth—that he was not just consorting with spice runners but had become one? He knew it didn't. He also knew his father would agree.

His father. What was Kes Dameron doing? What did he think? The idea—the *fact*, Poe knew—that his father was spending every waking hour worrying and searching for his son pained Poe. Had the NRSB figured out Poe's ruse? Poe wasn't sure he'd ever find out, or see his father or L'ulo again. The idea didn't sit well with him, and it had begun to ache more, like an unattended toothache, as time passed. It wasn't a coincidence that this painful longing for home—which Poe tried to suppress with enthusiasm for the future—grew as his menial chores increased. After a week or so, it began to grate on him. His interlude showing

Zorii how to fly helped ease his impatience temporarily, but soon enough the feeling returned.

"So this is the life of a spice runner?" Poe had asked at one point as he and Zorii made their way through another Sorgan swamp. He pulled his foot back, brown-green slime coating his pants like a second skin. "Getting eaten alive by whatever bugs live on this hunk of sludge, sweating through the only shirt I own, and mopping the ship every day because Vigilch can't keep his dinner down after a night of drinking?"

Zorii shook her head.

"You don't get it, do you?" she asked, her face smeared with dirt. She'd turned back slightly to look at Poe. She seemed more exhausted than upset—tired of having the same back and forth with him. "There's a way of doing things here. With the Spice Runners. A structure and hierarchy. We work together to get what we want. Some do tasks you think of as 'important.' Others, like us, have to do the rest. It's how we prove ourselves, Poe. It's how we show Tomasso and Vigilch and the rest of the people in charge that we deserve more responsibility and power. We earn our place, we don't inherit it."

Poe shrugged.

"No, I don't get it, okay?" he said. "I showed what I

can do. I got us out of a big jam. Instead of getting handed coordinates to the next thing, I get handed a bucket and a shovel. If I wanted to scoop up garbage and clean up after people, I—"

"Could've done it on Yavin Four. Yes, I get it," Zorii said, walking farther away from Poe, her back to him. She'd heard this sob story too many times. "But you made your choice. You're here now, and it's not going to be easy to go back to your quiet farm life now, is it? You have a taste for adventure. I can see it in your eyes—even here. When you're on that ship, you come alive. You'll never lose that."

"What is your story?" Poe asked, the question escaping before he could really decide if he wanted to ask it again. "You know almost everything about me—I'm an open datafile. But what about you, Zorii? I keep asking. What made you want to join the Spice Runners? Live this life? I mean, this doesn't strike me as a passing hobby for you."

The joke—meant to soften Poe's probing question—didn't land. Zorii froze and faced him, her expression cold.

"That's a story for another time," she said, her words delivered in a practiced monotone, as if read from a well-worn script. She turned and continued their trek. "Don't ask me again."

Poe opened his mouth to respond but found no words. He waited a moment before following Zorii farther into the swampy darkness.

The *Ragged Claw* was rocked by another onslaught of firepower, jarring Poe from his brief daydream. He checked his terminal. Zorii had knocked out a dozen or so of the tiny drones, but it seemed like more were coming from the Moraysian cruiser—angry insects bursting out of their hives, blood in their eyes.

"We have to get to that cruiser," Vigilch said, straining to keep his voice steady. "What are you thinking, Dameron?"

Poe noticed the subtle shift. No longer was he "pup" or "boy." Over the past month, he'd proven enough to their leader that Vigilch was willing to use his name, albeit begrudgingly. Poe tried to stifle a smile, even as laser fire rained down on them.

"I've got a plan."

CHAPTER 17

Sela Trune leaned back in the chair of her makeshift office in the main Yavin 4 Civilian Defense base. She rubbed her forehead, trying in vain to expel the headache that had set up shop in her skull for the past . . . days? Weeks? She'd lost track. Just like she'd lost track of herself. She hadn't planned on being on Yavin 4 this long. But little had gone as she'd hoped since her boots touched the dank ground of the moon's surface. Her hunt for any thread that could lead her to the leadership behind the Spice Runners had brought her here, where a small part of the gang had sought refuge after an impressive haul. But she hadn't moved fast enough. The small crew had managed to kidnap the son of a former rebel Pathfinder, using the boy to force their way off the moon and to who-knows-where. At least that was what they wanted her—and the New Republic—to believe.

Then . . . nothing. There'd been rumblings about a Spice Runners incident on Quintil but little that was quantifiable. Her team had found a member of the Spice Runners dead around the time Dameron's son was supposedly kidnapped—the Ishi Tib named Beke Mon'z, who also happened to be one of Trune's most valuable undercover assets—but little else. Trune still had visions of the small green figure, folded into himself. He had seemed more than dead. He had looked broken and defeated, as if death had been a final, merciful conclusion to a brutal life on the run. But Trune knew she was just speculating and trying to add details to a story that had few facts to support it. The reality was, she didn't know for sure if the Spice Runners had figured out that the Ishi Tib had been funneling intelligence to her, or had killed the pilot for some other, more mundane reason. L'ulo L'ampar had seemed much more definitive in his view. Either way, she wasn't surprised they'd resorted to murder. The Spice Runners were cold-blooded and hungry. They'd do anything if it meant getting a centimeter of real estate, a centimeter of power. While the arrival of the New Republic heralded an era of peace and democracy across the galaxy, Trune knew this was only partly true. There were areas the Republic could not reach, just as there were areas the Empire chose not to reach. Though, if Trune was being honest with herself, there seemed to be more of a problem under the New Republic. Much more of the galaxy was left to fend for itself—dark corners and distant planets and moons that dealt in the trades and violence that had outlasted many a regime.

Trune took a deep breath and opened her eyes. She tried not to dwell on the Spice Runners, tried to treat this like any other assignment, but she knew she was fooling no one. Not even herself. The hunt for the Spice Runners was the definition of personal. The rage that fueled her was unlike anything she'd ever experienced. She remembered the call as if it had just happened. It had been a little over five years earlier. Trune had just left her home planet of Yungbrii—a cold, rocky, and mountainous spot in the Opalok system in the Mid Rim—to join the New Republic Security Bureau. She was eager to serve and do some good in a galaxy that had been drowning in corruption and was still reeling from the Galactic Empire. She'd hungered to leave the cold, sparsely populated, and rough world where she'd been raised to see what else was out there, to experience the worlds and galaxy she'd only dreamt of as a child.

It had been hard. She was close to her mother. Her father was stoic and distant but also had moments of warmth. They didn't understand what their daughter wanted to do at such a young age. They were simple people. They worked their land, they helped their neighbors, they did service. The idea of their daughter leaving home—leaving the planet, even—was foreign and strange to them. Yungbriins were hardworking, not bogged down by the affairs of the worlds around them, unconcerned with galactic battles. But Trune wanted more. Saying goodbye to her parents, with the NRSB ship waiting in the background, had been difficult. But it had been even harder for Trune to crouch down and kiss her younger brother, Gaithel, goodbye. He was barely ten years old—but wise beyond his age. Smart, friendly, thoughtful. Gaithel was everything she was not and would never be. He was bursting with the hope and kindness she wanted to see across the galaxy. She would use him as her guiding light as she tried to bring some good to a universe that had longed for peace.

But then the call came. She'd been on duty for less than a month, still trying to find her way, feeling like a child pretending to be an adult. Despite that, Trune thought she was slowly getting some traction with her group. The work was hard, but she felt challenged—not overwhelmed. Basic training had been immersive, but she felt energized and eager to dive into her career.

Then the call.

She didn't recognize the voice on the other end. She'd never know who the person was, because the message they delivered was so seismic, so destructive to her world, their identity was irrelevant. The exact words were lost, mired in the bloodied visuals and nightmare scenario that flooded her mind's eye as the person spoke. Her parents were gone. Gaithel was gone. Gunned down in a firefight between a group of spice runners trying to find a hideout and her home planet's meager defense force. The skirmish had been quick, the caller said. Trune may have been new then, but she was not a complete novice. She understood what the caller was doing. Trying to soften what was certainly a gigantic tragedy. Later, when she researched the incident on her own, off the clock, she learned the truth.

The skirmish had been anything but quick—more like a massacre. A group of spice runners—she'd later learn they were members of the Kijimi faction and included a Klatooinian named Vigilch—had sought refuge on the planet, on the run from New Republic ships and looking for a place to lay low. They were soon cornered, right on the Trune family farm, and used Trune's mother and father as shields as they tried to escape. The gunfight was loud and bloody. Spice Runners, New Republic officers, and Trune's own family died in the battle. As the dust settled, the Spice Runners managed to escape on a stolen ship—and a New Republic officer was forced to make a call no one should ever have to.

"Do you need some time off?" her supervisor had asked, her eyes welling with tears. "You should go back home. Spend time with people you know."

But that held no interest for Trune. Everything was

gone. She had no family. No home. No, she did not want time off. She wanted vengeance. And she wanted it fast.

But such things don't come together easily, she knew. It was a project that materialized piece by piece as she moved up the ladder in the NRSB. Trune was not only innately talented, she was a quick study—and she climbed the ranks rapidly. She was often surrounded by colleagues and contemporaries a decade older or more. As she worked the case, she fostered connections, informants, spies, and leads that were strewn all over the known galaxy. Scoundrels and gangsters with mysterious loyalties and duplicitous natures that gave her a strong sense of who the Spice Runners of Kijimi were—and, more important, who was in charge. She didn't have all the answers yet. But she would soon. Her spies had been cautiously feeding her intel that was painting a clearer picture by the moment, getting closer to the final bit of intelligence that could make sense of everything. And on that day, she would take a visceral pleasure in choking the life out of the murderous organization's shadowy, vicious leader.

The chime at her door startled her momentarily. She stood up as the entrance to the office slid open to reveal Kes Dameron, looking like he hadn't slept in years, much less the past month.

"Dameron," Trune said with a nod. "Good to see you."

"You know what I'm going to ask you," Dameron said with less force than he'd probably hoped.

"There's no word," Trune said, trying to soften her response just as the New Republic officer had done for her years before. "I will let you know once I hear anything, I promise."

Trune noticed the man's shoulders slump slightly. It wasn't new to her. She'd seen this once-strong man fade into something else. Something lost and desperate. The strong jaw was coated with a thick beard now, the dark, piercing eyes saddled with purple bags underneath. The once flush face gaunt and stretched. He was slowly dying, and Trune was not being fully honest with him. But was the truth worth the life of this proud man? This hero who'd served the Rebellion in its darkest hour?

"Poe is in danger," Dameron said, his jaw clenching as he stepped into the office. "Every minute we spend here, doing nothing—it brings him closer to death. He could be anywhere. He needs help. I know it. I can feel it."

Trune felt a tug inside her. She'd managed to bury that part of her—the feeling, caring part—that showed weakness or empathy. It wouldn't serve her in the career she'd chosen. But this man—who reminded her so much of not only her father but herself, in his stoic, driven demeanor—didn't deserve to live in the darkness. No. Trune was tired of things that lurked in the shadows. It was on her to flush them out with the light.

"Your son is fine," she said, looking up to meet Dameron's gaze. "We have confirmation he's alive."

"He is?" Dameron said, his voice rising in pitch as he clasped Trune's shoulders. "Where? How? When can I see him?"

Trune gently removed Dameron's hands. He pulled back quickly, ashamed by the contact. He shook his head and began to pace around the cramped office.

"Where is he?" he asked. "Where is my son?"

"Your son seems fine, based on my intel," Trune said.

"Fine?" Dameron said, wheeling around. "How can he be fine? He was kidnapped. He's probably—"

"He's one of them, Kes," Trune said, finding it hard to believe her own words. But the facts were there. Her sources didn't lie. It wouldn't benefit them to lie. She knew it was true. And now he would, too.

"What?"

"You heard me," Trune said. "Your son is a spice runner. He's a criminal. Their kidnapping was a ruse to get away, and it worked too damn well. They tricked us."

Kes let out a coarse laugh.

"Are you mad? There's no way Poe would do that—would abandon everything. . . ."

"Really?" Trune said, trying to keep her tone soft and humble, trying to lessen the blow. The truth would do its own damage. "How many times did your son try to get off this moon, Kes? How many times did he scope out the docks and mingle with the transients to get an idea how to escape?"

Kes Dameron didn't reply. He didn't need to.

"I hate to be the bearer of bad news, Kes, but the truth is what it is. I learned a long time ago that you are who you associate with," Trune said. "And, as of right now, your son is a criminal."

Before Dameron could respond, Trune raised a hand. The signal coming in on her terminal was marked as urgent. She scanned the item quickly, her eyes widening at each word. It was a coded message, sent from deep cover—and it had details on just what the Spice Runners were up to next. Not what she'd expected. It was big. But she wanted to take them out on a big stage. It would make it all the sweeter.

"Gotcha," she whispered.

CHAPTER 18

"They're everywhere!"

Vigilch's guttural exclamation bounced off every surface in the *Ragged Claw* as another wave of fire from the tiny drone-like Moraysian ships sent their ship reeling. Poe's instruction to Zorii—to randomize her fire in the hopes of making it more unpredictable—had done some damage, but the miniature fleet was doing serious damage to the ship. They didn't have much time—and everyone knew it.

"You have a plan, I'm guessing," Zorii said, trying to mask the anxiety in her voice as she turned to meet Poe's eyes. "You always have a plan."

"I have a plan," Poe said. He did have . . . something. Not a plan, per se, but a thought. He just needed a minute. "Can you hold them off a bit longer?"

"Weapons are offline." Gen Tri's voice, usually stoic and placid, seemed agitated—another unnerving development. Without any weapons, the *Claw* was defenseless against the swarm's nonstop firepower. That meant they had even less time.

"Scratch that," Poe said.

He swallowed hard. His timeline had just been truncated. Badly.

"Everybody buckle up!" Poe yelled as he flicked a switch above him. He felt warm, the pressure sinking in. He gripped the controls and whispered a hurried "You've got this" before raising his voice for the crew to hear. "Hold on."

The *Claw* dipped steeply, as if in free fall, hurtling away from the Moraysian ships. As they started to adapt and give chase, Poe turned to Zorii.

"Hey, Copilot—your mission is simple," he said with a smile. "Get me some damn firepower, will you?"

Zorii nodded, her face frigid and focused. Over the past month, in between chores and their dirge-like existence on Sorgan, the two had grown closer—sharing long discussions about growing up, even if it was Poe doing most of the talking, and trading tips on their expertise. Flight for Poe, the thieving life for Zorii. He'd been pleasantly surprised by her willingness to learn and her ability to pick things up fast. Both were coming in handy already.

"Goin' up," Poe said, trying to keep his tone light. The *Ragged Claw* shuddered in pain as Poe took it up again, almost retracing its sudden descent down, causing the cluster of small ships to disperse and try to reassemble like a confused school of fish. "Hang tight, folks—it's gonna get worse before it gets better."

Poe knew the ship was in bad shape. Their deflector shields were fading fast, and he had no idea when—or if—the weapons would be back online. The *Claw* hadn't been built for this, Poe mused, but it was too late to bemoan their circumstances. All they could do was move.

"They're reforming under us," Zorii said, shaking her head almost imperceptibly as she tapped a few buttons on her console. She was cooler than Hoth, but the strain was showing. She was losing faith. "They're locking on to us now. What do you—"

Before she could finish, Poe had spun the *Claw* on its side and taken the ship careening left at a sharp angle, sending the drone ships past where the *Claw* had just been. If Poe had the ability to see two things at once, he would have enjoyed seeing the clustered warbirds bumbling into one another. He increased the *Claw*'s speed sharply. The thought had become an idea as he pulled the *Claw* out of its tailspin. Now it was a plan.

"We're heading straight for the Moraysian cruiser," Zorii said, more a question than a statement. But she hesitated, trying to keep Poe focused on whatever he was doing. "At this speed, it might be a good idea—"

"I've got a plan," Poe repeated. "Trust me on this."

Zorii nodded. She had come to trust him, Poe realized. Their time together—including the skirmish with the Zualjinn—had made their connection more than one born of necessity but one of friendship. That meant more than he could express in the moment.

Poe glanced at the cruiser from his terminal. The ship had an expansive hangar bay, from which the drones had sprung.

"What are you doing, Dameron?" Vigilch asked, lurching forward, his face centimeters from Poe's. "We're going to collide with that ship! We're within its weapons range. Are you mad?"

Poe ignored the Klatooinian's enraged panic.

"Stick with me. I know what I'm doing," Poe said. But Vigilch didn't hear him mutter the last two words under his breath. "I think."

The *Claw* continued to weave, turn, and sway through the space between the swarm and the Moraysian cruiser, which grew in size as they approached. Yet no laser fire seemed to emanate from the command ship. They were still taking fire from behind, but Poe tried his best to take their lumps where the shields were the most effective. If this plan didn't work, they were out of options. They were sitting ducks.

"We need to retreat." It was Gen Tri, walking toward

the four of them clustered at the front of the cockpit, their voice ominous and distant. Vigilch and Zorii turned to them briefly, panic and frustration in their eyes. "We got bad intel. Tomasso is steering us in the wrong—"

The *Claw* hurtled forward in a way that felt awkward and painful at once—a loud, metallic screeching sound cutting through the regular sounds of spaceflight. Poe winced. That was not good, he thought. Not good at all. A quick scan let him know the basics—thrusters almost gone, shields barely holding on, and a gaggle of armed ships chasing them down.

Poe gripped Zorii's arm and they locked eyes.

"See what you can give me in terms of speed," Poe said, trying to sound calm but aware of the desperation in his voice. "I'll try to evade them as best I can."

Zorii nodded and turned her attention to her terminal. Vigilch was not so easily swayed.

"We need to surrender, or we need to prepare to self-destruct," the pirate said. "They cannot board this ship. They cannot have our se—"

"The hangar . . ." Zorii said to herself, realization clicking in her brain. "You're leading them into the hangar. But the doors are closed. . . ."

Poe nodded, giving Zorii a momentary smile.

The *Claw* started to close in on the cruiser, with no

response from the massive ship as the tiny drones continued to pelt them with laser fire.

"We're losing power," Zorii said flatly. "Gonna be a struggle to make it. Shields will be down in seconds."

"Shut it off," Poe said, not looking up.

"Shut it off?"

"Yes, all power except life support, shut it off," Poe said. "Bring it to a full stop."

"We're meters away from the ship," Gen Tri said, confusion in their usually confident and distant tone. "What do we hope to accomplish here? A martyr's death?"

"What's the escape pod situation on this crate?" Marinda Gan quipped. "You do realize the hangar bay doors are closed? Your little plan was misguided from the start."

"All power except life support is down," Zorii said matter-of-factly. "We are defenseless."

"Great," Poe said.

"Great?" Vigilch asked, incredulous. "You've killed us, Poe. This is over."

"Not yet," Poe said. He turned to Zorii. "Where are our little friends?"

"Closing in fast," Zorii said. "They'll be on top of us in seconds."

The *Claw* shuddered, the ship rocking back and forth as

a few of the small attacking vessels fired single, warning-style shots at them—probably trying to gauge whether the *Claw* was still in a fighting mood as they sped toward their target.

"They're speeding up," Zorii said. Translation: *Now would be a great time for your plan to, well, happen.* "We should brace for impact."

Poe turned to the small crew.

"Get strapped in. We're going to move in a second."

"Move? We just shut everything down. They're droid ships, Poe. They're going to crash right into us," Vigilch said, shaking his head furiously. "This is how it ends. Why did I ever think you could pilot this ship?"

"T-minus ten seconds to impact . . . nine, eight," Zorii said.

Poe ignored her and flicked on the thrusters again, hoping he was timing this just right. Zorii's eyes lit up. Her faith had paid off.

"Gimme all the juice this ship can muster, Z," Poe said, wincing slightly as he pulled up on the ship's throttle. The *Claw* did an internal somersault, the ship's entire hull straining and wheezing as it made a jagged, sudden turn upward at full speed—or the closest it could get to full speed under its current, damaged conditions. The crew was tossed around the ship's small cockpit, Poe heard curses he hadn't even known existed, and he wasn't fully sure it had worked.

Until the explosions started.

Poe didn't wait for Vigilch, Marinda, or Gen Tri to respond as he deftly pulled the *Claw* into a complete loop, turning the ship around to face where it had been moments before—except what had been there had been replaced by a gigantic, still exploding fireball of destruction.

"Hot damn," Poe said, pulling the *Claw* into something close to a full stop as the ship closed in on the damage.

The docking bay doors were gone, and as the smoke cleared Poe saw that a gaping, uneven hole had replaced them. The Moraysian cruiser was rocking slightly to its side like a wounded purrgil.

Vigilch was struggling to his feet, one knee on the ground, the tall Klatooinian still wobbly as he gripped Poe's arm.

"You sly little bastard," he said, his one good eye almost staring into Poe's soul. "Well done."

"We're not clear yet," Gen Tri said, their usual cool and resolve back in place as they seemed to float to Zorii's terminal. "We have a job to do."

"What now?" Zorii asked, her eyes on Poe, a sly smile on her face. "Any other fancy ideas?"

"Nah, this one's simple," he said, tapping a few buttons. "We're going in."

The *Ragged Claw* sallied and sailed through the debris, the once pesky drones now an asteroid belt of burnt metal. The landing inside the disabled cruiser's docking bay wasn't smooth. Poe tried his best to minimize the bumps and scrapes, pulling the *Claw* into a clumsy but not altogether terrible landing. From what he could see, the docking bay was empty. As the adrenaline from the maneuver began to fade, Poe found it replaced by a sense of growing anxiety as the ship skidded into a full stop. That's when he noticed the handful of figures approaching the ship, blasters raised.

"Guys," Poe said. "I think we're surrounded."

CHAPTER 19

Zorii and Poe had to take cover almost immediately, the blaster fire coming from what seemed like all directions. Vigilch, Gen Tri, and Marinda Gan scattered, as well, using the already battered *Claw* as a shield.

The five figures, cloaked and carrying large blaster rifles, moved closer, not letting up with their fire as they approached. None of them tried to speak or hint to the Spice Runners what they wanted, or if there was any chance at some kind of agreement. It looked like this was to the death, one way or the other.

Poe gripped the small blaster Vigilch had tossed to him as they disembarked. This wasn't his area of expertise. He'd practiced, of course—his father had taken him out on the range many a time during his younger days, and he'd brushed up during the Zualjinn incident. His aim wasn't the problem. He just hadn't had much experience in live combat. His heart pounded—the buzz from their in-flight maneuver still coursing through him. Zorii tugged at his arm and moved them down the length of the *Claw*'s hull, looking for a few steps of cover as the foot soldiers continued to approach.

"We're evenly matched," Zorii said. "But outgunned."

"This is true," Poe said, crouching and taking aim. "Any suggestions?"

Then they heard the scream—primal, like a wild animal's. Out of the corner of his eye, Poe saw a figure move toward their attackers—twirling a long staff-like weapon.

"Marinda," Zorii said. She muttered a curse under her breath. "She's not good with patience."

Poe focused on Marinda Gan, wielding the Twi'lek lyaer'tsa—a traditional weapon equipped with a vibroblade at one end. She used the weapon carefully, disabling two of the attackers with swift, precise motions. In what felt like an instant, their blasters were sliced and the two grunts were on the floor, clutching their arms and midsections. Vigilch and Gen Tri approached from opposite sides, the former dragging another one of the cloaked attackers.

"Looks like this might be done before it starts," Poe said.

"Don't be so sure," Zorii said.

Poe heard a loud hiss and watched as a doorway at the other end of the docking area opened up, revealing another handful of cloaked attackers—each one armed and spreading out to fire on the *Claw*'s crew.

"Something's not right," Poe said. "Something doesn't click."

"We need to get out of this area and find Ledesmar," Zorii said. "We're cornered."

Poe ignored Zorii, sending a blast over Vigilch and their friends. It grazed one of the new arrivals, sending them backward. A crackle of blue energy sparked briefly as the figure hit the ground.

"Droids—enforcers. Not sure what kind, though," Poe said, to himself as much as Zorii. "There's no crew here."

"What?"

"Think about it," Poe said as he followed Zorii's lead—toward the far end of the *Claw*, opposite the incoming platoon of cloaked attackers—in search of better cover. "Those ships were unmanned—the ones that were attacking us. Now we get surrounded by mysterious henchmen who walk kind of funny, don't talk much, and just shoot. . . . It doesn't add up."

"You like to jump to conclusions a lot for someone who hadn't spent much time off-world as of a month ago," Zorii said, sending a few quick shots toward the group as they moved between the *Claw*, some cobbled-together

Uglies, and a collection of inactive, outdated droid tri-fighter ships that had seen better days.

Poe peeked at their comrades as he leaned his back against the nearest ship's exterior. It seemed Vigilch and Marinda were taking the direct approach—blasting and slicing at the heart of the attackers. There was no sign of Gen Tri, Poe noticed. The little he saw from the battle—as Vigilch took one down with a headshot and Marinda Gan speared another, sparks and shrapnel flying—confirmed for him they weren't dealing with living beings but a cadre of droids under someone's control. A lot of droids, though. A lot of angry droids.

"Not sure how long we can hold them—they look like a mix between protocol and Dac pirate droids. Never seen anything like it," Marinda Gan yelled, not turning her head. Poe understood she was talking to them, keeping their location vague to win them a few seconds. "Take point, get ahead of us. We'll do our best here. Find who—and what—we're after."

"Did she say *what* we're after?" Poe asked as they darted toward the main entrance, under cover of a few quick blasts from Zorii.

"So?" Zorii asked, tumbling toward the open doorway—the roll calculated and athletic, in stark contrast to Poe's clumsy stumble.

"They're behind us," one of the cloaked figures said, its voice mechanical and melodic in the way of most droids.

Zorii spun around, one knee still on the ground, and fired a volley of blaster fire toward the group of droids. Poe stood and made his way toward a small terminal on the other side of the doorway. He tried a few buttons. Nothing. He looked through the doorway and saw the droids approaching, Zorii trying to hold them off.

"Any luck?" she asked, not looking back.

"Well, to be honest, not really," Poe said, trying a different combination of buttons to no avail. "I'm thinking we might be better off just, well, running away."

The sound of enemy blaster fire increased. Poe thought he heard Vigilch curse. He tapped another combination of buttons and heard a slight beep, then the door began to close.

"Closing, closing," Poe said, trying to get Zorii's attention. She noticed the movement and scurried through the small opening that remained as the droids fired at the shuttered entryway.

"What'd you do?" she asked.

"I'm not really sure, if you must know."

Zorii shook her head.

"Should've handled that myself," she said. "You're a pilot, not a slicer."

"Hey, I got it to work, didn't I?" Poe said as Zorii cautiously walked down the hall, blaster drawn.

"What? That's it?" Poe continued as he caught up to her.

They'd reached an intersection. There were no signs of life. The halls echoed with their light footsteps. *Is there anyone else on this ship?* Poe wondered.

"Can you just be quiet for a minute?" Zorii hissed as she looked left, then right. "I'm trying to figure out where we are—and how to get to the bridge."

"What is it we're after, Zorii?" Poe asked, his energy levels waning. The rush and scramble to get on the cruiser and through the phalanx of droids had worn him out. "Ledesmar has something the Spice Runners want, right? It isn't just about knocking out a competitor. I mean, why risk so much for that?"

Zorii didn't respond, instead going farther down the hall, motioning for him to follow. Before Poe could reach her, he stopped—she'd raised her hand in alarm. She pointed to her ear. He heard something, too—a soft clanking. Had one of the cloaked droids made it through already? He doubted they were built for stealth.

"What is it?" Poe asked.

Zorii pointed down the hall. There, about midway, Poe noticed an EV-class droid leaning on the far wall at an awkward angle, its long legs buckling under its body.

"Well, it can only get better," the droid said to herself, her voice melodic and oddly cheerful.

Poe and Zorii shared a bemused look.

Poe grabbed his blaster and started down the hall, ignoring Zorii's whispered pleas to wait, which were followed by a string of curses Poe hadn't thought she knew.

"Hey, you all right?" Poe asked.

The droid looked up, her movements eager and quick.

"Hello, new friend," she said. "How did you find your way on this cruiser?"

"Look, I don't have time for a full download, but it seems like you need help," Poe said. "What's your, uh, name? Is that it?"

"I am Eevee-Sixbeesix," the droid said, taking Poe's offered hand and slowly getting to her feet. "I'm doing well, all things considered. Though I am overdue for a systems check."

Poe wasn't keen on droids. They weirded him out. He liked people. Living beings with personalities and foibles. Droids were just—odd. Poe hadn't had much chance to interact with droids back on Yavin 4, but he thought he had an idea what they were like. This droid was different, though. Almost . . . happy?

Even this brief exchange was giving him the creeps. But

if this droid knew how to get them to Ledesmar, then it would be worth it.

"Sure, I get it." Poe heard Zorii approaching behind him. "We need to find the bridge on this ship. Can you take us there?"

"I'd be happy to," EV-6B6 said. "But you should be careful. This is a Moraysian cruiser, you know. Some very bad stuff has been happening here lately, and it's really starting to make me reconsider—"

"Find a friend?" Zorii said. She wasn't joking. Her movements were jittery. She didn't like that they'd stopped in the hallway.

"Where is everyone on the ship?" Poe asked the droid, who'd managed to take a few hesitant steps down the hall. "Anyone else on board?"

"Yes, yes, plenty of people," EV-6B6 said. "Well, at least one. I hate to be negative, but she's not very nice. She's ensconced herself on the bridge. She seemed really upset at the people who owned the ship before. It was kind of violent and—"

"Ledesmar?" Zorii asked. "Can you take us to her?"

"I suppose so, but it might lead to a fight," the droid said. "And you both seem really nice, so I'm not sure I'd want you to get hurt—"

Poe gripped the droid by the shoulders.

"Listen, Eevee, buddy, it's been nice meeting you, but we're not joining a cult together just yet," Poe said. "We need to find Ledesmar. Fast. We have a handful of angry, violent droids waiting for us on the other side of that hangar door we'd like to avoid. So any help you can offer would be much appreciated, whether you want to give it to us or not."

"Well, when you put it that way," EV-6B6 said, "I guess I don't have much choice. Follow me."

With that, the droid spun around and began to make her way down the hall at a brisk pace. Zorii and Poe followed not far behind.

"You think she's running the entire ship alone?" Zorii asked as they continued to follow EV-6B6 farther down the winding hallway. "How is that even possible?"

"Think about it, Zee," Poe said. "Those ships were moving in an automated fashion—they were responding to what we did, but not in the way human pilots do. They didn't adapt or react in time."

"Huh," she grunted. "So that's why you were able to pull that trick off. They were heading for the *Claw* but had no idea what you might do—mostly because it was unpredictable."

"Right," Poe said with a nod, a bit unsure if Zorii was complimenting or insulting him. "And even after we got off the ship—we haven't seen another life-form. It's all automated."

"This way," EV-6B6 said with a wave. "My guess is she'll be upset, so you may want to draw your weapons just in case."

"Wait," Zorii said. "What's your story, droid? Why are you so keen to help us?"

"Well, helping is what I do," EV-6B6 said, her robotic expression pensive, though Poe could have sworn the mech was giving off an air of joy. "And this Zabrak woman, Ledesmar, hasn't been very nice to me. You have. My masters are gone. The people I knew on this ship are gone. It makes sense to help and be appreciated."

"Who was on this ship before?" Poe asked, stepping closer to the droid. "A full complement?"

"Oh, no, nothing like that," EV-6B6 said, shaking her head almost imperceptibly. "My masters were thieves, criminals—members of the Pyke organization. I guess they have a bad reputation, but they treated me well. Ledesmar stole this cruiser and its assortment of ships and eliminated the repair crew. It was not nice."

"So you're a droid that belonged to thieves?" Zorii said, raising an eyebrow slowly.

"Yes, and I feel very unhappy that things have to go this way," EV-6B6 said. It took Poe a second to realize what was going on. Then the doors on either side of the hallway opened and a squadron of the cloaked droids—armed with large blaster rifles—appeared. "I meant what I said. You both seem very nice. My story was true, but being the property of a thief, you learn the tricks of the scoundrel trade—including double crosses. My sincere apologies."

"Follow us if you want to live," the central droid said, motioning with its weapon.

"Droids," Poe muttered to Zorii. "I should've known. You can't trust these walking junk heaps."

"Shut up and get that brain of yours thinking," Zorii snapped back. "This isn't some Yavin Four swamp race you're losing—it's your life."

The enforcer droids led them onto a turbolift. A few boarded with them, leaving EV and the remaining droids behind. The one who'd spoken to them tapped a few buttons, and the lift shunted downward.

"What do you guys do for fun around here?" Poe asked.

None of the droids responded. In a few moments, the lift came to a stop and opened onto a sprawling bridge—that was completely barren of people. A few RX-series droids manned the essential stations, from what Poe could tell—the helm, a security terminal, and perhaps a general systems area. But it was as bare-bones as a ship of this size and class could get—probably risky considering the sheer number of things that could go wrong with a ship that was, in essence, a floating city.

At the center of the bridge, though, was a living person: a tall Zabrak woman draped in a flowing red cloak, her pale forehead framed by smallish horns above and around it. Designs decorated her face and visible skin. She wielded a long spearlike weapon with blades on each end. *Zhaboka,* Poe thought. His father had told him plenty of stories from his time out in space, one of them involving a Zabrak who claimed to be a Jedi, but Kes had never been sure. The zhaboka was a traditional Zabrak weapon, Poe knew. And it was deadly as hell.

Ledesmar stepped toward them with an air of confidence and ease. She was not threatened. In fact, based on her expression, Poe thought she was amused.

"This is what the famed Spice Runners of Kijimi have to offer me in terms of resistance?" Ledesmar said. "Two children? So trusting, you'd follow a droid into the mouth of the nexu?"

Ledesmar got closer, scanning Poe quickly but lingering over Zorii—her demeanor shifting from calm to slight concern.

"Could it be?" she said, squinting as if trying to see past Zorii. "How did *you* get here?"

"I should ask you the same thing," Zorii said. "You have something that belongs to us."

There it was, Poe thought. The real reason they were there. But why had Vigilch and his own teammates refused to clue him in on what it was? Did they not trust him yet? Probably not, and Poe understood—but it stung all the same.

"Do I?" Ledesmar said with a shrug as she continued to walk around them, the droids stepping back to allow her free rein. "That's funny, because I don't own much beyond this ship—which I stole myself, from the very people who enslaved me for most of my life—the Pykes, who, as far as I know, are sworn enemies of your people. Tell me, dear one, what is it you think I owe you, or the Spice Runners?"

Zorii gritted her teeth. Before she could say anything, a large boom caught the group off guard.

Poe, Zorii, Ledesmar, and the droids turned to face the explosion, which enveloped the far side of the bridge, smoke and flames growing quickly. Ledesmar raised a hand, warding off the droids.

A few moments passed, and three shadowy figures emerged from the wreckage. Vigilch, bruised and battered, a large gash across his already scarred face, and Marinda Gan and Gen Tri not far behind, looking about as bad. Marinda limped behind their leader, and Gen Tri's walk, which usually seemed more like floating, was stilted and awkward. They were messed up, Poe thought, but he'd never been happier to see them.

"Ah, the rest of your little crew," Ledesmar said with a sneer. "That makes things easier."

She leapt forward, and her speed took Poe off guard. Before he could register her movements, she'd sent the end of her weapon into Vigilch's midsection, causing the Klatooinian to bend forward and release a piercing, pain-drenched groan. She pulled the zhaboka out carelessly, sure to make the exit of the weapon as painful as the entrance. Vigilch folded into himself as he collapsed to the floor. Gen Tri and Marinda Gan seemed taken aback and stepped away from Ledesmar to regroup. But it was too late.

Poe realized they weren't the only ones entranced by the Zabrak murderer—the droids had shifted their focus to Ledesmar, their master, and were ignoring Zorii and Poe, whom they'd not bothered to disarm or bind in any way. Poe gripped his blaster and sent a few quick shots toward the combatants. One missed completely, but the other nailed Ledesmar's right leg mid-leap, sending the athletic thief twisting down a short flight of stairs and onto a lower level of the bridge, clutching the wounded limb.

It had bought them maybe five seconds, but it was enough time for Gen Tri and Marinda Gan to scatter, and for Poe and Zorii to take cover behind the ship's main navigation terminal—by design.

"They can't get too blaster-happy now," Zorii said. "They'll only hurt themselves by destroying the ship's controls. Even droids know that."

"They're mine," Ledesmar said, her voice booming from across the bridge. She wasn't talking about Marinda and Gen Tri, Poe knew. He watched as she leapt toward them, her agile body somersaulting over chairs and terminals to reach the far end of the bridge, where Zorii and Poe stood—blasters at the ready. They were both in a state of shock, not expecting Ledesmar to recover so quickly or to be able to reach them with such ease.

She swung the zhaboka as if it was an extra limb and knocked the blasters out of their hands in one precise motion, leaving Poe staring at his empty hand for a moment. A moment too long, he would soon learn.

He heard Zorii's angry scream before his pained one as the blade of Ledesmar's weapon slashed at his side, gouging deep. The blood came fast, and he crumpled to the floor, clutching his midsection. He tried not to look at the wound, but he couldn't help it—it was deep, the dark red blood already seeping through his clothing and covering the area, the pain and mess of it all spreading fast.

"Achhkk!" Poe grimaced as he rocked on the floor, waiting for Ledesmar to stand over him, weapon poised and ready to slam through his skull. His body was gripped by fear of a looming darkness—amplified by the blinding pain he felt in his side, which was quickly spreading all over him. He reached for the wound, immediately regretting the move. He looked down to see his hand coated in blood. His blood.

But his vision of Ledesmar finishing him off never came to be. Instead Poe's ears were shaken by another anger-fueled, bloodcurdling sound. It was Zorii again, but this scream wasn't laced with shock; it seemed to come from the base of her very soul—from a pure, animalistic hatred Poe would never have guessed her capable of.

He lifted his head slightly and saw the two figures sparring—Zorii had somehow knocked the spear from Ledesmar's grip, and the two were now clenched in hand-to-hand combat, Zorii pushing back on the Zabrak, her eyes fiery with rage. Ledesmar was momentarily caught off guard. Poe tried to get up, but an explosion of pain in his side sent him back down, doubled over.

"Your droids won't save you now," Zorii said through a

clenched jaw as she continued to press her advantage over Ledesmar. "Give me what we came here for."

"You've confused a momentary surprise with an advantage, little one," the Zabrak said, her knee pistoning upward and connecting with Zorii's chin, leaving her bloodied and disoriented for a moment. It was all Ledesmar needed. She sent two quick punches to Zorii's face, and she was down, arms up, like a fighter desperate to avoid the finishing blow.

Poe tried to reach for her, but he couldn't control his body, the pain enveloping him more tightly with each passing second. Was this the end of his story? A runaway child of the Rebellion, killed in the midst of some galactic gang war? Did he even know what he was fighting for?

No, but he did know *who* he was fighting for. He moved his leg and felt something at his left heel. The zhaboka. The weapon's long staff was tucked under Poe's boot. He lifted his head and saw Ledesmar standing over Zorii, who seemed on the brink of losing consciousness. He'd only have one chance.

The kick was strong and focused. Poe sent the weapon spinning in Zorii's direction. But it seemed hopeless, and Poe half expected to hear it rattle off the wrong way, based on how their luck had been playing out. He saw darkness on the edge of his vision, a blackness he knew wasn't sleep, though it beckoned to him like a warm, uninterrupted nap. He didn't hear the clanging of the weapon's blade as it rattled down the stairs. Didn't hear Ledesmar's laugh as she noticed Poe's feeble attempt to save his friend. Instead, he heard a thick, almost squishy *shunk*, followed by a watery rasp and Ledesmar's final words:

"This . . . this wasn't . . . the deal."

Then she fell to the ground, impaled by her own weapon. Zorii Wynn stood over her, not a drop of emotion on her blood-spattered face.

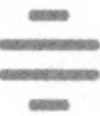

"He appears to be waking up."

"He'd better—for your sake," Zorii said as she stood over the droid who'd betrayed them.

"Well, we're in luck—I have some medical programming in my databanks," EV-6B6 said, backing away from Poe, who'd been laid out on the bridge's upper level. "Your wound has been sealed and I've stopped the bleeding. It appears Ledesmar didn't cause any permanent damage. It seems like it's your lucky day, Poe Dameron."

Zorii, Gen Tri, and Marinda Gan stood nearby as the droid finished patching him up. Poe could see Ledesmar's lifeless body in the background, and a cold sweat overtook him. He knew it wasn't a side effect of whatever the droid had done to revive him.

"How do you feel?" Marinda asked him, genuine concern on her face. She placed a cold hand on his cheek.

"I'm . . . I'm not sure," Poe said. He tried to get up and instantly regretted it. The pain in his side had lessened, but it was still there. Whatever the droid had done to him only softened it. He winced as he sat up. Zorii sat down next to him, her hands on his shoulders.

"Slow down," she said. "We almost lost you there."

"No such luck," Poe said, his expression a mix of forced humor and sharp pain. "Not yet, at least. What happened to Ledesmar's droids?"

"We silenced them," Gen Tri said, back to their usual ghostlike demeanor. They were a few paces away from the group and turned to survey the bridge. "That's how we found this droid—who seemed to be the only remnant of the previous crew."

"That is correct, my new masters," EV-6B6 said, nodding dutifully. "Not everything I relayed to you was a lie, despite my ultimate betrayal. Which, I may add, was born of necessity, not any dislike for you."

Poe got to his feet—gingerly, each movement clouded with the threat of more pain. But as he stood, he felt better, and he took a few hesitant steps onto the main bridge.

"Whatever you pumped into me, Eevee, it seems to be working," Poe said. "Guess not all droids are bad, even if you did give us up to Ledesmar."

"It was a decision I swiftly came to regret, Master Dameron," EV-6B6 said with a curt nod as she began to pack a small kit of medical supplies. "I do hope you come to understand, and forgive me."

Zorii approached Poe, a hand on his arm, her eyes focused and clear.

"You're very lucky, Poe," she said. "That was too close."

Poe nodded. No quips this time. She was right. But he did have a question.

"Why are we really here, Zorii? What are we after?" Poe asked. "What did Ledesmar mean when she said this wasn't the deal?"

She never got the chance to answer.

The Moraysian cruiser shook violently, lurching to the left, sending the Spice Runners tumbling toward the far wall of the bridge. As the massive cruiser righted itself, Poe winced as he scrambled to one of the navigation terminals, reaching for his side instinctively as Gen Tri hovered behind him.

"Looks like we missed a few ships dropping out of

hyperspace," Poe said, tapping buttons quickly—hoping to get a clearer picture of what was going on. "And they don't seem happy."

"Who are they?" Gen Tri asked. "Pykes? Moraysians after their own tech?"

Poe took a second longer than he needed, trying to confirm his information before he shared it with the group—hoping against hope that the intel he had was just wrong.

"They're . . . they're New Republic ships," Poe said, not fully believing his own words. "Lots of them, too."

CHAPTER 20

"Open fire," Gen Tri said, not a tinge of menace or anger in their voice. "And continue to fire at will."

Poe hesitated. If he followed Gen Tri's order, he'd be firing on his own people—was that really what he'd signed up for? He looked at Zorii, who seemed disgusted by Poe's lag. She shook her head at him as if to say, *Fire, Poe. It's who you are now. It's who we are.*

Marinda Gan's response was not as subtle.

"Out of the way, kid," she said, shoving Poe aside. "Let a real spice runner handle this."

Marinda took control of the terminal deftly, and before Poe could protest, she'd sent a volley of laser cannon fire toward the five New Republic ships, making contact with a few. But even with the weapons of the large Moraysian cruiser at their disposal, they were overmatched. The ship was old and had seen its share of scrums. It was not meant for full-on combat, especially with what amounted to an inexperienced skeleton crew running it. Their best bet was to distract and evade.

Gen Tri approached Marinda's terminal, their demeanor distant and defensive—more than usual.

"Can we withstand much?" they asked Marinda. But it was clear they knew the answer.

"Shields are a joke, even on a ship this big—they won't last much longer," Marinda said, shaking her head. "They got to fire first—and if this holds up, they'll fire last, too."

The ship shook, taking another wave of fire from the New Republic vessels. Poe dug his fingers into a nearby terminal, desperate to avoid being tossed across the bridge if he could help it. Zorii held on to him, doing the same. He thought he heard EV-6B6 squeal in the distance.

"Shields are offline," Marinda Gan said, tapping at her terminal with a desperate energy that did not inspire much faith in Poe. "Weapons systems are at twenty percent. We won't be able to access the hyperdrive, either, not unless—"

Marinda's update was interrupted by the static and crackle of a communications channel coming to life. The voice was unfamiliar, but the threat was clear.

"This is Sela Trune with the New Republic Security Bureau," she said. "Stand down and you will live. Prepare to be boarded or destroyed. The choice is yours."

CHAPTER 21

Something slammed into Poe's midsection, intensifying the tenderness in his side once more. His first thought was that he was under attack again, but when he looked down, it was a sturdy, gleaming silver case with an engraved handle. He looked up to see Gen Tri was holding on to it.

"This needs to get off this ship—as does Zorii Wynn," they said with a slight nod. "Do not betray our trust, Poe Dameron. The entire mission rests with you now."

Poe started to ask what it was but thought better of it. He took the case from Gen Tri and turned to see Zorii waiting for him.

"We have to get back to the hangar and hope there's a ship there that can get us out of here," she said, her words jumbling into each other. "We don't have much time. They're starting to get closer and they'll be on the ship in minutes."

Poe nodded and followed Zorii and EV-6B6 toward the turbolift. Before the doors closed, he made eye contact with Marinda Gan, who mouthed two words: *Good luck.*

They'd need more than luck to get off the ship, he knew.

The lift ride was short and rocky, the cramped space shaking forcefully as the Moraysian ship continued to be slammed by laser fire.

"Guess Gen Tri's dragging their feet on that whole 'surrender' thing," Poe quipped.

"Spice Runners aren't good at giving up," Zorii said, not meeting Poe's eyes.

"It is quite admirable, I think," EV-6B6 said. Zorii and Poe ignored her.

They stepped off the lift and ran down a familiar hallway, now littered with fallen droids—aftershocks from Vigilch and the crew's struggle to get on the bridge. *Vigilch*. Their leader was gone. Felled in one motion by Ledesmar, also gone. All this bloodshed, Poe thought. Was it worth it? The highs of this new life—the space tricks and battles, the subterfuge and trickery—seemed dulled by the losses. He wouldn't have considered the brusque Klatooinian a friend, or even much of an ally, really—but his loss still hurt. It was in moments like these that Poe realized he hadn't experienced enough. The tough skin hadn't fully formed. He'd never felt more sixteen than right then, scurrying down a strange ship's length, trying desperately to find a way off and into unknown space. He'd never felt farther from his father, from his home—from the life he'd come to take for granted. And for what? He wasn't sure. But he didn't have time to mull it over.

"Come on, follow me," Zorii said, tugging at Poe's arm, EV-6B6's slow metallic footsteps echoing behind them. "There's another hangar here, according to the schematic I looked over. We might get lucky."

They reached a final set of doors—closed. Poe punched one of the buttons, but nothing. He turned to Zorii.

"Let me see," she said, moving past him.

Zorii tapped a few buttons, then pulled out a small, thin silver dagger. She pressed it gently into the side of the panel, popping it off and revealing wires and cords. She yanked out a green and red wire, using the dagger to cut them. The doors hissed open.

"Follow me," she said, not waiting for any reaction. This wasn't Zorii Wynn's first break-in—or breakout.

The hangar was expansive, a handful of ships littering the wide, empty space.

"Hey, droid, what can you tell us about these ships? Any of them fit to fly?" Poe asked as they scanned the area. "We're on a bit of a time crunch."

"Well, I'm sorry to say my expertise isn't in—"

"Got one," Zorii said from a few meters away. She'd found a battered BTL-S3 Y-wing starfighter. "Assuming I can chip the rust off and we can get inside."

Poe approached the ship slowly, with some reverence.

"These ships are tough—nothing fancy, but this'll do," Poe said, nodding. "We're in luck."

These ships helped defeat the Empire, Poe almost blurted out, but thought better of it. The Y-wing would definitely fly, and it just might be able to outrun the New Republic corvette-size ships waiting outside. It would get Zorii out safely with their score, and that was Poe's top priority.

"Get in, Zorii," Poe said, trying to sound commanding. "This is your ticket off. I'm sure there are other ships I can—"

"Actually, it appears most of the ships here are not operational," EV-6B6 said, looking around the large space. "We might be able to find something else if we backtrack to the other hangar, but I can't be cer—"

The blaster fire started then, and the trio turned to see a group of New Republic officers shooting first and asking questions later. At the front of the team was a young, tall human woman with close-cropped blond hair. Trune.

"Step away from the ship, Dameron," Trune said, moving forward, her finger still squeezing the trigger, sending blaster fire around them. "And don't even think of returning fire."

"Thought you guys usually hit the bridge first, at least when you do the whole boarding of an enemy ship thing,"

Poe said, rolling to his right and sending a volley of fire back at Trune, hitting one of her men and sending him to his knees. One down. His blaster wasn't set to kill, he reminded himself—but it struck him nonetheless that he was firing on New Republic officers, who stood for the same ideals his parents had fought to establish.

"Your quips won't delay the inevitable," Trune said. "Though, it's nice to have my suspicions confirmed. Your pals on the bridge refused to say whether you'd joined their ranks."

Poe ignored the dig, though his internal alarms were going off. So Trune and her team had already been on the bridge. Where were Marinda Gan and Gen Tri, then? He sent another shot, hitting the officer to Trune's left. Two down.

Trune crouched and sent another trio of shots in Poe's direction, but he was able to slide behind one of the myriad zombie ships that were scattered around the hangar. It would only provide a brief refuge. He allowed himself a moment to peek around the ship to check on Zorii—who'd taken refuge inside the one ship that could probably get her to safety. He fought the urge to run to her and provide some kind of cover. Zorii Wynn was more than capable. She could handle herself.

"Your friends are dead, Poe Dameron," Trune said,

standing up and walking toward Poe's shelter. "Don't delay this and don't make me kill you. Your father would be even more disappointed than he already is."

She took a few more paces in Poe's direction.

"Either you come with me now and notify him yourself—let him know what you've decided to become," Trune said, "or I can handle it when I alert next of kin."

"Eevee, now!" Poe yelled. Trune jumped at the words, as if finally recognizing where Poe had been hiding. The realization didn't serve her for very long as the droid careened toward the New Republic officers, a loud, ear-piercing screech accompanying her mad run at the group. She was fast for a droid, Poe thought, and it took the New Republic officers too long to react to the new target. By the time they did, it was too late—EV-6B6's long arms had slammed into the two remaining officers, sending them back through the hangar doorway, presumably unconscious. That left Trune.

Trune spun around, as if just noticing her team had been disabled. Were those the only officers she'd boarded with? Poe hoped so, but he had learned over the past few weeks not to rely much on the luck of the draw. He sent a quick shot at Trune, which she dodged easily. Poe, despite the space between them, thought he heard her scoff.

"Your amateur colors are showing," Trune said, walking

in a slight, military-style crouch toward Poe, blaster raised. "You took a risky shot and just gave up where you are. I won't be as easy to drop as my men, Poe—remember that."

"I think he does," Zorii said, landing behind Trune and sending a focused kick at her head. The New Republic Security Bureau officer fell forward, hitting the cold ground with a loud thunk. She'd be out for a while.

Zorii made her way to Poe's corner and smiled.

"You're lucky I'm around," she said.

"I tell myself that a lot," he said, returning her smile. But as he looked at her more closely, he noticed something off in her movements. "Zorii—are you all right?"

She shrugged, but it was clear to Poe she was grimacing with each step. He moved toward her. He noticed the wound fast—a nasty gash on her side she was trying her best to cover with her hands.

"Let me see," Poe said.

"It's nothing," Zorii said defensively. "Just a strafe. Firefights are messy."

She tried to move away, but Poe gently pulled her hands from the wound. It looked bad, he thought.

"We need to get Eevee to look at this," Poe said.

EV-6B6 approached from the other end of the hangar.

"The assailants have been disposed of, Master Dameron, and they're alive—don't worry."

"Good work," Poe said, motioning for the droid to approach Zorii. "Can you give her a once-over? I think she got grazed badly—"

"Of course, I'm happy to help and quite sorry to hear Zorii was inju—"

"Enough."

Poe felt a hand grip his. Zorii's fingers were strong and cold. She moved his hand away from her side and took a step toward the droid.

"We need to get off this ship," Zorii said, her eyes locked on Poe. "I can get patched up once we're clear. Understood?"

He didn't agree, but knew Zorii wouldn't budge on this. Best to get her and EV-6B6 on their way and hope the droid could help her until they got some proper medical attention.

"Your call," Poe said, forcing a smile. "Did you buy what Trune said about Gen Tri and Marinda?"

"Yes—they're gone," Zorii said with a solemn nod. "At least it seems that way."

Poe hung his head for a second.

"I'm not sold. We have to be sure," Poe said, shaking his head slightly. "We can't leave them—"

"I think we might get lucky if we search the other hangar. Perhaps there's something more comfortable and spacious—"

"Can it for now, Eevee," Poe said. "You're going with

Zorii." He handed the droid the metallic case Gen Tri had entrusted to him. Poe tried not to think that would be the last time he'd see the tall, ethereal Pau'an. "Help Zorii get off this ship and into hyperspace fast, all right? Then do your best to patch her up. It's gonna be a bumpy ride."

EV-6B6 took the proffered case with as upbeat a look as a droid could muster.

"Understood. I will give it my strongest effort," EV-6B6 said as she passed the case to Zorii. "Good luck to you, Poe Dameron."

They made their way back to the small Y-wing, gingerly stepping over Trune's unconscious body. As they circled the ship, Poe watched Zorii step into the cockpit, a hesitant look on her face. He climbed up the ship's opposite side and crouched next to the pilot's seat.

"You should be coming with me, Poe," she said, concern flashing across her face. "You're injured, too. This is stupid."

"Stupid and me go well together," Poe said, trying to lighten the mood. Zorii's darkening glare told him he was taking the wrong approach. He responded with a quick sigh. "I can't leave them behind, okay? Not if there's a chance. I have to know."

She nodded quickly. Accepting, but not fully understanding.

"You think you can fly this thing?" Poe asked.

Zorii nodded as EV-6B6 started to climb aboard the ship and into the other seat.

"I can fly anything," she said with a broad smile. Suddenly, Poe was struck by his friend's simple beauty. He'd miss her if they never crossed paths again—which was a real possibility. "That's what my teacher always says."

Poe leaned forward into the ship's cockpit. They kissed, their touch electric and natural at the same time. Poe was surprised, and he could tell she was, too. It felt right, he knew that much—the culmination of weeks of kinetic energy dancing between them. Of lingering glances, knowing smiles, and a rapport that felt like more than just that of allies or teammates. The connection didn't last long, but Poe knew he'd never forget it.

"Smart guy, that teacher," Poe said, their faces still close. He kept his eyes on hers, unsure what was next but trying to remain in the moment for as long as he could.

Zorii pulled back, placing her palm on Poe's cheek.

"Do what you need to do. Then get yourself back to Sorgan, Poe," she said. "Or I'll have to come kill you myself."

Poe fought his instinct to kiss her again. To say something foolish he wasn't sure he meant. Something he might mean, if things were to go a certain way. He'd cared for people before—felt the flutter of excitement at something new with someone, only to see it dashed. Hope and romance were never guaranteed in the wilds of the galaxy. Even at sixteen, Poe Dameron knew that.

Instead, he slapped the hull of the ship and pointed at the EV droid, whom he'd come to admire more than he'd expected.

"Get her home safe, Eevee," Poe said, jumping back from the ship as it began to move. He thought he heard the droid respond in the affirmative, but any words were lost—overwhelmed by the sound of the ship's engines as it headed toward open space.

Poe thought he saw Zorii wave goodbye as the ship sped out of the opening hangar doors, but he could have just as easily imagined it. He didn't have much time to ponder, either, as he heard a rustling that could only mean one thing.

"You're not getting off this ship that easily," Sela Trune said, a sharp grimace on her bruised face. Her blaster was pointed squarely at Poe's head. "And if you do, you won't be breathing."

CHAPTER 22

It was a standoff.

Poe clutched his blaster, which was trained on Sela Trune, the focused, hard-nosed New Republic officer who also happened to have her blaster trained on him. He was wobbly, feeling feverish and weak from the injury Ledesmar had inflicted on him earlier. If Trune fired first, he'd return the favor. And vice versa. Mutually guaranteed destruction didn't strike Poe as the best way to ensure a healthy life.

"Whatever you're after, it's gone," Poe said, motioning with his head toward the closing hangar doors. "Your ships could've probably caught up to her, but I doubt they'd want to leave you here on this rusty bucket."

"You talk like a seasoned criminal, Poe," Trune said, taking a half step forward. "I wonder what your father—or L'ulo L'ampar—would say if they saw you now, making veiled threats against someone who serves the same side they do. The same side Shara Bey did."

Poe lunged at Trune. He didn't realize he was doing it until he was well on his way, blaster raised and fist moving toward her. The mention of his mother had been enough to shock an already frayed nerve into a fit of angry spasms. What did Sela Trune know of his life, of the people he cared about? Or why he'd fled Yavin 4?

What gave her the right?

His fist made contact with Trune's shoulder, sending her back and knocking her blaster out of her reach. She recovered fast, slamming her palm into Poe's chin, snapping his head back and loosening his grip on his blaster. They stood facing each other, both bloodied, only their hands to defend themselves. Angry, spent—but not dead.

"Bad choice of words, Dameron?" Trune said, the knowing smirk on her face almost driving Poe to take the offensive again. Who was this young woman? Why did she have such an obsession with him—and with the Spice Runners of Kijimi? "Does it sting to picture the people you care about learning how their golden boy left home to join up with one of the deadliest new crime syndicates in the galaxy? Did you think they were just friendly traders looking for a way off Yavin Four? Surely you can't be that dense."

"It's not what you think," Poe said, ashamed of his own defensiveness. "They're friends."

"Your friends are gone," Trune said. "Except for the girl you sent away. Vigilch, Gen Tri, Marinda Gan—they're all victims of this insane mission you're on. I would've savored arresting each of them. But I'm left with you—a kid who's lost his way."

Her words stung Poe because he felt the truth in them. As much as he wanted to think she was lying, Trune didn't need to trick Poe. The others were dead. He'd made a mistake staying, and he might pay for it with his life—or his freedom.

Poe pulled his arm away, but a greater force knocked them both back. The ship sank, its balance off, the vessels in the hangar moving along with the gravitational drop and sending the entire space into complete chaos. Trune regained her footing first but didn't reach for her blaster—instead she spoke into her wrist with an urgency that worried Poe.

"What is going on?" Trune said. "Report."

A harried-sounding male screamed on the other end. "The ship doesn't have much time," he said. "Think we hit it too hard—it seems like it's coming apart, Officer Trune. . . . We need to get you off, along with your team."

"I've got a prisoner," Trune said. "I need to be pulled out immediately."

"We need you back at the drop-off point. We cannot send another team in—again, I repeat, we cannot send in another—"

Trune cut the connection, but before she could return her attention to Poe, she was met with the butt of his blaster in the back of her head. The soft crunch of contact let Poe know he'd hit hard, and the speed with which Trune toppled to the floor confirmed he'd knocked her out. Had he truly been a spice runner, a ruthless space pirate as Trune had so easily suggested, he would have left her there—and rushed to find his way off the quickly imploding ship. But Poe couldn't bring himself to do that. He dragged Trune out of the hangar bay, groaning as he tried to minimize the damage he could cause by pulling her along with him. As he walked through the doors Zorii had disabled just a few minutes before, he found the two New Republic officers he'd stunned earlier. One of them was slowly getting to his feet. Poe spoke quickly and clearly.

"I've got your leader—she's hurt," he said. "You need to get back to your drop-off point or your crew won't be able to get you. Don't question me on this if you want to live."

The officer nodded as Poe handed Trune over to him. Poe noticed that the other stunned officer was waking.

"Where are you going?" the first officer said, shifting his weight to better carry his leader. "You can come with us. I'll mention that you saved Officer Trune."

"Don't worry about me," Poe said. "Good luck."

The first officer nodded as he and his colleague picked up Trune and started off down the hallway, in the opposite direction Poe needed to go.

The *Ragged Claw* looked almost docile as Poe approached the second hangar bay. He stepped aboard the ship, taking two steps at a time as the Moraysian cruiser lost control of itself more and more the longer he remained aboard. The ship was breaking down, scaffolding crashing to the floor, lights flickering on and off, doors unable to open. This was a gamble, Poe knew. The *Claw* hadn't exactly been in tip-top shape when they'd left Sorgan, nor had they landed it comfortably after Poe's maneuver outside the Moraysian cruiser.

He turned the power on and waited. The ship gurgled to life, the lights coming on with a flicker, like a reverse-dimmer effect. He did a quick status scan. Shields were barely there. Hyperdrive was working in theory. It could fly. That was all Poe needed. At least for now.

Another tremor, this one stronger. It didn't feel like the cruiser was under attack. It felt like the ship was destroying itself, years of wear and tear finally coming to collect their due. As he wove the *Claw* out of the hangar, he let his mind drift back to the Spice Runners—to Zorii, that kiss . . . to Vigilch and his crew, how he'd never see them again. A sharp jolt went through him. Of regret, and imbalance. He couldn't take the *Claw* back to Yavin. Those days were gone. But did he think the best thing to do was fly back to Sorgan? His gut said yes. He had unfinished business. He had to make sure Zorii had made it back safely. He had to see her again. This was his life now, and regardless of whether he regretted the journey so far, it was what he had to work with.

A quick scan of the perimeter showed Poe that the New Republic ships had made haste and left, escaping to tend to their wounded and avoid a massive explosion. Sound advice, he mused. He took the *Claw* out into open space and let the thrusters guide the banged-up ship as far as he could from the mammoth Moraysian vessel before kicking it into hyperspace.

"And away we go," Poe whispered to himself as the starship groaned into the jump.

The visions rushed past him as the *Ragged Claw* hurtled back to Sorgan—flashes from the past. Memories and dreams blended together like a feverish vision.

His mother, clutching him to her chest, his arm limp, shattered.

On the A-wing—her hands resting over his, showing him the subtle art of the barrel roll. He leaned back; their eyes met—a warm smile on her face. Her lips kissing the back of his head. *Mother.*

"I wonder what your father would say." Trune's words rang through his skull, shifting the visions from nostalgic to dark. He was back on Yavin 4, standing nose to nose with his father. Both men yelling, their faces red and spent from the effort. Both fighting an unwinnable battle they refused to back away from.

"I won't let you do this to yourself, Poe," Kes Dameron said, slamming a fist on their small dinner table. "The war is over. We don't need any more young men sacrificing themselves."

"But you did, Dad," Poe responded in his head, as he'd done many times before. "You and Mom both served the Rebellion."

"That is over!" Kes screamed, and the dream shifted, back onto the Moraysian cruiser—as Poe sent the handle of his blaster into the back of Sela Trune's head, knocking the New Republic officer unconscious. He had attacked someone who served the same cause his parents had fought for—and for what? To escape the ship as a fugitive, unable to ever return home?

"Not just yet," Poe said to himself.

Poe felt a great weight on his shoulders as he brought the *Ragged Claw* down on the soggy surface of Sorgan, the Spice Runners camp still intact despite the loss of so many just a few hours before. Poe looked down on the surface, half expecting to see no one but instead catching sight of two figures waiting for him as he disembarked. Zorii's wan smile and tired eyes were a welcome sight. Less so was the haggard, predatory stare of the man known as Tomasso. While Zorii's expression seemed almost joyous at the sight of Poe and the *Claw*, Tomasso's look was wary and disdainful. Poe longed to know what thoughts were taking up space in the older man's head, and what he'd been told about their struggles aboard the Moraysian cruiser.

He'd soon find out.

PART III: AWAKENINGS

CHAPTER 23

Poe pulled his long, thick coat tighter around his body as he walked up the steep staircase. The strong gusts of wind threatened to knock him and Tomasso off the rickety steps as they made their way up to the top of the mountain. Poe's eyes were teary from the whipping winds, and he squinted to avoid getting more dirt in them. Tomasso, on the other hand, seemed unperturbed, scurrying up the flimsy steps like a toddler chasing a toy. The Marimkes Mountains, of which Poe and Tomasso were scaling the largest peak, were the only notable landmark on the veritable wasteland that was the planet Elkeenar of the Penagosis system, which was as off the grid as one could get in the known galaxy. This suited Poe Dameron fine.

It had been three months since their bloody encounter with Sela Trune and Ledesmar on the Moraysian battle cruiser, and Poe still found himself reeling from it. The losses still stung—Vigilch, Marinda Gan, and Gen Tri—and the doubt that reared its head after those losses had yet to fade away. He no longer grappled with whether he'd made the right decision to leave Yavin 4—he just dealt with the aftershocks, which were strong and ever present. Moments after Poe had landed their ship, the *Ragged Claw*, on the swamp planet Sorgan, Poe and Zorii Wynn had been ushered to myriad Spice Runners safe houses around the Outer Rim—a few days here, a week there, never longer than that. The Spice Runners knew they were on the New Republic's sensors, Tomasso had explained, and their numbers were depleted in the wake of the battle with Ledesmar. It was time to regroup—and to learn on the go.

"Pick up the pace, Poe Dameron," Tomasso called from the top of the makeshift stairs, motioning to Poe. "We don't have much time."

Time. Poe had once thought of time as a flowing river—endless and always moving. But his friends' deaths had slowed the flow to a trickle. Every second counted more. Every moment moved a bit faster than he'd have liked. For years, he'd lived life like a repetitive, soul-draining chore—the same things, the same people, the same moon. He loved his father and his family, of course. His friends and routines. But he'd hungered for something different and livelier. He'd gotten it in spades. Now he wasn't sure where he'd lay his head to sleep from one night to the next, whether he'd be piloting the *Ragged Claw* into a pitched battle or roasting nerf meat over a fire on any given day. He'd gone from zero to another numeric system altogether in the span of a minute—just by agreeing to pilot the *Ragged Claw* off Yavin 4.

As he gripped the railing and pulled himself to the top of the mountain, he found Tomasso standing nearby, looking relaxed, as if climbing a massive rock was just another routine task in the life of the Spice Runners of Kijimi's second-in-command. They'd been on Elkeenar for a few days, mostly spent working on the *Claw* and waiting for word from Kijimi, which would naturally come to Tomasso first and filter down to Poe and Zorii in a slow drip.

Poe thought back to that moment on the Moraysian cruiser. It had been a spur-of-the-moment decision, to lean in and kiss her. It had felt right then and still felt right. But Poe wasn't exactly experienced in the ways of the heart, and he'd probably managed to screw things up somehow. He'd messed up relationships with people before. His dynamic with Zorii hadn't changed, exactly. There'd been other intimate moments—hands clasped together, lingering kisses, quick longing glances—but they seemed more like an extension of the warmth he knew they shared, not necessarily a sign of what was to be.

Poe pushed the thoughts away as he approached Tomasso. These things would shake out on their own, whether he wanted them to or not, and as much as he cared for Zorii, he couldn't make them be something else.

He reached the older man and nodded, trying not to seem as winded and exhausted as he felt.

"Here we are," Poe said. "You wanted to chat? Doesn't get more secluded than this."

Tomasso nodded and Poe followed him toward a small hut-like structure. The space inside was barren and not much warmer than outside. Tomasso took a small chair and motioned for Poe to take the only other seat. For a split second Poe wondered if this was the end—if Tomasso had taken him up there to kill him and solve the lingering problem the Spice Runners had been struggling with since Yavin 4. But he tried to ignore the thought. If that was true, it would be too late to stave it off anyway.

"Sit, sit," Tomasso said. "Don't worry. I've come here to praise you, not punish you."

Poe tried not to exhale too loudly. He'd come to admire the aging spice runner over the past few months—first out of sheer intimidation, then out of a respect born of long hours spent watching the leader at work. Tomasso acted in the way he expected others to, and seemed to treat all—from the lowest members of the organization to the one person above him—with the same level of care and kindness. But there was a sharp edge beneath the soft exterior, which was truly befitting a thief. You could respect Tomasso, but you could never fully trust him. The definition of a scoundrel, Poe thought as he looked at the man across from him.

"Funny way of showing it, Tomasso," Poe said, scratching at the awkward stubble that had begun to grow on his face. "You had me worried there for a second. Maybe longer."

"Understandable," Tomasso said. "But no. We are quite happy with your work, and with Zorii's. You both share a great future as members of our growing organization. Our leader has taken a very special interest in this small but active branch of the Spice Runners."

"Well, they sent you here to train us, so that's a good sign," Poe said. "Right?"

"Indeed, as you've probably noticed—it's my duty to ensure you and Zorii learn the tools of the trade so you can not only serve the Spice Runners well now but in the future," Tomasso said, nodding to himself. "There is also the question of trust."

"Trust?"

"Yes, yes. The events of the last few months were worrisome beyond the death toll, you see," Tomasso said, wincing at his own words. "That knowledge—of what you and the team were doing, and who you were after—was known by only a small, tight circle. By the leader of the

Spice Runners of Kijimi, myself, and your immediate teammates."

Poe let Tomasso's words sink in. The elder thief was being very clear. Someone had betrayed the Spice Runners—and it was someone Poe knew and worked with closely.

"But why would anyone betray us to end up dead?" Poe asked. "If it was Vigilch, Gen Tri, or Marinda Gan—they're gone. They died fighting Ledesmar and Trune. Seems like a not-so-great payoff for a risky betrayal, you know?"

"That is the mystery, young Poe," Tomasso said, a dry laugh crossing his chapped lips. "Who, indeed? I have no reason to doubt your loyalties. I certainly don't doubt those of young Zorii Wynn. So that begs the question, was the traitor double-crossed in some way? Or . . ."

Poe waited, but the older man lingered on the word. After a few moments he continued, his voice growing hoarse and raw.

". . . is the double cross still coming?"

CHAPTER 24

"This station could use a little cheering up."

Poe and Zorii rolled their eyes at each other as EV-6B6 followed them down Ankot Station's central walkway, which would—according to the schematics Tomasso had handed them—lead to a large promenade. It had been a few days since Poe's chilly—in terms of temperature and in terms of mood—meeting with their leader, and it felt good to be off Elkeenar and away from the machinations of the Spice Runners, even if Poe was once again in the dark when it came to why they were doing what they were doing.

They walked slowly, their steps echoing down the winding hallway. Ankot Station had seen it all, even from its perch on the inner fringe of the Outer Rim. Once a highly trafficked base for the Galactic Empire, after the Battles of Endor and Jakku, it had fallen under the thrall of various spice-running gangs before being taken over formally by the New Republic. But the control was in name only, as Zorii didn't hesitate to clarify for Poe.

"The New Republic can't patrol everything everywhere," she'd said with a scoff. "They don't have the time or energy to care about the Outer Rim. Surely you know that by now."

Poe gave her midsection a friendly jab. She swatted his hand away playfully before leaning into him, her lips landing softly on his. The kiss was tender but brief, ending as Poe pulled back for a moment. They looked at each other briefly and hesitated, stepping apart and continuing on their way, as if the kiss had been a short detour. Poe tried not to focus on these missed signals as much anymore, but something hadn't happened after that kiss on the doomed Moraysian cruiser. While the feelings were there—and while they sometimes found themselves in intimate contact—it rarely evolved beyond that, as if stopped by some unseen barrier. Poe wasn't sure if he'd put it up or if she had, but it was there nonetheless, and he was unsure how to get past it.

In his darker moments, alone, lying in whatever bed he called his own on a given night, Poe wondered if it was hesitation that stemmed from that moment on the Moraysian bridge—when Gen Tri had ordered him to fire on the New Republic ships and he'd paused for a second or two too long, just enough for Marinda Gan to step in. Did Zorii think him weak? Or perhaps not loyal to her cause? Possibly, Poe thought. Possibly because it was true.

As if in response to his thoughts, Zorii gripped his

hand—her fingers tightening around his for just a moment and then releasing them—and it meant *something*, Poe knew. Their eyes met. Zorii gave him a devious smile.

It was clear to Poe that Zorii reveled in their current life—on the run from the New Republic, hopping from base to base, learning the tricks of the trade from one of the best thieves in the galaxy in Tomasso, and taking orders right from the top of the Spice Runners of Kijimi food chain. This was what Zorii had dreamt of since birth, and she didn't hesitate to tell Poe that when they had moments together—lying by the fire and sharing stories of their childhood, in the pilot's seat of the *Ragged Claw* as Poe guided Zorii's hands over the controls, or as Zorii walked Poe through the various tools in her compact but versatile lock-picking kit. Over time, she'd become a more than serviceable pilot, and he could do a passable imitation of a scoundrel.

"Kind of odd to be here, on our own," Poe said, his eyes darting around the space station. "I mean, aside from Eevee."

"I'm very happy to be here with you," EV-6B6 chirped. "It is truly an—"

"Tomasso trusts us," Zorii said as she continued to lead them down the walkway. "That means a lot."

Tomasso, despite his legendary status among thieves

and within the Spice Runners gang, had become a bit like a bemused surrogate father to them, putting up with their moods, bad habits, and quirks with a chagrined smile and unexpected patience. But when business beckoned, he was quick to revert to the role of Tomasso, second-in-command of the Spice Runners of Kijimi, and abandon the doting foster father act. Zorii and Poe had sensed the shift happening earlier that morning, when he asked them to meet outside of his ramshackle shed to discuss their orders.

"Hope we find this guy fast," Poe said. "This place isn't what I'd call cozy."

"This guy" was a noted smuggler named Alfris Sotin, who'd relayed to the Spice Runners—and various other potential buyers, Tomasso was sure—that he'd come into a large supply of chak-root and a cache of "mint-condition" Imperial weaponry and ships, apparently forgotten in a holding area only Sotin could access. Sotin was a Fiumarian—with a pale, pinkish complexion, pupilless eyes, and a long, sloping forehead. From what Tomasso had told them, Fiumarians were also deceptively fast and adept at closing deals—their ability to remain neutral during even the most heated negotiations serving them well as diplomats and smugglers.

The goal was to negotiate a suitable price with Sotin and then relay word to Tomasso and the rest of the Spice

Runners, who'd come and collect the fleet. Then, with just one deal, the organization would take a gigantic leap in terms of size and firepower—the kind of game-changing development that could alter the galaxy's criminal underworld for generations. But Tomasso had been clear as they left about the potential downside.

"One thing you'll learn over time is that often a deal seems too good to be true," Tomasso said, folding his hands together. "And that's because it is. Be wary. Listen and be patient. If anything feels strange, step back, reconsider, and wait."

Tomasso's warning was ringing through Poe's mind as they reached the end of the hallway. He wasn't sure why.

"We appear to be closing in on the meeting point, Master Poe and Mistress Zorii," EV-6B6 said, slowing down her pace. "I believe there's a—"

"I see him," Poe said. He'd come to almost tolerate the droid, but at moments like these, he regretted saving the hunk of metal. He wasn't really up for having every step of the journey narrated by a bubbly machine. "Hang back and let Zorii and me handle this."

"Certainly. I'm here to serve," EV-6B6 said with a cheerful bounce that seemed out of place.

The figure stood at the far end of the abandoned promenade—empty storefronts and outdated machinery littering a space that had once housed a lively and active common area. The station, abandoned for years now, had changed hands so many times there were markings and signage from the many regimes that had held sway over it—Imperial propaganda, New Republic optimism, and the bare-bones and direct bartering language of spice runners and thieves.

Alfris Sotin stood alone on the far edge of the central promenade—thin, medium build, his limbs long and almost slithery. His dark eyes darted around as Poe and Zorii approached, a wry smile on his face. His clothing was baggy and simple, the gray jumper giving off the air of a prison inmate or medical patient, Poe thought.

"Ah, the fabled Spice Runners sent me their very best hatchlings, eh?" he said smugly. "I'm glad we could make this happen on such short notice. Tomasso seemed very intrigued by my offer."

"We all are," Zorii said, stepping forward. "We have your payment. Where are the ships?"

Poe knew she was going to take point on the negotiations. It was her area of expertise, not his. Still, his unease grew as they got closer to the smuggler.

"Patience, patience, young lady," Sotin said with a wave of his hand. "The art of the deal and all that. Part of the fun is the conversation, don't you think?"

"Not really," Zorii said, her tone muted and all business. "You asked for us, we came. Now let's trade. Isn't that your business, smuggler?"

"Oh, *smuggler*, such a dirty word," Sotin said with a grimace, shaking his head. "I prefer *dealer*—or *facilitator*. I bring people together, or bring things to people that want them, is all. I'd heard through my channels that the Spice Runners of Kijimi might be on the lookout for some, well, added firepower, shall we say? Prepping for a big battle, are we?"

"What do you care?" Poe said, stepping in front of Zorii. "Let's just make the deal as offered and be on our way."

He regretted it almost immediately. He'd ruined her momentum. He felt her hand on his shoulder.

"Let me handle it, Poe," she whispered in his ear. "Okay?"

He nodded. She pushed him back gently and moved closer to the Fiumarian.

"Please forgive my, um, partner," she said. "He's a little overeager."

"It happens—especially with one so young," he said. "Not to worry."

He looked around the promenade. His demeanor was skittish and strange, Poe thought. Something was up.

"Can we discuss next steps?" Zorii said, trying to push the conversation forward. "We're ready to help you. Are you able to return the favor? Let's get this over with."

Sotin smiled his unnerving smile, the deep blackness of his eyes almost hypnotic. He looked amused at Poe and Zorii's impatience. This Fiumarian known for his negotiating prowess and speedy dealmaking seemed content to sit back and watch them squirm.

It gave Poe a moment to scan the base around them—the crumbling architecture and untended walls and floors. It looked like something discarded, just pulled out of the trash and dusted off in the hopes of salvation. An isolated point where two groups of thieves met to make deals and try to survive the galactic jungle they both called home.

Krat. Scritch. Scrit.

The noises seemed like the usual creaking-space-machinery sounds, Poe tried to tell himself—just standard, nothing-to-worry-about reverberations. The station was old, falling apart. But his gut said something else. His gut screamed one word:

Run.

"Eevee, what's that noise?" Poe whispered to their droid companion as Zorii continued to try to get Sotin to close the deal. "Do you hear it?"

"I do, yes, but I've decided to keep comments to myself, based on how my last few—"

"Eevee, cut the crap, will you?" Poe hissed. "There's no time for moping. Can you hear the sounds or not?"

Poe looked up to see Zorii turning around, her face stricken with panic.

"What?" Poe asked. "What is it?"

"It's a trap," Zorii said.

"Oh, don't take it so personally," Sotin said. "You can't be surprised, can you?"

"Sotin," Zorii said. "What's going on here?"

"He double-crossed us," Poe said. "You sold us out?"

"I'm a businessman, you know. So when the Guavians offered me a healthy sum, well, it just made sense. I mean, I am in quite some debt to them, so—"

The words sent a jolt of terror through Poe's body. In his months with the Spice Runners, he'd gotten a crash course on the criminal landscape of the galaxy—from Pykes to the Hutt empire to other spice runner groups, it all seemed pretty intuitive. While most of the gangs—despite being competitors—had a sense of understanding of how they fit in with the others, the one exception was the Guavian Death Gang—a cabal chased out of the Core Worlds by their fellow thieves, murderers, and bounty hunters. They were too bad to even be considered part of the bad guys, Poe thought as Tomasso had relayed the story. The Guavian soldiers underwent surgical procedures to augment their physical attributes with cybernetic implants—mechanical reservoirs that pumped chemicals into their bloodstreams to amplify their rage and speed. Most frightening of all, the Death Gang members didn't make much noise when they approached—communicating with each other via some kind of high-frequency comlink.

It was too late, Poe realized as he looked around to see the red-armor-clad figures surrounding them. The sound Poe and EV-6B6 had heard was the scraping of the Guavians' metal boots on the gravel-coated space station floor—the only giveaway that these faceless killers of killers were coming for them.

But why? Poe wondered. To what end? What did they have that the Guavians wanted? And who, aside from Tomasso, knew they were coming?

"What do you want?" Poe asked. "What's the meaning of this?"

A trilling chuckle escaped Sotin's pale lips.

"Hand over the girl," Sotin said as the lead Death Gang member, his completely masked face tilting slightly as he pointed at Zorii, stepped forward. "And I'm sure they'll make your death less painful."

Zorii. They were after Zorii Wynn.

CHAPTER 25

"I've been at this game a long time, young man," Sotin said to Poe. "If I cared about you or your pretty friend, I'd apologize."

Sotin took a satisfied breath before continuing.

"I don't. This good deed pulled me out of a nasty chit I owed our quiet friends here," he said. "And that is worth much more than any relationship with the Spice Runners of Kijimi, or Tomasso."

"That's not very nice," EV-6B6 said, shaking her head. "You don't seem like a good person."

Before the Guavians—about six of them—could begin to close in, Zorii was on the move, shooting first. It was in moments like these that Poe felt closest to her—saw the fire in her eyes and admired how little she hesitated when it was time to take action.

Zorii pointed her blaster above the crowd and sent up three quick shots. The blasts loosened pieces of the base's shoddy ceiling, sending chunks of plaster and metal hurtling down toward them. Poe and Zorii were able to lunge backward as the debris began to fall. It wasn't enough to disable the Guavians—that would prove to be a bigger challenge on any day—but it did give them the one thing they desperately needed: a head start.

"Go, go," Zorii said, pulling Poe by the arm, leading him and EV-6B6 down another entryway opposite the hallway they'd come in from. "We don't have much time."

"Smart move there, with the ceiling," Poe said, out of breath, trying to keep pace. "But I hate to remind you this is not the way we came—the *Claw* is in the other direction."

"I know," she said, turning around and sending a few hasty shots in the opposite direction. "We're not going backwards."

The fire caused a series of doors to close, which would only delay the Guavians for a few moments—but that might just be enough.

"It appears we are heading toward the central control terminal, but I must remind you, Mistress Zorii—"

EV-6B6 didn't get to finish her sentence before Zorii cut left down another hallway. Poe knew better than to question her at times like this. Even with the distractions and well-timed blaster shots, he could still hear the Guavians making their way toward them. They couldn't risk getting caught. Getting caught was a death sentence: immediate execution for Poe and EV-6B6, and something longer and more painful for Zorii—depending on why they were after her and who was paying them to take her.

What is so special about Zorii Wynn? Poe thought as they reached a set of thick double doors. It wasn't just about the Guavians hunting her down. It was other, smaller things, too. A comment made by Tomasso in passing. Gen Tri asking Poe to ensure Zorii got back to Sorgan safe. A knowing look between Gen Tri and Vigilch aboard the *Ragged Claw*.

He tried to ignore the pieces floating in front of his vision. Surely he should know whatever her secret was by now. They'd been so close—more than friends. She knew all there was to know about Poe Dameron—but did he know everything about Zorii?

She knelt in front of a small terminal to the right of the doors and pulled out her lock-picking kit. The Guavians were maybe ten or fifteen seconds away, Poe guessed.

"I'll try to cover you," he said, turning to face the empty hallway. "Eevee, help Zorii with whatever she needs."

"I've got this," she said, applying her tools to the exposed and glitchy wiring. "Let me concentrate."

Ankot Station was old and beat-up, which meant it wasn't going to be a simple rewiring job—transferring power from one area of the base to another to enact a given command, like "open these doors"—it would take a bit more finessing. Poe wasn't sure they had the time for that.

The steps were growing louder. A few errant blasts. Then a large group of red shapes, turning and realizing their targets had gone left.

"They see us," Poe said, crouching and opening fire. "And that's bad, in case I need to remind you."

The Guavians took their positions and returned fire. Poe had little room to hide, a small inset wall the only bit of cover he could get. But Zorii was wide open. She seemed indifferent to the wave of incoming fire, her eyes locked on the panel, tiny blue sparks flickering off her tools as she tried different methods to get the doors open.

"Whenever you're ready, Zorii," Poe said as he leaned out and sent off a quick volley of blaster fire, landing a blow against one of the lead Guavians. But it had little effect, as the target got back on his feet moments later.

"They don't seem to be taking much damage from your blaster, Master Poe," EV-6B6 said. "Maybe we should try something else? Just a thought."

"Yeah, Eevee? What do you suggest? Maybe I should use the laser cannon I've been holding in reserve?"

"I'm just trying to be helpful," EV-6B6 said, her voice oddly soothing. "But I see my words have made this more stressful for you. I'm sorry."

Before they could continue, a loud hiss interrupted them. Poe wheeled around to see Zorii darting through the open doors to the main control terminal. She was motioning for them to follow her.

"Hurry, before they catch up," she said. "I got it open, but I'm not sure I can close the doors in time."

They followed. Poe turned quickly and did his best to try to give her cover, but the Guavians were coming in hard and fast. Poe took a glancing shot, his arm burning from the close call.

He got off another few blasts, but the Guavians had given up on trench warfare. Instead, they were just making their way toward the doorway, ignoring Poe's blaster fire. Some would fall, but the rest would keep coming, unrelenting.

"They're not stopping," Poe said, his nerves coming through in a singsong he hated. "This is not good."

"Poe, be quiet," Zorii snapped, not looking at him. She leaned into the terminal, elbows jutting out at weird angles, brow furrowed. "I've . . . almost . . ."

One of the Guavians crossed the threshold. Poe blasted him back, but another took his place. This was how it would end, Poe guessed. Cornered by a pack of murderers on a dead space station, looking for Imperial weaponry that never existed.

"Got it!"

The doors closed at an accelerated rate, the huge metal

slabs crushing the unlucky Guavian's leg, leaving the lower half in the control room with them, the rest of him writhing in pain on the other side.

The red-plated leg smeared blood on the doors as it slid to the ground with an empty clank.

"That's disgusting," Poe said, averting his eyes.

"You're welcome," Zorii said as she walked farther into the room. "We don't have much time. They'll regroup and figure out another way inside."

Poe caught up with Zorii and placed a hand on her shoulder. She brushed him off, surprised at the touch.

"Zorii, why are these goons after you?" Poe asked. She wouldn't meet his eyes, but he pressed. "What is going on?"

" 'What is going on?' " she said, turning to face him. "I'm trying to save your life, that's what's going on. Now let me do my job and then you can do yours—flying us off this godsforsaken base."

Poe backed up, hands raised in surrender as Zorii took a seat in front of a large monitor and began typing feverishly. That was when the thumping noises on the other side of the door began. Then the blaster fire. The Guavians weren't known for giving up.

Poe stood behind Zorii, trying to stay out of her way but curious to see what she was doing. On the terminal were numerous real-time cam feeds, showing them different angles and views from around the base. Most were barren—no people, no movement, just broken-down equipment and empty rooms. But the one she enlarged and zoomed in on was familiar—the hallway they'd just evacuated. It showed the gang of Guavians taking turns blasting the door while others seemed to be working on a bigger weapon, a long cannon-like cylinder protruding from a tripod base.

"What is that?" Poe asked.

"It appears to be some kind of portable drilling tool," EV-6B6 said, standing next to Poe. "I imagine it's quite powerful, which means they'll be here pretty swiftly."

Poe turned to the droid.

"You're a fan of stating the obvious, huh?"

"I like to help," the droid said without a hint of emotion. "I just want to make sure we're all working together as a team. It's the best way to be."

Poe didn't respond, turning his attention back to the screen.

"Let's see how they like this," Zorii said, tapping a quick succession of keys—the final one with a brief, knowing smile.

Poe moved closer and watched as two small panels on the ceiling above the Guavians opened. Moments after, a green mist was sprayed from the space. It didn't take long to figure out what the gas was meant to do. The Guavians began to spasm, gripping their helmets and contorting on the ground. After a few more moments, they were immobile. Unconscious or . . . ?

"They're alive," Zorii said, as if reading Poe's worried expression. She stood up and moved to the opposite end of the room. "Not that they deserve to live. But I know how squeamish you can get about that sort of thing."

"How did you know to—to do that?" Poe asked.

"I studied the schematics Tomasso gave us," Zorii said, only looking at Poe briefly. "Did you?"

"Where are you going?" Poe asked, ignoring Zorii's question. He was walking after her, with EV-6B6 a few paces behind. "We're done. This was a wash. Let's get back to the *Claw* and connect with Tomasso. There's nothing for us here."

"Wrong," she said, sliding into another terminal and typing away feverishly. "We have to get what we came for. I'm not going back empty-handed."

Poe moved closer to her, trying to make eye contact.

"Zorii, it was a trap," Poe said. "There's nothing here. We need to go back and talk to Tomasso, see why they were after you in particular. Doesn't that worry you?"

She met his eyes.

"Of course it does," she said. "But I'm also worried about not completing our mission. Doesn't that worry you?"

She looked away and continued to type, checking the screen above the terminal every few moments. After a while, she spoke, not looking at Poe or EV-6B6.

"Sotin's ship is still docked," she said. "Looks like the Guavians took him out while we escaped."

"Guess he got a raw deal after all," Poe said.

"Couldn't have happened to a nicer smuggler," she said, leaning in to check something else. "Okay, let's head to his ship. That's where we'll find the goods, I think."

"But why would he double-cross us and still have what he promised?" Poe asked. "That seems backwards."

"Any smuggler worth his weight in mirkanite has some kind of goods on them," Zorii said, standing up and tapping the door on the far wall of the control room, opposite the sliding doors that had crushed the Guavian. "We find his ship, we find something of value—which ensures this trip wasn't a complete waste of our time and money."

Poe didn't respond, letting his mind process what was going on. What he'd gotten himself into—that day and ever since he'd agreed to join the Spice Runners on Yavin 4.

Zorii noticed his silence and kept going, saying words that would haunt Poe Dameron for the rest of his life.

"We have to get what we came for."

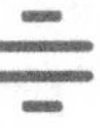

They found Sotin—alive and bound—near his ship. His pale face was bruised and bloodied, but the smuggler was otherwise intact. Poe pulled out his blaster and approached him, his own face flush with anger.

"How'd you wriggle your way out of this, Sotin?" Poe asked.

Sotin looked up, his eyes glassy, as if he was just waking up from a long nightmare.

"Oh, it's you," Sotin said, trying to force a grin. "I wondered who'd find me. If anyone would."

"The Guavians left you to die?" Zorii asked. "How sad for you."

"Oh, not to die, not exactly. Even Guavians have a code, my dear," Sotin said. "It's what makes us all thieves and criminals, no? I tipped them off to you, and they felt that was enough to let me live. Who am I to argue?"

Poe swung the handle of his blaster into Sotin's face, the soft crunch of the Fiumarian's jaw bringing him some minor satisfaction. He grabbed Sotin by the neck as his head snapped forward, yellowish blood caked on his mouth.

"Why are the Guavians after Zorii?" Poe asked, shaking Sotin with every other word. "What did they want?"

"Are you mad?" Sotin spat, his expression baffled and pained. "I'm close enough to death as is. If I tell you that, I might as well jump out of this hangar myself."

Poe shoved the smuggler back, watching as his head slammed into the cold ground of the space station.

He felt Zorii's hand on his arm, pulling him toward Sotin's stout Corellian freighter—a G9 Rigger. EV-6B6 was already making her way up the loading steps and into the ship's main storage area.

"Come on," Zorii said. "Let's go."

She seemed softer somehow, as if she felt bad for Poe but also sympathized with his anger—or was drawn to it. But there was something else, something that was left unsaid. Poe tried to shake it off as he moved a half step behind her.

As they boarded the ship, Zorii got on her knees and began feeling the floor—running her hand over certain areas, almost as if she was wiping it down. Poe and EV-6B6 crouched down and tried to see what she was looking at but came up empty.

"Um, Zorii?" Poe asked. "Are you okay?"

"Trying to find something," she said, almost to herself. "Every ship has one. Every smuggler needs one."

"Needs . . . what, exactly?"

"A secret compartment," she said, grunting to herself as her fingers latched on to something. "There . . . this is it. Help me out here."

"A secret compartment for what, though?"

"Poe, can you think for a second?" Zorii said, exasperated. "He's a smuggler. Smugglers steal and, well, smuggle things. How else do you think people like Sotin transfer goods illegally?"

Before Poe could respond, a loud, sharp screech filled the storage area and Zorii fell backward, a panel in her hands. Beneath where the panel had been was a long tunnel with a ladder embedded in it. Where it led was anyone's guess. Poe didn't have much time to ponder, though. Zorii started to climb down, unfazed by the ladder to nowhere. Poe followed, telling EV-6B6 to stay topside.

A few moments after they started their descent, Poe heard noises. The buzz of voices. A chorus of nervous whispers. Eventually sobs. *What is down here?* he thought. *Who is down here?*

What had Sotin been doing?

Zorii heard the same sounds but remained stoic as they reached the end of the ladder and a lower level—dark and claustrophobic. The sense of falling deeper into a hole with no sure way of getting back out hovered in the back of Poe's mind. The smell hit them hard. Dank and dirty. Waste and soiled clothing. They both pulled out their blasters and walked down a low and narrow hallway, dust and grime coating the walls. It didn't take long for them to reach the main holding area—the secret compartment Zorii had hoped to find. But she hadn't hoped to find this, Poe knew.

The space was not large—perhaps the size of the entire *Ragged Claw*—and full of people, all kinds. Human, Kubaz, Yarkora, a Dressellian or two, Crolute, and a Duros in the background. They ranged in age from teenagers to the elderly. Various genders. Each one of them was chained to the wall—and it looked like they'd been down there for some time.

"What is this?" Poe asked.

"Prisoners to be sold into slavery," Zorii said, moving toward the first row of captives.

She started blasting the connections holding their bonds together. With each blast, a handful of them were freed, rubbing their hands, muttering thanks in their native tongues. Zorii nodded and moved on to the next row, repeating her action. Poe moved past the crowd of people forming around Zorii—those who were freed and looking for a way off the ship, and those still chained in place, desperately tugging and moving closer to freedom.

"Slavery?" Poe said. "How is that possible?"

"Look around you, Poe," Zorii said, continuing with her task, not slowing down. "What other explanation is there?"

"So Sotin is a slaver?"

Zorii didn't answer. *Another obvious question*, Poe thought. He continued anyway.

"We have to take him in, or—do something, destroy this ship," Poe said. "Or, I dunno, we have to—"

Zorii spun around, eyes wide, blaster in hand.

"What, Poe? We have to what? Kill Sotin?" she asked harshly. "To what end?"

"So we do nothing?"

Zorii scoffed, offended.

"No, we free these people, take them somewhere, and move on," she said, destroying the last batch of restraints. The crowd was beginning to get unruly, desperate to get out of the cramped, soiled chamber.

"Sotin needs to pay for this," Poe said, surprised by the chill in his own voice. "This is wrong."

Zorii smirked and looked up at Poe. She patted his cheek. It was not a gesture of affection.

"Poe, you have much to learn, even after all this time together," she said. "Do you really think killing Sotin—which, wow, is that what you're suggesting?—will fix anything?"

Poe bristled.

"Of course it will," he said, stepping into Zorii's space, his anger bubbling out with every word. "He won't do it again. It will make others hesitate, too. It's the right thing to do."

"Sotin is scum," Zorii said, waving her hand to gesture at the people in the holding area. "This is wrong, yes. But do you really think by destroying him—his ship, or his operation—we'll win? That we'll eradicate all the bad things in the galaxy? Someone else—someone much worse—will come along. And then what, Poe Dameron? Do we stop being Spice Runners and start being heroes?"

"So, what? We just let him go?" Poe said. He was in her face. They weren't talking anymore; they were yelling. "We just resign ourselves to being part of this? To doing business with people like him?"

Zorii shook her head and backed away.

"If we let him go, we deal with the devil we know. The Spice Runners have worked with Sotin for a long time, Poe. We need him around. We free these people now, and we do some good. He knows he cheated us, and I don't expect it to happen again. That's how these things work. Thieves double-cross thieves who double-cross scoundrels. It's the world we live in," Zorii said. "It's not our call anyway. Tomasso spoke to Zeva directly about this, and she sent us because she thought we could handle ourselves. Coming back and saying we killed Sotin without at least trying to get their okay first doesn't make sense. What if the Spice Runners leadership knows something we don't? We can't just act on our own. Sometimes you have to let things go."

Poe slammed his fist into the ship's wall before he even realized he was going to do it. The pain helped—gave him something else to feel, to think about. Something besides rage and helplessness.

"This isn't you, Zorii," Poe said, his voice hollow and soft.

She cut through the people who'd begun to crowd around them and jabbed him in the chest with her fingers, pushing him back.

"This is us," she said, baring her teeth. "This is how things work out here, Poe, on the edges of the galaxy. There are no black-and-white answers or simple choices. It's all gray and complicated. You can't just swoop in, play hero, and leave. You have to live in this world."

"This arguing is making me very uncomfortable," EV-6B6 said. They ignored her.

Poe started to respond, but Zorii cut him off.

"What did you think you were doing when you got on the *Ragged Claw*, Poe? Saving the galaxy?" she said. She moved farther into the holding cell, motioning with her blaster for the group to follow her. "I'll meet you back at the base once I figure out what to do with these people. How to do some actual good, instead of daydreaming."

A moment later, Zorii Wynn was gone, leading the group of prisoners down the walkway and to the ladder, to freedom. Poe Dameron stood alone in the dank holding cell, his hand bruised and bleeding and his world in pieces.

CHAPTER 26

"You're going to fly us through the Torch Nebula?" Zorii asked, her voice rising above the chaos swirling around them. "Are you insane?"

Poe shook his head. No, he was not insane. But he was desperate. He was piloting the *Vondel*, Sotin's old ship, at maximum speed and it still wasn't enough. He felt the space between their ship and their pursuers closing. Along with Zorii, he had Tomasso and the EV droid, but he wasn't sure any of them could help him.

There were three slim and fast *Karura*-class ships hot on their heels—enforcers for the bloodthirsty Osako space pirates, hell-bent on getting their hands on what the Spice Runners of Kijimi had just made off with. It had been a busy few hours. He shot a quick glance at Zorii, who was frantically checking her terminal to try to find some kind of lost reserve, any forgotten button or switch that might get them ahead for a few moments while the hyperdrive slowly came back online. *If* it came back, Poe mused.

Six months had passed since the incident on the Moraysian cruiser. Eight months since Poe Dameron left his home on Yavin 4 and signed up with the Spice Runners of Kijimi. Much had changed over that time, Poe thought, perhaps too much. Ever since Zorii and Poe had parted ways on Ankot Station—she taking Sotin's prisoners on the *Vondel*, Poe and EV-6B6 returning to Tomasso with the *Ragged Claw*—a chill had permeated their relationship. A tension appeared, fully formed, replacing the warmth and intimacy Poe had come to rely on during his first few months away from home. While there had been glimmers of the Zorii he first came to know, her default setting was now one of distance. It had made Poe's new life that much lonelier, and he longed for the chance to sit and talk it out with the woman he considered his closest friend.

But that conversation would require time and peace, two things the Spice Runners had in short supply these days. After Sotin's betrayal and the Guavian attempt on Zorii, Tomasso—on orders from the mysterious, secret leadership of the Spice Runners—kept the team moving. He was vague and evasive about the need to continue changing locations, but Poe picked up enough. They were at risk, and despite the fact they'd let Sotin live, there were people eager to find out where this specific cell of the Spice Runners was hiding. Even if, on some level, it made sense, for Poe the plan proved haphazard and disruptive. He was surprised at how much he needed a home base—a place to call his own, routines to fall back on, and people he could trust. Instead, he was thrust into a nonstop world of subterfuge, shady dealings, and murky morals, without ever coming up for air. Poe was slowly realizing his thirst for adventure only stretched so far. Sure, put him on a ship and he would do his best to pilot it out of any jam. But he was becoming less and less interested in navigating the corrupt and confusing worlds that populated the Outer Rim.

Poe was torn. He fed off the adventure—the shootouts, the high-stakes space battles, the last-minute escapes. It was what he'd dreamt of since before his mother died, even before he desperately longed for a life outside of the constraints of Yavin 4. But at what cost? He often found himself wondering that as he laid down to get a few hours of sleep on any given night.

The incident inside the *Vondel* was the most egregious, but it wasn't the only one, Poe knew. His days were littered with them. Firing on New Republic ships. The murder of Ledesmar. Moments when he felt his new life tugging at the very fabric of who he was. His mind often skittered back to his confrontation with Sela Trune, aboard the Moraysian cruiser—when she'd asked him what his father and L'ulo L'ampar would think of what he'd become. What *would* they think? He tried not to dwell on it. There were more pressing issues at hand.

"They're closing in," Zorii said, not looking up from her terminal. "I hope you have a better idea than just sending us through that nebula, Poe. We'll be flying blind."

Truth was, he didn't. The best they could hope for was losing the Osako pirates in the space anomaly, which would send all their sensors off the grid and leave them to rely on their own, very limited senses—not the safest way to navigate the galaxy.

The order had come from the top of the Spice Runners organization, according to Tomasso—from the mysterious commander only referred to directly as Zeva or "our leader." They were to steal a handful of rare, previously-believed-to-be-destroyed star maps known as the Letters of Where and When, which—legend had it—carved out the best, most effective smuggling routes in the galaxy, the kind of paths that couldn't be weathered even by time and technology. They worked the galactic terrain and were the kind of head start any smuggler—especially an up-and-coming gang like the Spice Runners of Kijimi—would literally kill for.

According to the information passed down to Tomasso, the maps were being kept on the planet Guat'a, a barren, dank rock known mainly as a hub of chaos and bloodshed—a haven for spice runners, smugglers, bounty hunters, and anyone else who took refuge in the underbelly of the galaxy.

The maps were in the possession of the warlord Smaatku, a large, bloated, and slow-moving green-skinned Gordelian who hailed from the Nishmar system on the fringes of the Unknown Regions. Gordelians were often considered lazy and rarely seen away from their homeworld, but Smaatku was a rare exception, having built a strong organization on Guat'a aligned with the Osako pirates. The new confederacy didn't yet pose a major threat to the Spice Runners or other organizations of that tier, but Smaatku had also refused to pay his proper tithe to the gangs above him on the food chain. Add to that the fact that, despite being unclear on how to decipher the fabled maps, he had them in his hands and could very easily begin using them to his great advantage, and Smaatku's new group was evolving from minor annoyance to viable threat. That meant it was time for the Spice Runners to take Smaatku's shiny toy and use it for their own means.

"Let's teach them a bit about what we do," Poe said with a grin, tapping his terminal as if he was playing a valachord. "This is where you clap confidently, Zorii."

She gave him a forced smile. He felt Tomasso's hand grip his shoulder.

"We cannot afford to lose this prize, as you know," the older man said. "I should also note that the Osako pirates are not known for their kindness to prisoners. In fact, I have yet to hear of a time when they took prisoners."

Poe swallowed hard. Tomasso wasn't one to mince words.

They'd managed to land the *Vondel* on Guat'a with little fanfare—they'd purposely used Sotin's ship so as not to raise alarms. The *Ragged Claw* had become too closely identified with the Spice Runners of Kijimi. The hope was that word about their run-in with Sotin hadn't spread that far into the Outer Rim. They'd been wrong, but they hadn't known that yet.

Tomasso and EV-6B6 had stayed behind as Zorii and Poe entered Guat'a's main trading post, a market-style area known as Alshuey—half town, half trading post, and for all intents and purposes a festering dump. Everything looked and smelled worn down. Little eye contact was made, and the entire stretch of land seemed pelted by sounds from every corner—loud, droning music; unintelligible screams; the staccato rhythms of bartering, pleading, and dealmaking.

"Smaatku holds court at the center of this area," Zorii said, taking point. "It's about a two-minute walk from here."

They'd adopted the attire of seasoned smugglers, unaffiliated and looking to deal. Both Zorii and Poe's faces were covered by colorful scarves, only revealing their eyes. If anyone looked close enough, they'd be able to tell the two were human, but the hope was no one would have enough time to stare.

It wasn't hard for Poe to figure out where they were headed. Every stand, store, terminal, and workshop seemed to be built around another, larger building. For a split second, Poe thought he was back on Yavin 4, heading toward Gully's. He could almost hear Fontis's hissing tone, smell the wood chips and ale-coated floorboards. But they were very far from Yavin 4, and Poe wasn't sure he'd ever see Fontis—or his father—again. The thought hit him like a strong wave. He tried to shake it off, but Zorii noticed his hesitation, taking a step or two ahead of him before turning around.

"Poe, let's go—we don't have time for soul-searching," she said, keeping her voice low. "In and out, that's what Tomasso said."

He nodded. A few months earlier, he would have tried to debate Zorii—push back on her criticism, eager to have her believe he was as into this life as she was. But those days were gone, he realized. He wondered if there was a path back to what they'd been or had—to those two eager teenagers savoring their new, exciting life. Maybe they could figure that out at some point—decide if being part of the Spice Runners was really what they both wanted. Perhaps they could strike out on their own. Poe almost laughed. Who was he kidding? This life was all Zorii had ever wanted. He knew it in his soul.

Smaatku's base of operations was a social club, according to Tomasso—a place for people to meet, share stories, have a laugh, and listen to music. But from the outside it looked like any other dive cantina or dead-end bar Poe had seen. It made Gully's look like a vacation spot. He followed Zorii as she entered the place called Rugova's, and instantly his sense of smell was assaulted: the odor of bodies cramped together, of cheap overcooked food, of stale liquor and unkempt counters and floors. It reminded Poe of the outhouse on his dad's farm after a few days of negligence. He looked at Zorii for a similar reaction but saw none. Stoic and unfeeling as ever, she was playing a role—a desperate smuggler looking for the next deal. Poe hoped no one had seen him wince as he stepped in. They'd be out of there soon, he reasoned, if everything went according to plan.

The place was sprawling and labyrinthine—and though it was full of people, each group had enough space to huddle up in their own corner or hunch over their tables, whispering to each other or screaming for another beverage. Poe could make out a central staging area, with a number of uniformed guards standing around a throne-like seat. Zorii leaned in, her mouth close to his ear.

"There he is," she said. "We need to get close to him. He keeps the maps on his body."

Smaatku was a large, bulbous, and imposing figure who was also impressive in his physique, not just slovenly but stocky and strong—a being of power and clearly the leader, even there in that mixed company. He sat ramrod straight in his chair, scanning the venue and nodding to himself, the dark black bags under his large eyes in stark contrast to his greenish skin. He drank from a large silver goblet, long sloppy pulls that spilled almost as much as he managed to swallow. He wiped at his mouth with his bare arm and smiled in Poe's direction. Poe almost froze, thinking the gang leader had spotted him, but soon realized Smaatku was merely entranced with the entire spectacle of Rugova's. This was his element, and he felt at home with his people and his business associates. The perfect time to strike, Tomasso had said—when someone is most relaxed and expects it the least.

Zorii motioned with her head for Poe to follow her as she circled the large central bar and moved to the left, toward a less trafficked hallway that seemed to be for staff. They made it a few paces before they were stalled by a towering Guat'a guard with two masked figures behind him, smaller in size but eager to point their blasters at Zorii and Poe.

"You're not allowed back here," the Guat'a guard said, his voice gruff and low. "Go back to the bar. Mind your business, strangers."

They hadn't discussed what to do if they were intercepted, but for Poe, this was the fun part.

"Hey, no worries, friend. We get it," Poe said, muffling his voice and raising a hand in a sign of peace. "Totally get it. In fact, we were just here to give you a heads-up about the Dressellians that just walked in. They're shaking down the barkeep and it's getting violent. They don't seem to, well, fit with the vibe here."

The large Guat'a guard grunted in the direction of the bar, nostrils flaring.

"Dressellians? Attacking Jarv?" he said, sounding more annoyed than surprised. He muttered something unintelligible but decidedly impolite before brushing past them and into the main bar area.

That left Poe and Zorii plus the two masked guards. They'd kept their blasters locked on target.

"You can move along now," the first one said, moving his blaster toward the bar. "You've done your good deed for the day."

"Happy to help," Poe said, turning around slightly. "We'll be on our way."

Out of the corner of his eye, he saw the guards lower their weapons, expecting the two strangers to wander back into the crowd. Instead, Poe and Zorii both crouched and shot out their feet in a unified pair of kicks, each one hitting their respective guard in the lower leg. Both guards crumbled fast, following a soft crack as the kicks made contact. Their moans of pain were muted, muffled by the dark leather masks they wore. In the time it took them to recover, the blasters the guards had been pointing at Poe and Zorii were squarely pointed at them instead.

"Don't say another word," Zorii said.

The main doors to Rugova's slid open as Zorii and Poe walked out of the musky watering hole and made for a batch of landspeeders parked near the entrance. They were not moving casually—quite the opposite. Poe's heart pounded as he gripped the embroidered case close. After evading the initial coterie of guards, Zorii and Poe had slinked toward Smaatku and his throne. The overlord held the case tightly in his lap, and Poe knew they'd only get one shot at grabbing it. With Poe serving as a distraction—bellowing "It's a raid!" turned more than a few heads—Zorii grabbed the goods and they made a beeline for the exit. They weren't surprised when the gang gave chase. Poe heard Zorii a few steps behind him as they hit the open air, followed by a loud, gut-wrenching scream.

"Do not let them escape!" Smaatku bellowed, the final syllable more a roar than an actual word. He was surrounded by about a dozen more masked guards, all of them chasing Zorii and Poe on foot. "Do not let them steal from us!"

Poe took cover behind one of the landspeeders and sent over a few blaster shots. It didn't slow down the horde much, but it bought him and Zorii enough time to hop on the farthest speeder—with Poe behind the wheel and Zorii clutching his midsection, turning her body to fire behind them. But the benefit of the small vehicle wasn't paying dividends just yet, and the guards were closing in.

"Can this thing go any faster?" Zorii asked, out of

breath, each word matched by the sound of her blaster going off. "We're not going to get far enough to avoid getting blown up."

"Patience, patience," Poe said. He was trying his best to hide the anxiety in his voice as he slammed his foot down on the accelerator, the tiny landspeeder bumping on the ground as he tried to keep it steady and prevent it from flipping over. "Just keep me covered."

"I've got one blaster," Zorii said, one arm wrapped around his torso so she could lean backward and send a few more shots in the direction of the guards, who were now a handful of meters away. "They have dozens. That's bad math, Poe."

For a moment, a long shadow overtook them. Poe and Zorii glanced upward.

Then the explosions started.

Their landspeeder trembled as a trio of blaster cannon shots landed behind them, obliterating the bulk of their pursuers. Poe, Zorii still gripping him, wheeled the speeder around and caught a glimpse of the carnage through the black smoke and fire. Screams of pain rose from the crater created by the cannon. Poe saw shadowy forms trying to rise but collapsing to the ground, unable to stand. The moans and pained sounds formed a chorus of anguish that Poe couldn't shake, even as he pulled his eyes away and upward to see the *Vondel* hovering above the scene. Tomasso.

"Was . . . was that . . . ?" Poe said, faltering. "Why?"

Zorii pulled him off the landspeeder, trying to get his attention as the ship landed and the rear hatch opened.

"What did you want to happen?" Zorii said with a snap. "We had to make sure we could get away clean. Stop being so precious."

He didn't respond. It was an argument Poe knew he couldn't win—and he was tired of trying. Poe understood that lives were lost—but this wasn't war in the same sense as the battles his parents fought in. This was murder, Poe realized. But Tomasso—and Zorii—were not as concerned with the loss of life, especially when the people being taken down were those they considered the enemy: rivals who would just as easily slide a dagger into their backs as make a deal face to face. In their eyes, they'd gotten what they wanted. At the same time, they were able to gut a potential threat—Smaatku and his gang—before they gained much traction. Win-win for them. But was it right?

Poe knew the answer as he followed Zorii up the ramp, and it made his stomach turn.

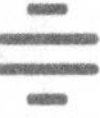

"Now entering the Torch Nebula," Poe said as he pivoted the *Vondel* into the astral anomaly. Tomasso, Zorii, and EV-6B6 had strapped into their seats. "Gonna get bumpy pretty fast."

"Osako ships aren't far behind," Zorii said.

"I've never been through a nebula before," EV-6B6 said excitedly. "It should be interesting at the very least."

Poe fought the urge to turn around and just stare at the droid. But there was no time to ponder the awkward optimism of EV-6B6—they had to avoid getting overtaken by pirates. Just another day in the life of a spice runner, Poe thought.

"They're in pursuit," Zorii said, checking a reading on her display. "Sensors are flickering. We should expect them to go offline any second."

The gamble had failed. Poe had hoped that by jetting into the nebula, he'd catch the pirates off guard, but they predicted his move. It made him feel like an amateur. But he wasn't ready to give up. There was still a chance to lose them. If the *Vondel*'s sensors were fading, so were those on the three ships chasing it. But Poe was flying blind, and that put them all at risk every moment they wandered through the dust-filled, asteroid-heavy nebula. The Torch Nebula was far from a random space anomaly. Also known as the Torch sector, the nebula was a massive part of the territories populating the Outer Rim. It was so large that on a given night, you could spot it from the surface of nearby planets, like Guat'a and Shownar, creating a fireworks display of colorful lights. Poe was leading them through a tourist attraction, basically—except it wasn't as pretty from the inside and could cost them their lives.

Poe looked over his shoulder at Tomasso. His eyes seemed wild, hungry.

"Tomasso, can you decipher those maps?" Poe asked, his body poised to turn back around at a moment's notice. "Is there anything we can use?"

"In terms of what, son?" Tomasso asked, getting out of his seat and moving toward Poe. "These maps—they're about smuggling, how to get around. . . . Wait, I see what you mean."

The *Vondel* shuddered as Poe swung back around in his seat, squinting as he tried to make out what had hit them. Then it shuddered again.

"They're firing at us," Zorii said, shaking her head. "That one barely made contact—they're flying blind, too. But eventually they'll connect."

A few moments of silence passed. Poe did his best to steer the ship—using his own vision to guide it around a batch of debris and a large asteroid chunk—but he knew this wasn't sustainable. Eventually something would be impossible to dodge.

"Yes, yes, how could I forget?" Tomasso said to himself as he made his way back to his seat, a small screen in his hands. "The Llanic Spice Run—it's near here."

He handed the screen to Poe, pointing to the top of the map that dominated the visual.

"This is where we are," Tomasso said excitedly. "And this is where the Llanic Run intersects with the Triellus Trade Route—near the planet Llanic."

"How does that help us?" Poe said, trying to divide his attention between Tomasso and guiding the *Vondel* around the floating debris that made up most of the nebula. "I mean, it's nice that those routes are there, but . . ."

"The route is cleared, Poe—it's a pathway for thieves and our kind to ferry goods, even through the thick of a nebula," Tomasso said with a knowing grin. "It may not save us completely, but it'll certainly help."

Poe felt his face grow hot, and a shot of shame passed through him for questioning the older man. Tomasso was no one's fool, and while he took Poe's defensiveness in stride, Poe still felt like he'd offended the spice runner. But the sentimental apologies would have to wait, he thought.

Poe punched in the coordinates and guided the ship as best he could, knowing that the *Vondel*'s long-range sensors were unreliable at best, the short-range ones completely shot.

"The pirates are trying to match our course change, but it's taking them a second," Zorii said, a sliver of hope in her voice. "They're not quitting."

"Neither are we," Poe said, more to himself than anyone else. He was surprised to feel Zorii's hand grip his, the touch brief but true. Their eyes met before they returned their attention to their respective terminals.

The ship shook again. A glancing shot but a hit nonetheless.

"They're strafing now, trying to get as many shots off as they can muster in one direction, hoping to make contact," Zorii said. "Hard to dodge."

"I believe in you," EV-6B6 said.

"Why do these pirates have a deal with Smaatku?" Poe wondered aloud. It'd bothered him since Tomasso had picked them up from Guat'a with the *Vondel*. He knew Smaatku's operation was small and growing—but was it big enough to partner with the Osako pirates? Wouldn't they see it as helping a competitor?

"You think they're helping Smaatku?" Zorii said, a quick scoff escaping her mouth. "Not quite. They know what Smaatku has—well, had. Word travels fast in places like Rugova's. The easier thing to believe is they figured out what we did and realized they wanted those maps, too."

Poe nodded. Zorii's explanation made sense, but there was still a piece of the puzzle missing. He didn't have much to go on beyond his own gut, and that wasn't enough to spar with Zorii Wynn—something he'd had his fill of lately.

The ship wobbled more violently, almost spinning out. Poe gripped the controls fiercely. His body was shoved forward, and he had to strain to stay in his seat.

"What the hell was that?" Poe asked, pushing the *Vondel* downward to avoid a batch of debris. "We're closing in on the spice run. Should be there momentarily, if I'm eyeballing this right."

"They're still shooting," Zorii said. "That felt like a direct hit. I can't get a good lock on where they are, though."

"Which means they can't lock on us, either," Poe said. The ship spasmed again as Poe wove the *Vondel* around a few more errant meteors—hopefully confusing their pursuers a bit more. "Let's keep that going."

The ship continued to shake and shimmy as Poe took it through its paces—diving deep, jerking left, right, and up again. It made for a stomach-turning ride.

"This is almost enjoyable," EV-6B6 said.

A few minutes passed and Poe leveled out the ship's trajectory. It was oddly quiet.

"I don't see them," Zorii said. "But that doesn't mean they're not around."

"We're taking the run now," Poe said, a drop of hope in his voice. If they managed to make it through the Llanic Spice Run, they'd be free of the Torch Nebula and in open space—which would give them a chance to jump to hyperspace and find their way home. If the drive was functional in time. "Hang on."

The *Vondel* groaned as it picked up speed, inertia pushing everyone back into their seats with a jolt. Poe let out a long breath. He didn't realize he'd been holding it until that moment. Could they have lost the pirates? The ride smoothed out as the ship cruised through the last leg of the Llanic Run. In the distance, Poe thought he could see the end of the Torch Nebula. Once they were clear, they could pivot home and see to it that the head of the Spice Runners of Kijimi got the loot they'd snagged from Smaatku.

Poe squinted as he poured on a bit more speed. The clearing changed shape a bit. What he'd first thought was an opening—a sign that the galactic anomaly was ending, was actually something else. Something big.

"Is—is that a ship?" Poe asked.

Zorii frantically pecked at her terminal, looking up every so often.

"Sensors are still mostly offline," she said. "But a bit better now that we're picking up speed. It seems like that's . . . not one of the pirate ships, though. Whatever it is, it's not moving."

"Perhaps they're here to help," EV-6B6 said, her voice upbeat and curious. "That would be quite opportune."

Poe ignored the hyper-positive droid and pulled back on the speed, but it was too late. They were closing in, and as they moved toward the mysterious object, it came into focus.

"Oh boy," Poe said, the memory of their last encounter with the ship in front of them flooding his mind. "This isn't good."

The giant Moraysian cruiser seemed to sense their recognition as it swiveled slightly to face the *Vondel*. It looked much improved from the last time Poe had seen it, when the ship had been seconds from complete destruction. Someone—something—had taken the time to repair it. But who? And to what end?

"Getting a message," Zorii said. She seemed shaken. Surprised. The one thing Zorii Wynn hated, Poe knew, was to be surprised. "They're not hailing us, just sending us a transmission. First . . . a set of coordinates . . . then the words 'Land your ship immediately if you want to live.' "

Poe steeled himself. They'd beaten this ship before. There had to be a way out.

Zorii turned to face him.

"I know that look," she said. "What are you thinking?"

"Just going over our options," Poe said. "That's all."

"We're outgunned here, Poe," Tomasso said. "Our best option is to get planetside and see who we're up against, then make a move."

Poe nodded. But it was half-hearted. Surrender wasn't in his makeup. The *Vondel* still had weapons, still had some speed. And—most important—it still had Poe in the pilot's seat.

He was running through the alternatives in his head—despite Tomasso's order, despite Zorii's fears—when the first wave of fire hit. From behind.

"The pirates," Zorii said, struggling to stay in her seat as the ship shook violently, smoke bursting from a panel above them. "They found us."

"Maybe we need to rethink our strategy," EV-6B6 said. "Just some soft criticism. You're all doing a good job."

"Now is not the time, Eevee," Poe said, trying to avoid the second wave of laser cannon fire from behind. "Got bigger things to worry about right now."

The *Vondel* lurched down, dodging a new barrage from

the tiny ships. Poe heard Tomasso take a tumble behind him as the ship was rocked by another hit—this one coming from a different direction.

"The Moraysian ship just cut loose on us," Zorii said, shaking her head. "Our weapons systems are down. They targeted our—"

Before Zorii could finish, the *Vondel* took another hit, and the ship was sent spinning out, the wounded starship no longer in Poe's control. Poe fell back, slamming his head on the floor and sliding to the edge of the small bridge area, a deep cut on his forehead. Smoke and fire filled the space. He saw Zorii trying to climb back into her seat. Tomasso was out cold, with EV-6B6 attempting to revive him. Alerts, beeps, and emergency symbols flickered and blared at them. Even from the floor, Poe could see the massive shadow cast by the cruiser. Then it hit him as their pirate pursuers appeared to back off.

"They're not killing us," Poe said. "They're working together."

"They want what we have, Poe," Zorii said, wincing as she took her position again, a hand outstretched to help Poe do the same. "I told you this."

"No, look," Poe said, pointing out into space. "Those pirate ships—they're circling the cruiser. They're on the same side. This was a trap."

A loud crackle of static interrupted them, then went quiet. A barely intelligible voice cut through the dead air, low and coarse.

"We will not warn you again, Spice Runners," the voice said. "Land on the planet or die on your ship. The decision is yours."

The choice was clear. The *Vondel* was barely functional. Poe punched in the coordinates of the planet—a small hunk of rock named Judakann that could've passed for an asteroid. The surface looked jagged, a dank, inhospitable mess—not the kind of place Poe envisioned spending his final moments. Out of the corner of his eye, he saw a small Moraysian shuttle mirroring their descent. They'd meet their eventual captors soon, Poe thought.

"There's got to be a way out of this," Zorii said.

She was standing over Poe, a hand on his shoulder as if to say, *Don't give up hope yet*. But Poe was struggling not to lose the sliver of hope he had left. Their ship had no weapons or hyperdrive, Tomasso was unconscious, and their droid was unhelpful. It didn't bode well for a miraculous escape. He shook his head. No. He wouldn't fall into despair. He was the son of two of the bravest people who'd ever fought for the Rebellion, he told himself. They'd faced off against a Death Star. They'd saved the galaxy. Surely he could con his way out of the grip of a few rankled space criminals. Right?

Tomasso came to, and they disembarked from the *Vondel* slowly, Tomasso leaning on EV-6B6 for support.

"We just might run into some lurkers here," EV-6B6 said. "If I recall correctly, this is their planet of origin. I don't think they're friendly, which is a shame because they seem very—"

"Lurkers?" Poe asked.

"They're carrion eaters that thrive in this kind of environment," the droid said. "They're amphibious and very, very—"

"Enough," Tomasso said, the exhaustion in his voice evident as he waved off the droid's information download. They reached the end of the *Vondel*'s plank. Poe and Zorii followed soon after, with eyes open wide and blasters drawn.

The Moraysian shuttle landed and its rear hatch opened slowly. Two dark figures emerged, their features not discernible yet. Poe and Zorii approached, ready for a shootout.

"All right, folks," Poe said. "You have the bigger guns. You got us down here. Now tell us what you want. Let's make this easy for everyone."

"Yes, let's make this easy," one figure said. The voice sent a wave of fear through Poe, the tone and sound intimately familiar. *No, it can't be.*

The figure stepped into the planet's gray, muted light and Poe's throat tightened. It became hard to breathe. The second figure followed, and the sight almost sent him to his knees.

He reached out to Zorii, gripping her arm. Tried to keep his balance. *How is this possible?*

"Poe—what? What is it?" Zorii said, her tone desperate. "What's wrong? What's the matter?"

"What we want," the first figure said, arm outstretched, a sad, somber look on his face, "is for you to come home, Poe."

Poe crumbled, tears streaming down his face as he looked up at Kes Dameron and L'ulo L'ampar standing over him. His father and the closest thing he'd ever have to an uncle. They'd found him. They'd crossed the galaxy to reach him. They were here.

"Father . . . Dad. But—but," Poe said, his voice a feeble croak. "How . . . ?"

"What? Wait, wait a second," Zorii said, her tone harsh and surprised, Poe's hand still clamped around her arm. "Your . . . *dad*?"

CHAPTER 27

It had been almost a year, but Sela Trune never lost hope—never lost sight of her targets. Finally, her patience was vindicated. She tried to stop the smile from forming on her face as she walked briskly down the illuminated corridor of the space station, but she couldn't help it. The dam had begun to crack. Soon it would break.

Trune had always been playing the long game with the Spice Runners of Kijimi, even before they were little more than a gang of criminals with no allegiance to anyone but themselves. From the moment she heard the news—about her family, about how they died—she knew what had to be done. She would do whatever was in her power not only to destroy the Spice Runners but to make their destruction painful and impossible to ignore. It would send a message across the galaxy—to the darkest, most nefarious corners, to the people who thought the New Republic wasn't paying attention, who figured there were other, bigger problems for the New Republic to deal with. They were wrong. Trune believed in justice. If she managed to get a little vengeance along the way, so be it.

The chatter from her spies and double agents had gone quiet months before but seemed to crackle back into existence recently—as the activity of Tomasso's cell of the Spice Runners of Kijimi increased, with young Poe Dameron in tow. She felt a twinge of sympathy for the boy—she knew what it was like to be young, lost, and eagerly following an ethos you weren't sure you believed in just yet. The problem was, the lifestyle he was embracing was one that stood in stark contrast to her own ethos—and the laws of the New Republic. If her intelligence was right, the trail leading her to not only Poe Dameron but Zorii Wynn—an asset of unimaginable importance—was getting much warmer. It would soon boil over if Trune played things right.

Her subtle smile morphed into a grimace as her thoughts drifted from Poe to his father, Kes. The elder Dameron had tried every fading connection he had over the past months to find Poe—had worked every angle and called in every favor, to no avail. Trune was as eager as he was to find the boy, but for a greater reason. She didn't want Poe Dameron back so she could hug him and chastise him for being bad, as she imagined Kes did. She wanted to toss him in a cell and use whatever information he had about the inner workings of the Spice Runners to hunt for bigger game. Kes Dameron knew this, of course. Which explained why he and his friend L'ampar had gone rogue, chartering a ship and sailing into the fringes of the Outer Rim to find a boy who clearly didn't want to be found. But as it turned out, Kes Dameron's meddling had proven helpful. And combined with another angle she'd been working, it could give her the final bit of information she needed to take the fight right to the Spice Runners' leader—a force so dark, unknown, and hidden from view that sometimes Trune felt the mastermind didn't exist. But she knew better. As much as she admired the aging pirate Tomasso—and as much as she knew about his bloodied hands and murderous exploits—she couldn't bring herself to believe he was atop the Spice Runners food chain. She'd heard rumblings about someone else—a woman named Zeva. But it was all rumor and conjecture at this point. Trune needed more than that to move on it.

I've been surprised before, though, she mused as she picked up her pace. Trune absentmindedly rubbed her fingers over the bridge of her nose—which featured an added ridge where she had broken it, falling over unconscious on the Moraysian cruiser. Some things never healed right.

Good officers knew when they'd been beaten, too—and Trune was not invincible. She'd missed her chance to snare Poe and the girl known as Zorii Wynn aboard the Moraysian ship, despite her best efforts to set a palatable trap with Ledesmar.

She ignored the knowing nods and salutes as she made her way to a massive office area packed with bustling New Republic Security Bureau officers and staff, each person moving on to their next task with a speed and eagerness Trune could only admire. She approached the central operations area, where she was met by a cheerful Sullustan named Pheeb. Her large eyes receded into the jowls that covered most of her face as Trune approached, the smile gone long before.

"Trune, good to see you," Pheeb said in the thick accent of her native tongue. "I hope all is well?"

"Is the prisoner awake?" Trune asked, not in the mood for pleasantries.

Pheeb smiled curtly. Two security officers appeared and nodded at Trune, a signal that she should follow them. She did, down a winding corridor that took her past two security checkpoints and another staging area. After a few more turns, the guards walked her to a door that was situated at the far end of the station. One of the guards tapped a few numbers on a panel to the left of the door and it hissed open. Trune stepped in.

The figure was at the opposite end of the room, back turned to Trune, facing the only source of light in the space—a tiny circular window.

"They tell me you're ready to talk," Trune said.

The prisoner turned around, her long, fleshy lekku framing her face as she took notice of her visitor.

"Ah, the young Officer Trune," Marinda Gan said, her voice eager. "I'm more than ready. I'll tell you everything, if it means I can get out of here."

Trune kept her expression flat. This was standard. She wasn't going to bargain with Marinda Gan until she knew what the Twi'lek had in her hand. After all this time, she wondered if the scoundrel had anything worth sharing.

"Let's see what you've got," Trune said. "Then we can talk about compensation."

Marinda Gan smiled a toothy grin, her tongue sliding over her teeth before she spoke again. "What, pray tell, do you know about the upcoming Kijimi summit?"

CHAPTER 28

Kes Dameron pulled his son to his feet and embraced him. Poe's eyes watered again as he breathed in the familiar scent—of trees, the outdoors, home. It was really him, Poe thought, even though he couldn't believe it. He felt a hand grip his shoulder. *L'ulo*. How had the two men tracked him down?

Poe stepped back, wiping at his eyes with a rough swipe before beginning to speak, his voice halting and nervous. He knew Zorii and Tomasso were close enough to hear everything he said. He had to choose every word with care.

"Dad . . . what are you doing here?" Poe asked. "How did you find us?"

"Poe," Kes Dameron said, placing two hands on his son's shoulders. "Nothing could keep me from you. Nothing. I used every bit of power, every bit of intelligence and contacts—everything I had. It took a while. But we made it."

Poe was shoved aside. He turned to find Zorii Wynn facing his father, her eyes aflame as she pointed a finger at him.

"What is the meaning of this?" Zorii said. "You

bartered with space pirates to track down your son? For what? Poe is one of us now—he's a Spice Runner. There's no going back from that. It's a life, not a hobby."

Kes turned to look at Poe, his expression saying *Who is this?* Poe didn't flinch. This was between father and son, and Poe knew he had to figure out his next move. But Zorii's verbal barrage was helping delay that decision. The fire with which Zorii slung her words at Kes had also surprised Poe.

"You're right, Miss—" Kes started.

"Zorii," she said. "My name is Zorii. Who are you?"

"This is Kes Dameron, Poe's father," L'ulo said, stepping forward. "My name is L'ulo L'ampar. We're old hands from the Rebel Alliance days. We had a few tricks up our sleeves when it came to locating your friend Poe, here."

Zorii shook her head. She was locked in. Poe knew this was not something she was going to give up on.

"So, let me get this straight," she said, tilting her head a bit as if trying to get a better look at Kes Dameron—as if she was straining to see the resemblance between him and Poe. "You were so desperate to find your son—a man who'd left your backwater moon of his own free will—that you made a deal with a group of murderers like the Osako pirates to corner us? That doesn't seem very New Republic to me."

Kes's smile was gone. Poe could see he was growing tired of Zorii. He wanted to take his son home, not get into an ethical debate with a girl half his age.

"I almost lost my farm, almost sold it off to some scammers for a scrap of information that I thought might lead me to you," Kes said, pointing at Poe. "That was just one of many things I did that were new. Things that were desperate."

Zorii shook her head again.

"I can't believe we're being chased down by your dad," she said, looking at Poe for what seemed like the first time since they set foot on the desolate rock. "We could have been killed. Our ship is barely functional. And I doubt those pirates are just going to let us fly home when we do get off—"

"You're not leaving with my son," Kes said.

"Excuse me?" Zorii responded. "That's not your call."

"Zorii," Poe started, trying to get between his past and his present. "Let's just—"

"No, let's not," Zorii said, glaring at Kes Dameron. "What makes you think you can just stroll into our lives and take Poe from us? He's a Spice Runner now. You think just because you called in a few favors with your old cronies you can do as you please? The New Republic's tentacles don't stretch out this far, old man. And even if they did, we follow a different set of rules."

"Fathers will do whatever they need to do to find their sons," Kes said, his voice low and his speech methodical, clearly not wanting anything he said to be misinterpreted. He turned to look at Poe, eyebrows raised. "Poe, we want you to come home. It's been too long. We can talk about it all on the way back."

Tomasso spoke. His voice boomed over everyone, giving off a strength and seniority Poe had come to appreciate over time.

"Poe Dameron is not a boy, nor is he a piece of property," Tomasso said, stepping forward, losing whatever limp he'd acquired on the way down to the planet's surface. His air was regal with a dash of menace. "He is a Spice Runner, by choice and by virtue. We do not simply surrender people when their relatives come calling."

L'ulo drew his blaster and pointed it at Tomasso.

"Tomasso," L'ulo said. "I've heard of you. One of the most feared spice runners of the galaxy. I'm not impressed. We're not asking you to let us take him. We're telling you that Poe is coming with us, understand?"

Poe looked at Zorii, her eyes distant, rimmed with red. Was she expecting Poe to go back to Yavin 4, the place he was desperate to escape when they first met? Was she experiencing a tinge of regret over the past few months? Poe turned his gaze to his father and was equally surprised at what he saw there: a look of utter confusion. This was not going as Kes had planned. He'd expected Poe to leap into his arms and run back home. Instead, there was hesitation—and in front of him was a man, not a wandering boy. And this man had become something Kes Dameron had not expected.

Kes broke the silence.

"Son, everything is forgiven," he said, reaching out a hand to Poe. "Just come with us. Get on this ship. It's been too long, all right?"

Before Poe could answer, Tomasso broke in again—his voice sharpened by an unexpected, haunting chill.

"We appear to be surrounded."

The long, high-pitched hiss froze Poe in his tracks. It had taken him a second to process Tomasso's warning—but he could see now. They were everywhere. Small, stocky amphibious-looking creatures lurking a few meters away from them, all making that terrifying sound as they stepped closer and closer.

"What are they?" Zorii asked, whipping out her blaster and taking a defensive stance. "They don't seem to be—aware? I mean, they clearly want to murder us, but—"

"These are the lurkers I mentioned. What a coincidence," EV-6B6 said with genuine surprise in her voice. "Nonsentient but very, very dangerous creatures native to this planet. It'd be a shame to hurt them, but they do seem a little angry."

The first lurker leapt onto EV-6B6 and began slamming its large, webbed hands into her head, sending the droid backward, screaming as she toppled to the ground.

Kes took a few shots at the monster, knocking it off EV-6B6. But it was just the first. Soon the area was swarming with the high-jumping predators—and they were not there to make friends. Some spat a highly acidic liquid from their mouths, which caused painful, deep burns. Others had sharp, jagged teeth capable of tearing through most anything. They were fighting to kill, and there were a lot of them.

Zorii and Poe found themselves back to back, knee-deep in a dark, brownish-green puddle, surrounded by marsh and buzzing flies. Most important, there were at least a half dozen lurkers making their way toward them—their long tongues lolling out of their mouths, the muted yellow of their eyes dull and distant in the fading Belsavis sun.

"They're pretty fast for their size," Poe said as he sent a few blaster shots at a leaping lurker. He landed two hits, knocking the animal down mid-jump. It gave a pained wail as it splashed into a nearby creek. "And they seem to keep coming—"

Zorii sent off strafing shots at three of the lurkers lunging toward her, disabling them momentarily.

"I can't believe you're considering leaving," she said, keeping her eyes on the remaining lurkers, now wary of approaching her. "After all we've been through, Poe."

"Do we have to talk about this now?" Poe said, ducking to avoid a kick from the closest lurker. He sent an elbow into the green-skinned monster's face—a satisfying crack emanating from the impact. "It feels like a not-so-great time to talk about us."

"It's not about us," Zorii said, flinging a lurker back into the larger group of attackers, sending a few of them tumbling into each other. "It's bigger than that. Don't make this so emotional. That's what you always do."

Poe fired a few more shots at the two or three remaining lurkers on his side, keeping them at bay. He was bruised and battered, a deep gash on his right side from a lurker that got too close, his face caked with dirt and blood. But all things considered—he was standing and could've been much worse, he rationalized.

"I'm a sensitive guy, what can I say? It's part of my charm. Isn't it?"

Zorii didn't respond, instead sending a short kick into the remaining lurker's face as it tried to grab at her. It went down and didn't show any signs of getting back up. Zorii wheeled around and fired a quick flurry of shots into the other lurkers creeping on Poe. They fell fast and loud. Poe and Zorii stood for a moment, unsure where to go next.

Their momentary indecision was shaken by the sound of a pained human scream.

"Dad," Poe said, his tone frantic.

"I will kill you myself if you betray us, Poe Dameron," Zorii said, taking off in the direction of the scream. Poe followed.

He wanted to think she was joking, that she understood why he'd consider going back home. But in the time he'd known Zorii Wynn he'd learned a few things. First and foremost—Zorii Wynn did not joke around when it came to the Spice Runners of Kijimi. But he didn't have time to care.

He caught up with her as the second scream started. Then they broke into a run.

When Poe and Zorii made it back to the *Vondel*, they found Kes Dameron on the ground, a deep wound in his midsection—dark red seeping through his tunic as L'ulo tried to tend to him. About a dozen dead lurkers were spread out around the group. Tomasso and EV-6B6, scratched up but still functional, stood on the fringe, blasters at the ready.

"Dad," Poe said, reaching his father and falling to his knees. He took the older Dameron's hand and looked into his eyes. "Dad, what happened?"

Kes Dameron coughed, a wet, slushy sound.

"Those green things . . . sure can get at you," Kes said, stifling another cough. "Guess I'm . . . out of practice."

Poe grabbed L'ulo, surprising his old friend with his strength.

"I'm doing the best I can, Poe," L'ulo said, trying to remain calm. But he was unable to hide his fear. Kes had lost a lot of blood. "That droid of yours patched him up a bit, but that's about all we can do from here. Once I get him back to the cruiser, we should be fine. But we need to leave now. We needed to leave five minutes ago, but your father refused to go without you."

Poe felt Zorii's eyes boring a hole into the back of his skull. He had to decide. He had to make a choice that would affect his life forever. If his father died on that Moraysian cruiser, he would never forgive himself. But was he ready to give up on everything he'd started to build with Zorii and Tomasso as a Spice Runner? Would they let him?

"This isn't for you, Poe," Kes said, his voice shaky. He winced as another wave of pain hit him. "It's . . . it's not safe for you. I can't risk this . . . can't risk losing you, too . . . not after . . ."

Poe crouched down closer, his face next to his father's—their eyes locked.

"I'm not Mom, Dad," Poe said. "This is different, okay? I know you want to protect me, but you can't. You have to let me learn on my own. You and Mom and L'ulo did your best for me. Now I have to use that to do what's best for me, all right?"

Kes let out a long sigh. He tried to sit up but was seized by a wave of coughs. He collapsed into Poe's arms, wheezing. He cleared his throat and tried to force a wan smile onto his face.

"If I wasn't laid up like this, I'd throw you in that shuttle and we'd figure it out on the way home," he said, his breathing shallow and quick. "But you're a lot more like your mother than you know. She was stubborn, too. She wanted to experience everything. Wanted to be part of the bigger story. Me? I was happy living a quiet life on Yavin Four. I'd done my bit for the Republic. But I can't force you."

Kes sagged in his son's arms, his eyelids fluttering. Poe looked at L'ulo.

"He needs to go, now," L'ulo said, hoisting his friend up. Poe stood with him. L'ulo laid a hand on Poe's shoulder. "We are always here for you, son. You know that. But you have to think for yourself. You have to ask yourself if this is what you want. If this is truly what you were meant to do with your life. You're an amazing pilot. I hope you'll learn to use those skills for the greater good, before it's too late. I'd keep arguing with you, Poe, if there were time. But I have to get your father help. He's dying."

All Poe could muster was a brief nod before L'ulo pulled him in for a tight embrace.

"Don't let anyone change who you are, Poe," L'ulo whispered in his ear as he held Poe close. "Be true to yourself."

As they broke the hug, a cold wind hit them. They all looked up to see a massive ship hovering above, preparing to land.

"What is that?" Kes croaked.

"The Moraysian cruiser only had a few shuttles," L'ulo said. "And that's not one of them."

"It is one of ours," Tomasso said, a tone of admiration and confidence in his voice. "So I suggest you two get off this planet now, if you want to avoid the full wrath of the Spice Runners of Kijimi."

Poe couldn't fight the sinking, dark feeling that he'd never see his father or L'ulo alive again.

CHAPTER 29

"That is something else."

Kes Dameron's hoarse words would haunt Poe for a long time. But for now they just served as an astute observation as they all stared upward at the massive unknown ship making its descent to the planet's surface.

Poe turned to face Tomasso, who had a knowing, creepy grin on his face.

"You said that's one of ours?" Poe asked. He looked at Zorii, whose expression had gone blank—an empty stare in her eyes. It took Poe a few moments before he realized she was paralyzed with fear. "Zorii, what—what is that? Who is that?"

She didn't respond. She didn't look at Poe. She remained focused on the ship, her expression frozen.

Poe looked back at his father, who was slouched in L'ulo's arms, looking ashen. He felt like he could read the older Dameron's mind. Kes didn't want to leave. But that was a death sentence.

"L'ulo," Poe said, "you have to get Dad off this planet. Now."

L'ulo nodded. "Your father doesn't seem to agree."

Kes Dameron struggled, trying to break free from L'ulo's grasp. But he was too weak. The lurker's bite—probably rife with poison—was impeding his every movement.

"No, Poe—no," Kes said, but his words were slow and slurred. "Come with us."

Poe and L'ulo's eyes met. They heard the loud thump of the new ship landing, and a strong gust of wind buffeted them. Time was running out.

"Take him, L'ulo," Poe said, his eyes wet with tears. "Take him now. He'll never forgive us, but it's the right thing to do. I'll find my way back to you."

L'ulo didn't speak. Instead he dragged Kes, half conscious, toward their shuttle.

"Don't make your promise a lie, Poe," L'ulo shouted as they boarded the ship.

Poe couldn't muster the words to respond.

By the time the small Moraysian shuttle was in the air, heading up to the cruiser, the massive new ship had completed its landing—and a small coterie of guards had begun to walk down a long boarding ramp, armed to the teeth. They weren't uniformed or organized—their look was ragtag—but they were each imposing in their own way, a mix of humanoids and non-humanoids from across the galaxy, all with looks of danger in their eyes. Poe turned to his remaining friends—Zorii, EV-6B6, and Tomasso. Zorii's expression remained fearful. The droid muttered to herself in an oddly cheerful tone.

Only Tomasso seemed content, as if anticipating a great gift. He wore a relaxed smile on his face.

"What's going on, Tomasso?" Poe asked. "Who's on that ship?"

The last figure to disembark the ship was a tall, wiry woman wearing a luminescent golden helmet with a long protruding visor. Her demeanor—menacing and distant—screamed that she was in charge. The entire squad of guards deferred to her, scanning the planet's surface with an eye on protection as they waited for her to step to the ground. Her helmet's plasteel shell and bronzium finish shone in the planet's unfiltered sunlight. A flowing violet cape billowed behind her as she turned to face the Spice Runners.

"Zeva Bliss," Tomasso whispered, the words barely audible.

"Who?" Poe asked.

"Our leader, young Poe," Tomasso said. "A name only muttered in shadows. The ruthless, genius leader of the Spice Runners of Kijimi."

"My mother," Zorii said.

CHAPTER 30

The woman known as Zeva Bliss approached them, sword dangling carelessly in its scabbard at her side. Her smooth golden helmet moved as she scanned the group before stopping on Tomasso. She nodded at the older man. The dark visor that covered most of the front of her headgear revealed nothing of the face inside.

"Old friend," she said, her voice sounding distant and mechanical, as if spoken through a filter. "It's been too long."

"My duties keep me quite busy," Tomasso said with a wry smile. "As you know all too well, Zeva."

"Indeed, I do."

"What brings the leader of the Spice Runners of Kijimi to the far end of the Llanic Spice Run?" Tomasso asked, genuine curiosity in his tone. "All is well, I hope?"

Zeva's visor shifted to Zorii, who returned the stare—her look defiant but respectful. Though it was clear to Poe his friend was afraid, he admired her efforts to look the opposite. But if Zeva Bliss was indeed Zorii Wynn's mother, she had probably picked up on that, too.

"All is not well, Tomasso," Zeva said, still looking at her daughter. "Unfortunately."

As Poe watched the two women size each other up, he felt a wave of betrayal. How, in all the time he'd spent with Zorii—intimate moments, moments of friendship, and tense, fearful moments—had she not mentioned she was the daughter of the leader of the Spice Runners of Kijimi? Why had she kept it a secret? Did he even have a right to ask?

Zorii looked at Poe—her eyes softening a bit as if to say, *I'll explain this, trust me.* Poe nodded, the past few months spent sniping at each other melting away in this one, brief flicker of humanity between them.

He was transported back to a few moments earlier—to his fateful choice to remain with the Spice Runners of Kijimi—and he realized how much of that decision was tied to Zorii, to that look of fear and uncertainty on her face as Zeva Bliss arrived. Poe knew—deep inside—that he had to help her get through whatever was coming, and his own journey would have to wait. At least until he sorted out his feelings for Zorii. Not so much his romantic feelings—though that was part of it, if he was being honest with himself—but their bond as friends and partners. He hoped he'd made the right call.

Zeva Bliss tilted her head slightly as she faced them.

"You will accompany me to Kijimi, immediately," she said. "The time for training is over. You, Poe Dameron of Yavin Four, and my daughter, Zorii Bliss, have proven yourselves capable enough. You will be welcomed on Kijimi as full members of the Spice Runners, with all the amenities, respect, and responsibility that role brings. There is a mission that I can only give to people I trust with my life."

"This is, of course, your decision, Exalted One, but, if I may ask," Tomasso said, confusion dripping from every word, "what of my services? Surely I can be—"

Before Tomasso could finish, Zeva buried her sword hilt-deep in the older man's midsection. Tomasso sputtered, blood flowing out of his mouth, an expression of pure surprise and betrayal on his face.

Zeva pulled the sword back, the curved blade coated in Tomasso's blood. He collapsed to his knees, his eyes still wide.

"No!" Poe screamed as he tried to lunge for the older man. He was held back, his arms pinned by Zeva's guards. "Tomasso!"

"You swore an oath to the Spice Runners, Tomasso," Zeva said as her second-in-command crumpled to the wet, swampy ground. "You swore your undying loyalty to all that we do, forever. You betrayed that oath."

Before Poe could say anything else, Zeva spun around

and marched back toward her ship, her guards lining up behind her. She caught a glimpse of EV-6B6 bending over to tend to Tomasso. Zeva looked at Poe.

"Where did you get this droid?" she asked.

It took Poe a moment to formulate a response. "The Moraysian . . . the cruiser," Poe said. Why did she care?

"Ledesmar's ship?" Zeva asked, a knowing ring to her words. "The property of a competitor? I see."

The leader of the Spice Runners of Kijimi pivoted back and continued toward her ship. She turned to one of her guards and nodded. The foot soldier pulled out his blaster and sent a few shots into EV-6B6's back, destroying the droid's midsection.

Poe, released by the guards as they followed Zeva onto the ship, fell to his knees. His body began to shake as he stared down at his two friends—one dead, the other destroyed. He sensed Zorii standing above him. He looked up to see her, shaken, struggling to remain stoic as she locked eyes with her murdered mentor, a pool of blood forming around his lifeless body.

CHAPTER 31

"You didn't think to tell me?"

Poe's words hung between them in Zorii's quarters on Zeva Bliss's massive ship. The starship felt like a city unto itself—long, winding hallways meshed with massive atria and meeting rooms and docking areas. Though not as huge as the Moraysian cruiser, the Kijimi-bound ship seemed to do more with less—giving Zeva Bliss's *Centurion*-class battlecruiser a sprawling, endless feeling. Or maybe Poe was just reeling from all that had happened in the past two hours.

"Zorii," Poe continued. "When were you going to tell me your mother ran the entire operation?"

"You're one to criticize, Poe," Zorii said, as if seeing him for the first time. "When were you going to tell us—your friends and teammates—that your own father was after us? That he'd fought in the Rebel Alliance? When would we learn that?"

"That's completely different," Poe protested. "And I didn't even know he was coming after me."

"Is it, though?" Zorii said, one eyebrow arched. "That's convenient."

"Is this why the Guavians were after you?" Poe asked. "Why Ledesmar recognized you? Why Gen Tri was so concerned with getting you off the Moraysian cruiser safely?"

"Points to the farm boy from Yavin Four," Zorii said, not trying to hide any hurt feelings or anger anymore. The stoic façade had faded once Zeva Bliss had left them alone. "You figured it out. So what?"

"You could have said something," Poe said softly, trying to lower his defenses—to show Zorii he was still with her. It seemed to work. She stepped toward him. "I'm your friend. You know that."

Zorii nodded as she looked around the cramped space, as if trying to come to terms with all that had happened to them.

"I couldn't find the right time, honestly," she said. "It felt like too much—especially with everything going on. It just seemed like an added burden to share."

"But why . . . why did your mom put you through this?" Poe said motioning out toward space. "Why not train you herself?"

"I didn't want that," Zorii said. "I didn't want special treatment. Some people knew, of course. My mother wouldn't send her only child out into the galaxy alone.

Tomasso and Gen Tri were there to ensure my safety. But I didn't want anyone else to know or coddle me. I wanted to learn, to get better, to become the best at this."

Poe shook his head. So much had happened. So much had changed. He'd seen his own father and L'ulo, and that felt like it had happened years before. EV-6B6 destroyed. Tomasso dead. Zorii's mother. It was too much. Poe felt like he needed a month to process it all. But he didn't have that luxury. They were on their way to Kijimi, like it or not.

"If we're being honest now, Poe, if we're laying it all out on the table," Zorii said, stepping closer, more into his space, "I should ask you the same thing." Her expression was intense—a mix of anger and passion. "Why are you here? What keeps you with us? Do you really believe in what the Spice Runners are about? Or did you just want to run away from a boring life tending to your dad's farm?"

Poe gripped Zorii's arm but wasn't sure what it meant. They'd had moments like this before—like on the Moraysian cruiser—when the intensity of whatever was going on brought them physically closer. The intimacy was always charged and fleeting, but the energy lingered. But this felt more focused, like they were airing everything in the hopes that what was left was something they'd want to hold on to.

"At first, yes. I just wanted something else," Poe said, nodding. "I wanted off Yavin Four. I wanted to experience the galaxy. To fly and fight and risk my life for something, like my mother had. Like my father had, before he lost the fire."

"Then what?" Zorii asked. "What changed your mind?"

"Then I got to know you. You're . . . important to me," Poe said, caressing Zorii's face. "I figured after a while we could score our own haul—that maybe you and I could break away, leave all of this behind. It was our friendship—this bond—that kept me around, Zorii. We make a good team."

Zorii pulled away with a jerk.

"That's not enough. I'm not looking to be rescued, Poe Dameron," she said. "Don't you see? This—the Spice Runners of Kijimi—it's not just a lark or a joyride for me. It's my life. It's what I was born to do. You're a great pilot—maybe the best I've ever seen. You're smart. You're brave. But you're a hothead. A silly romantic. You get caught up in being some kind of galactic hero when what we need—what I need—is a comrade, someone I know is going to be here forever, in the trenches, because this is where they want to be."

"Someone like Tomasso?" Poe said.

He regretted the words the second they left his mouth.

The punch landed fast and hard, a blow that showed Poe the full force of Zorii Bliss's strength. It came from a place of simmering rage—a reaction that she'd kept in check for a long time. He reached for his face, felt the hot skin that would surely bruise. She stood in front of him for a second, registering the pure shock in his eyes, before she stormed out of the tiny cabin without looking back.

After a few minutes, Poe walked out of the room, rubbing the side of his face gingerly. He'd ice it for a while, giving Zorii time to cool off, then find her and talk it out. He'd messed up. He knew how close she was to Tomasso, knew she was broken up about what happened. He'd poked a raw nerve and deserved the shock of pain.

"She has a temper," someone said. He turned around to find Zeva Bliss, still wearing her massive helmet, standing behind him, half shrouded in darkness.

"You'd know best," Poe said, not in the mood for ominous warnings or threats, "fearless leader."

Zeva Bliss stepped out of the shadows and Poe sensed a tinge of fear in the back of his mind. He suddenly felt very much a young man, standing in the company of unadulterated power. Zeva Bliss had more than an air about her—she had presence.

"Watch your tongue, boy," Zeva said, her mechanized voice weighted with years of experience and more battles than Poe could imagine. "I will humor you for only so long."

Poe nodded.

"I'm sorry," he said. "It's been an eventful few hours."

"Yes, I can see that," she said, moving closer to him. "You were close with Tomasso, no?"

Poe winced, enough of an answer.

"Despite his failing at the end, I could not have asked for a better second-in-command," she said, some regret filtering through her helmet. "But he made a fateful mistake. And I did not rise to this position by forgiving traitors. He'd have taken us all down with him."

"You'd been watching us the whole time," Poe said, not a question—a statement of fact. The pieces had begun to click together, the stray bits of string weaving into something he could make out. "That case—the one we stole from Ledesmar. What was it? Why were you so desperate for us to get it?"

Zeva Bliss tapped her helmet.

"It was the most important item I own—a symbol of everything I stand for," she said. "And it had been taken from me. I sent in my best people to get it. Only a few survived."

"No one knew it'd been taken," Poe said.

She shook her head.

A few moments passed before Zeva Bliss spoke again.

"You've done well for us, Poe Dameron," she said. "But mastering your training is one thing. You now have to prove more than that."

She reached for him, and her cold armored hands weighed heavily on his shoulders as she continued.

"You have to show me that you're not only someone who could someday be a proficient thief and smuggler but that you are one, right now," she said. "That this is the life you've chosen, and that this is the group you've decided to pledge your allegiance—your entire being—to. If this is the path you want, there will be no past life for you, Poe. Yavin Four, your family, your dreams—they disappear. There will only be the Spice Runners of Kijimi, and nothing else. I will be your only reason and purpose."

"I'll stand by Zorii," Poe said, surprising himself with his own words—words that had only existed as strange thoughts and concepts in the ether of his mind before then. "I'll do whatever I can to help her."

Zeva Bliss paused, processing what Poe had just said, hesitating for a moment.

"Let's hope that is enough, then," she said. "Or you, like others, will have to be dealt with . . . accordingly."

Zeva Bliss turned and began to walk toward the ship's bridge.

"What's next?" Poe asked. He'd be respectful of Zeva Bliss and her world—he had enough of a survival instinct to understand what was expected of him—but he wouldn't be passive. He wanted to know what was in store for them. *Had* to know.

She turned around and seemed to size Poe up.

"What's next?" Zeva Bliss said, her voice rising, even through the robotic filter of her helmet. "The death and rebirth of Zorii Bliss and Poe Dameron, the newest Spice Runners of Kijimi."

PART IV: FALLOUT

CHAPTER 32

Zorii Bliss walked down the dark, ice-coated alley, her face speckled with snow. Even the hood of her cloak couldn't protect her from Kijimi's painful, frigid weather. Her boots sloshed as she stepped over the obstacles she'd quickly forgotten after leaving her home planet—along with the sleeping derelicts, the fast-talking con artists, the shadowy thieves waiting to pounce. But they knew. They all should know. Who she was. And who she was destined to be.

She made a sharp left turn, slipping slightly on the worn cobblestones mostly hidden by snow and patches of ice, and stepped down a winding flight of stairs. It felt strange to be back. *With Poe*. The thought entered her mind without warning, but she couldn't deny the truth it held. When she first met the boy—well, man—from Yavin 4, she hadn't expected much of him. A means to get off the moon, really. But over time she'd come to care for him. He was insufferable, she wouldn't deny that. But he was also charming. The thrill of those early days was like a tonic to Zorii. The memories of hands clasped together, longing kisses after everyone else was asleep, the twinkle in his eyes as an idea took shape—it all seemed like a vivid dream as their worlds had grown darker, more fraught.

"Hey-hey, Zorii is you?"

The gravelly yet still high-pitched voice seemed to come from nowhere as Zorii reached the bottom of the stairs. The space was a workshop, with half-finished droid bodies lining the walls, and tools and other machinery covering a massive workbench at the center of the room. But Zorii was no stranger to this place—or its owner. A tiny figure popped up, seemingly from within the droid parts scattered around the table. The Anzellan's mashed-together features and tiny build didn't immediately make one think of a master droidsmith, but that's who Zorii was in the presence of now. Babu Frik—whose mastery over all things mechanical was second to none.

"Babu," Zorii said, skipping the last few steps as she approached her old friend. "How are you?"

"I is good, good, yes," he said, continuing to work on the droid as if Zorii wasn't there. "Zorii return Kijimi, Babu glad."

"I missed you, old friend," she said, giving the droidsmith a gentle pat.

Babu looked up at her.

"I miss, too," he said with a quick nod. "Your mama, miss Zorii, her own way."

Zorii didn't respond. She wasn't sure her mother could miss anyone. But she was wary of speaking out—even in the slightest way—against Zeva Bliss. Many others had done so. Few had survived the experience. And Zorii knew her mother's spies were everywhere.

"Here-here, sit with Babu," he said, waving a tiny hand toward a stool. "Chat-chat."

Zorii took the seat and let out a long sigh.

"Wow-wow, says many that sound, eh?" Babu said, not looking at Zorii. "You home, but frowns, no joy I see."

Zorii opened her mouth but stopped short of talking. She wasn't ready, she thought.

Babu turned around, a frown on his already puckered tiny face.

"Busy busy, much to do," he said, the annoyance in his voice obvious. "Zorii-Z, special to Babu. But not much time. Work is everywhere, yeah-yeah."

Zorii looked around the cluttered workspace. The room had been like a second home to Zorii growing up—an escape from the demands and expectations of her mother. A place where she wasn't Zorii Bliss, daughter of the feared Zeva Bliss, leader of the Spice Runners. She was just Zorii, a kid with kid problems and daydreams. In contrast to the bleak, freezing world outside Babu's door, his workshop was an oasis of calm and freedom.

"My mother wants to sit with me today—to talk about the future. My future," Zorii said, the words picking up speed as she progressed. It was a relief to let it out, even if just here, to Babu Frik. These were things she couldn't share with anyone else—not even Poe, and certainly not her mother. Neither would understand. "I don't know what she's going to say. But I have a feeling it won't be good. That she'll want me to pledge myself to her, more than I already have, even. And I'm fine with that—I love my mother. And I love being a Spice Runner. But it feels like so much to, I don't know, to have everything decided for me so early. Is my story already written? Am I just going through the paces? What if I want to do something else—"

Babu gave a slight shake of his small head. "Spice Runners we always, and always be. Zeva not just leader big boss, she mama to you. Make hard. What of boy?"

"Poe?" Zorii asked. "I—I don't know. He's strong-willed. Smart. Cunning. He'd make a great Spice Runner—"

"He on Kijimi, so he Spice Runner," Babu said matter-of-factly. "Not?"

"Yes, I suppose he is," Zorii said, a tinge of uncertainty in her voice. "But there's something . . . a hesitation. I can see it in him. I worry that we're just a means to an end, Babu. A path off his homeworld, a way to learn how to survive."

"You like boy, I think," Babu said, pointing a long, sharp tool at the protocol droid parts strewn over his table. "If Poe go, what is Zorii? Must think."

Zorii didn't answer. It wasn't the first time she'd pondered the question. Though she'd felt a Kijimi-like chill settle over her bond with Poe since the revelation of her mother and Poe's father, she still thought of him often. Still spent hours with him each day. It was easy to fall into familiar routines, even now. What would she do if he ran? Would she leave everything behind? She wasn't sure.

"Enough about that," Zorii said, forcing a smile. "I have a favor to ask of you, dear Babu."

"Zorii I do help help, no worry," Babu said, shuffling closer to Zorii's hand and welcoming another tender pat. "Friend to you."

The cavernous battle room was empty and dark as Zorii stepped inside, a slight, cold wind hitting her. She could make out a figure at the other end of the large room, the glint from the helmet the only clue as to who it was. Zeva Bliss didn't turn as Zorii approached, her footsteps echoing as she made her way toward her mother.

As she reached Zeva, Zorii ducked, barely dodging the

first blow from her mother's long staff. She wasn't so lucky on the second one, the tip of the weapon connecting with her chin and sending her on her back, the battle room's cold, rocky surface scraping through her tunic. She winced but didn't make a sound.

Zeva Bliss, staff pointed at Zorii's face like a sword, approached, her expression unreadable behind her helmet's large visor. Her voice was filtered but still clear enough to be understood. She didn't even sound winded.

"An attack can come from any direction, dear daughter," Zeva said, shaking her head. "You must always be ready. Always on guard."

Zorii pushed her mother's staff aside and got to her feet, wiping her mouth and finding no blood on her sleeve.

"You wanted to see me . . . Mother?"

"Yes," Zeva said, pacing around her daughter. "I felt it was high time we spoke—freely and honestly—about you, Zorii Bliss."

The name still shook her. She'd been Zorii Wynn for so long, she'd become used to the ruse. But Zorii Wynn was gone now, and all that remained was Zorii Bliss, daughter to the leader of the Spice Runners of Kijimi.

"I'm here," Zorii said, trying to keep her tone neutral. "As you desire."

"As my daughter, you are weighed down by great expectations already, so I say this not without some understanding," Zeva said, her pace slowing as she turned to face Zorii. "But we all face challenges we must defend against, and this is one such time—for you and me."

Zorii nodded, unsure of her mother's point but certain she would not appreciate being interrupted.

"Tomasso is gone, his betrayal a surprise that I will never recover from," Zeva said. "He was like family to us. But over the years, his resentment grew and, by the time I killed him, he'd been serving as an informant to our enemies in the New Republic for months, if not longer. Word was beginning to spread within the Spice Runners and, had I not acted, my own hold on power would have weakened. Do you understand?"

Zorii didn't respond. She understood her mother's logic—but she couldn't believe it to be true. Tomasso had always been stern—but also kind, generous, and a fountain of experience and information. He didn't have an opportunistic bone in his old body, unless he was moving to benefit the Spice Runners as a whole. She would have never thought him capable of betrayal—much less on the scale her mother suggested.

"I don't need to be your mother to see the doubt in your eyes," Zeva said. "But take my word, young one. Tomasso saw his time ending. He sought to find meaning for his life and ended up in the hands of the New Republic. I saw the evidence with my own eyes."

Zorii looked away, unable to meet her mother's gaze, even through the dark visor that shielded her face from the world.

Zeva approached and placed a hand on her shoulder.

"I have things coming together very soon, things that will alter not only the lives of our crew but the entire landscape of the galaxy," Zeva said. "And I need people I trust close to me. Family. I once thought Tomasso was family. Like a brother. But I was wrong. His death . . ."

She trailed off. *His murder*, Zorii thought before Zeva continued.

"It leaves a vacancy only you can fill, Zorii," she said. "I need a second-in-command. I need my daughter standing by my side. Will you do that? Are you ready?"

Zorii met her mother's gaze, her eyes fierce and focused.

"I am ready," she said. "I have been ready."

Zeva stepped back with a nod.

"Good," she said. "As I expected."

She placed a hand under her helmet, near where her chin was, and there was a soft hiss. She lifted the helmet up over her head, revealing her true face—her sharp green eyes standing out from her snowy skin; a long, aging scar running down her right cheek; the pitch-black hair falling to her shoulders. Her expression was focused on the task at hand, but Zorii found the move jarring. She'd of course seen her mother's face—as a child, over the years—but not in some time. Not since Zeva had ascended to her role as leader of the Spice Runners of Kijimi. It was disconcerting to see that visage—of the woman who raised her, nurtured her—underneath the helmet of the cold, cruel overlord known as Zeva Bliss.

"There will come a time, dear one, when I will step back—or be taken back," Zeva said, her eyebrows raised in anticipation as she moved closer to Zorii. "And this will be yours. Not merely the garb of the leader of the Spice Runners, but the power—and the responsibility."

Zorii held the helmet—her hands on it alongside her mother's—and felt a jolt of something. Power. Rage. Excitement? She wasn't sure. This was all she'd ever wanted. At least until . . .

Poe.

When she thought back on this moment in the years that followed, she could never pinpoint what made her turn around just then. A cough? A scraping of boots on the floor? No. It was something deeper than that. A feeling within her that signaled they were not alone. They hadn't been for a while. Someone had been listening intently, afraid to even move.

Her eyes met Poe's as she looked back, and she knew things would never be the same.

CHAPTER 33

Being a Spice Runner of Kijimi wasn't something you could put on hold. It wasn't something you could freeze while you pondered what you'd gotten yourself into. Poe Dameron knew this. Had been grappling with it for a good, long while. But it had never been as stark as in this moment.

Spice running waited for no one.

The scene from a few weeks back, of Zorii Bliss hoisting her mother's helmet up, still haunted Poe. The vision was frozen in his mind. He still had questions. He still wanted to talk to Zorii—to get to the root of what was happening. But it would have to wait. They had a mission. For Zorii Bliss, the mission always came first.

These thoughts bounced through Poe's mind as he crouched down, trying to move stealthily. The only sounds he could hear were his and Zorii's heavy breathing as they made their way across the frigid plateau on the outskirts of Kijimi City, capital of the planet Kijimi, home to the Spice Runners. He pulled out his macrobinoculars and looked down at their target—the Dai Bendu Monastery. He could hear EV-6B6's metallic footsteps stop behind them.

Kijimi City rested atop a plateau tucked next to the massive Mount Izukika, where the monastery could be found. Built a thousand years before, the city was often raided and overthrown by various factions. The monks themselves were long gone, but their buildings and signature remained. Poe looked at Zorii and made a quick motion with his hand. It was time to head in.

They'd been in Kijimi for a little over a month, by Poe's count, and he still felt unhinged and out of place. From what Poe could tell—through his own explorations and research—Kijimi had once been a spiritual center, the landscape of the capital city littered with abandoned relics and temples. But those days were over. Kijimi was now a hotbed for criminals, a safe haven for those looking to skirt the eye of the New Republic and continue their illicit activities.

There was only so much the New Republic, years after the Battles of Endor and Jakku, could do. The leadership was stretched thin, and the struggle to tamp down any remaining Imperial Remnants took the wind out of the first few years of the new galactic government. They just weren't able to stem the tide of the underworld, which created a wave of apathy in the galaxy when it came to the new regime. Kijimi—cold, frigid, remote, and mountainous—had become an ideal headquarters for an organization that dealt primarily in the shadows and gray areas of the galaxy, and for anyone looking to lay low and get off the grid. There was no central government or ruling body in Kijimi, which was—for all intents and purposes—an anarchy that had achieved some level of social stability, as everyone's own criminal self-interests kept the civilization afloat.

Upon arriving, and after getting his first taste for life on the cold, barren planet, Poe found himself wondering just how long this criminal paradise could last. How long the New Republic would seemingly turn a blind eye toward an entire planet dedicated to bending and breaking whatever laws got in its way.

Poe was still troubled by Zorii's quick, biting scoff when he had asked her about it.

"It's only going to get stronger," Zorii had said. "The New Republic doesn't care about what goes on here, and Kijimi can tell. They don't have the firepower to pacify worlds on the fringe, or places that aren't cosmopolitan or of strategic value. That will come back to haunt them."

"Kind of weird that a planet like Kijimi is decorated with so many religious structures," Poe said, trying to break the silence between him and Zorii as they approached the monastery. Whatever tempers had flared during their confrontation on Zeva's ship had settled into a professional distance, only made more awkward by what Poe had seen in the battle room and the subsequent argument with Zorii a few weeks back. Zorii wasn't just his friend on this journey, she was the next in line to run the entire operation. This was, in every aspect, Zorii's life, more than Poe had even realized. Did Poe feel the same way? He wondered if there was a chance for them to retrieve even a fragment of the friendship—the relationship—they'd once had. And if not, where did that leave Poe Dameron?

"Criminals are a cowardly, superstitious lot. But you know that," Zorii said, not meeting Poe's eyes, her tone flat and unfriendly. "Smugglers and mercenaries might believe in the gray areas of life, but they also tend to regard monuments like this with a strange reverence."

"Spice Runners are complicated people," Poe said innocently, a desperate attempt to regain the rapport he knew, deep inside, would never return.

"You're one of us. Don't try to distance yourself," Zorii snapped, turning to face Poe. "Whether you like it or not, Poe Dameron, you've made your bones with the Spice Runners. You belong to us."

Poe's anxious thoughts were disrupted by the soft trill of the droid's voice.

"I can't imagine there's a better view of Kijimi City than this one," EV-6B6 exclaimed as she tried to keep up with Poe and Zorii on their approach to the monastery.

"Eevee, pipe down, okay?" Poe said in a harsh whisper. "We're trying to stay incognito."

"I'm just appreciating the scenery," EV-6B6 said, sounding puzzled by Poe's snippy command. "But I'll keep my enthusiasm at a lower volume if it makes you feel better, Master Poe."

The droid's melodic voice sent Poe back to one of his first days on Kijimi—following Zorii through the capital city's famed Thieves Quarter, both of them wearing baggy, layered clothing that masked their faces and intentions. They were lugging what was left of EV-6B6, but Zorii refused to explain why. *A droid burial?* Poe had wondered as they wove through the cobblestone streets of Kijimi City, strange looks and whispered threats creating a tense, anxious soundtrack to their every step.

The small workshop appeared out of thin air, and Zorii pulled Poe down the stairs and into the cramped, warm space with unexpected force. The bag loaded with EV-6B6's remains clunked and clanged as Poe dragged it toward a long wooden table. A diminutive, rodent-like being popped up from behind the table. He looked to Zorii, who pointed at Poe.

"Babu Frik, I'd like you to meet my friend Poe Dameron," Zorii said. "And that bag holds the droid I mentioned to you."

Babu nodded as Poe approached him.

"Poe-Poe, hey hey!" he said. "Zorii friend is mine friend, yeah."

Poe had heard Zorii mention Babu from time to time. The first time, Poe had felt a pang of jealousy. Later it had become clear Babu was just a friend, but he hadn't expected this. Babu Frik, as he'd learn, was Anzellan and one of the best techs on the Outer Rim, not to mention one of the most loyal members of the Spice Runners of Kijimi.

"Zorii say droid gone, but never Babu see droid he not bring back," Babu Frik said with a raspy chuckle.

"How'd . . . how did you know?" Poe asked, looking at Zorii.

She responded with a warm smile.

"You wear everything on your sleeve, Poe," she said. "I heard you trying to fix Eevee, even if you didn't think anyone was listening."

He leaned his face into hers, hesitatingly at first—because it felt like so much time had passed since the last moment like this—then more naturally, as if they were back on Sorgan, just two teenagers learning about the galaxy and each other. She welcomed it, returning the kiss with a passion he hadn't expected. But a tiny throat clearing interrupted them.

"Babu here, remember me," Babu said, banging a tool on a shattered droid arm, the clanging sound bringing them back to reality. "Not invite you here for the kissy-kissy, no-no."

Poe and Zorii stifled laughs, their faces reddening. Babu's interruption brought Poe back to why they were there—why Zorii had brought him there. He looked down at the bag of droid parts that had once been EV-6B6.

Zorii was right. He'd spent the better part of his first few nights on the frigid planet attempting, with little if any success, to piece together the droid he never thought he'd even liked. But the truth was, he'd come to appreciate her cheerful, optimistic perspective on life—and Zeva Bliss's sudden, unexpected order to silence her had rankled Poe. He'd carefully collected as much of EV-6B6 as he could before they boarded Zeva's ship, unsure of what his plans were. When he'd repeatedly failed to piece her together, he figured that was that. He'd been surprised by his own sadness. He didn't even like droids. Did he?

"Gimme to see," Babu Frik said as he motioned for Poe to bring EV-6B6's remains to him. "Need know what droid is like."

Poe carefully spread the pieces and parts over the long,

worn wooden table. Babu Frik shook his head without saying a word, just emitting a low growl that said plenty. Poe knew it was bad. A direct, up-close blaster shot to EV-6B6's midsection couldn't be an easy fix.

Poe turned to look at Zorii, who was staring intently as the droidsmith got to work—roughly sorting through boxes of tools, positioning the droid's various parts into something that resembled what the droid once looked like, muttering under his breath. Poe felt a wave of warmth toward Zorii in that moment. He imagined her watching his futile efforts to rebuild EV-6B6 and realized that, despite her distant and defensive behavior toward Poe over the past few months, she still cared. The kiss was physical proof of that, but the gesture—bringing Poe to Babu's workshop—said even more. She looked up to see him watching her and responded with a surprised but welcome smile.

It would be a memory Poe would hold on to for years to come.

But it was also forever tainted by another set of remembrances—of Zorii and Zeva. Visions that revealed more truth than Poe ever wanted to know about the world of the Spice Runners of Kijimi.

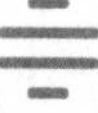

Zorii urged Poe and EV-6B6 forward, closer to the monastery—and to their destination. The words shook Poe out of his trance, and back to the task at hand.

"Snap out of it. We don't have time to waste," she said, her tone distant and harsh. "Move."

They all did, in unison, for a moment—but then she raised a hand to signal them to freeze.

"Do we need to go over the plan?" she asked, clearly frustrated. "Again?"

Had it been a few months back, Poe would have balked at the slight—but this was Zorii now. The wide-eyed and eager teen had been swiftly replaced by a strong, focused, and driven woman. Poe understood. This was all Zorii cared about. But he didn't have to like it.

"I think we're all set," Poe said, his tone snippy. He waited for her to shrug and turn around before he continued behind her.

The immediate plan, at least in Poe's mind, had a lot to do with the Spice Runners as a whole—a subject he'd gotten to know a lot about during his brief stay in Kijimi City. Now that he and Zorii had, for lack of a better term, graduated to full membership, he'd become privy to more about the organization and the world it sprang from.

Kijimi was unlike anything Poe had ever imagined—dark, dangerous, and subzero in both temperature and feeling. It was a thieves' planet run by thieves' rules, where anything went as long as you stole it fairly—which was a moving target, in and of itself. Every corner seemed packed and fraught with possibility—a deal, double cross, or threat. The planet's icy weather made for endless nights and brief, fleeting bursts of daylight, which only served to showcase the grime and cracks that made up the world's aging, ancient infrastructure. Poe couldn't shake the unease he felt walking the streets of the capital city, even when accompanied by Zorii—who was treated with a fearful reverence Poe found almost equally unnerving. This was not just a place the Spice Runners called home—it was a planet ruled and run by the Spice Runners' laws and traditions.

Zorii slipped slightly on an icy embankment, her knees scraping on the jagged rock. Poe rushed to her side, extending a hand. She winced as she got to her feet, only recognizing the gesture with a curt nod.

"Sorry," she said as they continued, not looking at him, focused on what lay ahead. "I . . . have a lot on my mind."

"I can imagine," Poe said. He hadn't meant it as a jab, but realized how Zorii might take it. "I mean, you've got a lot to worry about."

"What's that supposed to mean?"

"Nothing, nothing," Poe said, raising his hands in

surrender. "I just know you've had some added pressure, is all. I mean, my mom isn't in charge of this whole operation, but I think if she—"

"I'm not loyal to the Spice Runners because my mom is in charge, Poe," Zorii said, her voice sounding defeated and tired. "All of us—including you—are sworn to stand by her, by what she's done. It's more than just a moneymaking enterprise."

Poe understood. He'd seen the belief in action in his brief time on Kijimi. The planet was a testament to the strength of the Spice Runners that they could not only run one of the deadliest criminal organizations in the galaxy but also unite its membership with a zealotry that encompassed an entire planet. But even the most stable criminal organizations had dissent, and the Spice Runners—under Zeva Bliss's leadership—understood that not every satellite operation saw things in the same way she did. And while Zeva Bliss was patient, she was not a fool. If other smugglers and criminals wanted to tap into what the Spice Runners had going, they had to pay a toll, a fee—and they had to abide by the rules. Or else.

"So, once we get there, what's the idea?" Poe asked, trying to chip away at the strange silence that had formed. "Or are we just playing security detail?"

"We'll get our next orders when we arrive," Zorii said.

The words sounded evasive to Poe, but he chalked it up to Zorii's natural defensiveness.

"It'll be a nice spice runner reunion, that's for sure," Poe quipped. Zorii ignored him.

He was only half joking. He knew they were heading into something unique and potentially dangerous. Something had spurred Zeva Bliss to invite a wide selection of warlords, smugglers, slave traders, mercenaries, and chieftains to Kijimi for a summit. She'd described it as a chance to air grievances and compare notes, to work together to foster their growing, mutual criminal enterprises—for a price, of course. The meeting would serve as a peace offering in a business that was not known for dialogue or diplomacy. Zeva Bliss certainly wasn't known for it.

They continued to trudge forward, EV-6B6 a few paces behind, having more trouble with the terrain than Zorii or Poe but refusing to complain. Poe was glad the droid was back. He'd missed her more than he thought possible.

"This seems like a big moment for Zeva," Poe said, trying to keep pace with Zorii. "For all of us."

The reference to Spice Runners unity thawed Zorii's mood for a moment. She turned her face to Poe, seeming almost happy—but something stopped her before she spoke.

"It is," she said slowly, squinting slightly, as if trying

to see past some kind of defense Poe had set up between them. "Zeva Bliss has been working toward this for . . . for a very long time."

Poe felt a sharp pang of unease as the trio crept closer to the target. Something seemed wrong to Poe. Something just didn't fit. Over the years, Zeva Bliss had made partnerships, expanding the reach of the Spice Runners of Kijimi, solidifying her role as head of the criminal organization. But at the same time, she'd made her fair share of enemies. And she had invited all of them to gather on Kijimi.

"Huh," Poe said to himself.

Zorii looked back at him for a moment before continuing the course.

The question hit Poe fully as they reached the far edge of the monastery, like a gust of wind colder than the frigid air of Kijimi that chilled his very soul.

Why are we sneaking into our own meeting?

CHAPTER 34

Zeva Bliss strode into the monastery's atrium-like war room, her long cape flowing behind her. She turned to her guards and made a quick motion with her hands. They spread out around the room, a few standing on each side of the table, their blasters motionless. They wouldn't need their weapons now, she thought. The time for battle was over. This was something else.

This was her moment—the Spice Runners' moment. Her helmet heightened her vision and gave her a schematic look at the space—wide, open, uncluttered. But it wasn't the technical that interested her now. It was the personal.

The buzz of conversation had quieted to a low mutter as those in attendance began to take notice. The attendees were made up of allies, enemies, and acquaintances—the entire spectrum was present at this meeting. She could feel the tension, like a mist slowly thickening as she entered the space. Heads turned. Her heightened senses picked up slight scoffs and one or two quick tongue clicks. Her eyes—through her helmet's long visor—scanned the room.

It was like a recap of every backroom deal or threatening exchange she'd ever experienced, dating back to her earliest days as a young member of the small gang that would grow and evolve into the Spice Runners of Kijimi. This was her entire life, in one room—every scrum, every alliance, every betrayal, every murder—as if the gods wanted to give Zeva Bliss one final moment of introspection before she entered the next phase. It was fitting, she thought, as she took her seat at the head of the table. Almost too perfect.

Before her was a mix of some of the deadliest smugglers and bounty hunters the galaxy had to offer. They'd come here on Zeva Bliss's invitation, in hopes of bringing the various tentacles of organized crime together to forge a new path to subvert and sidestep the New Republic and to launch a golden era for their "business," in a way they could only imagine under the harsh regime of the Empire.

There was BoShek, a human Corellian thief who was often a thorn in the Spice Runners of Kijimi's hide when it came to transporting goods. She knew little else about him, and that was fine by Zeva Bliss. To his left were Alfris Sotin, apparently recovered from the skirmish at Ankot Station; the grumpy Iakaru spice dealer Alugomes; and Caryn, a human smuggler and fence who'd done business on the fringes of the Galactic Civil War. Like BoShek, she was mysterious and spoke little—traits of a successful smuggler, Bliss mused. Across from Caryn was the helmeted pirate Woan Barso. A refugee who only believed in his own battered orange vac-suit, Barso was in deep conversation with an Abednedo named Sarb Iltage, whose dangling mouth tendrils and nostrils seemed to be flaring in surprise or anger. Zeva wasn't sure which. No matter.

Astrid Fenris, another human smuggler, smiled as Zeva's gaze reached her. Zeva nodded, but they both knew she held Fenris in low regard—considered her a fraud and poseur. But it was important she be there. To her left was a slinking, skittish Arconan dealer named Adlerber. To her right was Adlerber's partner, a goggled and hooded Kubaz female named Monigallgh. At the other end of the table, sandwiched between Vranki and the Rodian Civian Bain, sat the rugged pirate Tarand Crowe. His perpetual smirk softened, replaced with a knowing nod, as he noticed Zeva Bliss take her seat.

"My friends," Zeva Bliss said, her voice silencing the hushed whispers and murmurs still popping up. "I appreciate you coming here, on my invitation. I appreciate that, despite our past disagreements, we can sit down and be open to what's to come. To the future. To our future."

Zeva Bliss stood up, a smooth, quick motion that

took the other attendees off guard. That was the idea, she thought.

"We are, at best, friendly rivals. At worst, bloodthirsty enemies. But those days must end now," she continued, walking around the long table with a slow, calculated precision. She took a moment to nod or recognize each of the smugglers and thieves at their seats as she walked by, trying to make sure they all felt seen and recognized. "The Battles of Endor and Jakku have created a new galactic order, and over the past few years, we have come to learn ways to subvert and sidestep the New Republic, in many of the same ways we profited off the mistakes of the Empire. But I am here to tell you that there is much more profit to be made a different way. Together."

Slight murmuring as Zeva Bliss paused. She'd expected this—a little dissent before her point was even made. But she'd come ready.

"I hear your dry laughter," she said. "I understand the hesitation. What is there to gain from pooling our resources? From sharing information? Why not continue to cut the corners and skim from the top as we've all done for generations? I'll tell you why."

She slammed her fist down on the table, the blow echoing off the room's high ceilings and spacious décor.

"We can do better," she hissed. "And our time is now,

as the New Republic continues to fumble, continues to focus on other things."

She continued to pace, faster, angrier.

"The fact is, the New Republic does not care about us, or about the worlds on the Mid or Outer Rim," Zeva Bliss said. "It is our time to seize control of what is rightfully ours. What we deserve."

"This is all nice and cozy, but so what?" It was Crowe speaking, with an ever-present shrug. "What can the Spice Runners of Kijimi offer me that I can't do for myself?"

Zeva Bliss smiled under her golden helmet.

She strode toward Crowe, and the buzzing conversations ceased. This was what everyone had expected, to some degree: A confrontation. A battle. The ruse of Zeva's invitation revealed to be nothing more than a trap. But she stopped short and stood over Crowe, who stared up at her, a bemused expression on his gruff, worn face.

"An excellent question," she said. "And the answer is simple: the Spice Runners of Kijimi are ready to become more than just a fast-rising gang looking to fill a void. We want to be more than your competition. We want to be your partners. If we pool our resources—intelligence, weaponry, routes—we can become richer than we'd ever imagined."

Crowe shook his head.

"I don't get it," he said with a scoff. "Why would the Spice Runners want to give me their secrets? For what? A cut? Why not just do it yourselves?"

Zeva Bliss placed a gloved hand on Crowe's shoulder, taking the smuggler by surprise.

"We are not invincible. We are still learning ourselves. The Spice Runners of Kijimi cannot be everywhere," Zeva Bliss said. "But we see opportunity. We see a path to riches and a world where our organizations can live and thrive next to the simpleminded governance of the New Republic."

She took her hand off Crowe and turned to address the entire group.

"Tell me you haven't seen it, too, my friends. The New Republic is stretched too thin. They're more concerned with eliminating ghosts from the past than looking toward the future—and determining what they'd like the galaxy to be. Now that role must fall on us, and I want to share my vision with you, to make sure we seize it faster than any of us could do alone."

Barso spoke next, not bothering to raise his hand or call for attention.

"We've tried everything else, you know?" he said.

"We've tried being at each other's throats. We've tried ignoring each other. Why not see what comes of working together?"

Adlerber chimed in. "Are you mad? The Spice Runners of Kijimi have never hesitated to double-cross us before. Why should we believe them now?"

Then Sotin spoke.

"I'm not one to judge too harshly. I know it's a dangerous galaxy out there—the idea of partnership is nice, charming even," the smuggler said. "But I come here more out of curiosity than a genuine desire to believe. The second thieves start to trust each other, we've lost, no?"

The room bubbled up into a heated exchange, all decorum lost as voices rose and some of the attendees stood up to be heard. Zeva had seen this kind of incident before. It wouldn't be long before the gathered criminals were at each other's throats. No matter, she thought as she quietly moved toward the exit. The plan was the plan. She gave one of her security officers the signal as she stepped out of the room slowly, so as not to raise any alarms.

"This feels wrong," Poe said as he followed Zorii down a worn path outside of the monastery's weathered exterior.

He pulled his coat tighter, trying to fight off the biting Kijimi City winds. He heard EV-6B6's clunking footfalls behind them.

"What do you mean?" Zorii said as Poe caught up with her, their backs to the monastery's wall. "Second thoughts?"

"You could say that," Poe said. "But more like thoughts, period. Why are we sneaking around if this meeting is supposed to be about bringing people together?"

"If you have a question, Poe, ask it," Zorii said, craning her head around a doorway, then signaling it was clear. "I don't have time to crack a code."

They followed her down a short, dark hallway before reaching an empty room—the only furniture two small cots and a tiny control terminal that seemed out of place in the ancient structure.

"This seems quaint and cozy," EV-6B6 said, pacing around the small room. She glanced at the control terminal. "What does this do? It seems to be a surveillance device of some sort. . . ."

Poe grabbed Zorii's shoulder, and she turned around to face him, her face red with anger. She was frustrated—but it was more than that, Poe realized. She was struggling with something else. Something stronger.

Shame?

"This isn't a meeting to form alliances, is it?" Poe asked.

Zorii's silence was more than enough of an answer. They weren't helping Zeva Bliss enact a masterful, unifying plan to bring the myriad criminal organizations into closer alignment. They weren't there to ensure the safety of their guests or to make sure Zeva Bliss was able to get her message across. No. It was something much more cunning—and much, much deadlier.

"It's a trap," Poe said. "And we're the ones pulling the trigger."

CHAPTER 35

The conversation that would alter the course of Sela Trune's life started off quietly, just one of many mundane tasks she had to oversee as part of her duties in the New Republic Security Bureau. But her supervisor's final words jumped out at her—and would haunt her until she died.

"We have to shut down this hunt you have going, Trune. We have other targets aside from the Spice Runners. We need our best people focused elsewhere."

"You can't be serious," she'd responded. Had she been able to hold a mirror up to her face, Trune was certain she would have found her mouth agape.

Trune's words hung over the comm, the silence on the other end saying more than the head of New Republic Intelligence, Tolo Mandah, could with words.

"You have your orders, Trune," Mandah said, finally breaking the silence. Her demeanor was stern but not without empathy. Sela Trune's passion for this mission was no secret. "I realize this might not be what you—"

"It's a mistake."

"Excuse me?"

"We're making a terrible mistake," Trune said. "I have intelligence—good intelligence—on a major event that could alter the landscape of the galaxy's criminal underworld, and it directly implicates the Spice Runners of Kijimi. I just need a few ships. A dozen men, maybe less, and we will—"

Mandah cleared her throat.

"We don't have the resources," she said, her words tougher now. "We're stretched beyond our means, Trune. I know you understand that. I know you have a personal stake in this—believe me, we all have to bring some passion into this cause. But it's not our battle now. Perhaps in a few months . . ."

"Don't humor me, sir," Trune said flatly. "I deserve better than that."

She could tell Mandah hadn't expected so much pushback. Despite her young age, Trune had earned a reputation as an officer who knew and stuck to the rules. This defiance was out of character, and Mandah wanted to cut it off fast.

"I expect a report on how we'll reallocate resources as soon as you can," Mandah continued. "I don't mean to be harsh here, Trune, but if we're not seeing eye to eye on this, that's a problem. Do you understand?"

"I understand," Trune responded. She was being

truthful. She did understand. But it wasn't what Mandah was referring to.

"Good," she said. "Now, if this is a problem—you need to get it out of your system fast. We have to move to deal with this bounty hunter situation before it becomes a bigger obstacle."

Silence.

"Trune?" Mandah said. "Are you there?"

"Yes."

Mandah's patience was wearing thin, Trune could tell. She didn't really give a damn.

"Let me be clear, and I'm only saying this because I respect you and the work you've done for the NRSB," Mandah said. "If you don't show me things are going to move away from this obsession you have with these Kijimi spice runners, and do it fast—we're going to have a big issue. I don't want to have to reassign you, understood?"

"I understand," Trune said again, with no emotion in her voice.

"Good," Mandah said. "I look forward to your report."

She signed off. A charged silence filled Trune's cramped workspace.

There would be no report for Tolo Mandah. Trune knew this as she placed her datapad and identikit on the table. There would be a shift change at the docking station in about an hour. She would make her way there. She would have an innocuous conversation with the officer on duty. She'd find a ship—a small, fast ship, one that could get her where she needed to go. And that would be that.

She loved the New Republic. Loved everything it stood for. She felt a weight on her heart as what she planned to do set in. But she had no choice.

Zeva Bliss had to face justice.

CHAPTER 36

The visions swept into Poe's mind, like a flood of memories, dreams, and possibilities. For a moment, he was on an A-wing, battling back TIE fighters in Endor's orbit—a giant Death Star looming in the background. Then he was on the surface, walking through the planet's dense forests, surrounded by a team of Pathfinders and Ewoks, dodging fire from a cadre of stormtroopers. Then he was somewhere else on Yavin 4, running down a barren, vine-strewn road, his footsteps falling in the same rhythm as his pursuers'—an authoritarian voice booming behind him: "We know it was you, Poe Dameron! Slow down and turn yourself in!" Then he was a boy again, his sheets pulled up to his chin, his mother's outline looming above him, her soft hand on his cheek as she hummed a familiar lullaby. Why couldn't he see her? Then darkness, the only sound a low, moaning cry. He was in his house, but older, walking through the main hallway toward the pained sound. The living room was dark; he could only make out a hunched form. It was his father—racked with sobs, a picture of Poe's mother, Shara Bey, in his quivering hands.

His vision cut to a field, blood on his chin, another boy behind him—his mother's voice running through his young brain as a group of older kids approached. "Help when you can, Poe. We're a family of helpers. We try our best to do the right thing, no matter how hard it can be. Don't ever forget that."

Then he was older, on a landspeeder on Yavin 4, the wind slapping his face, L'ulo L'ampar driving at top speed. He didn't remember how or why, but he'd been with his mother's oldest friend when L'ulo got a call. L'ulo didn't hesitate. "Stay here, don't say anything," L'ulo had commanded as he kicked the small Civilian Defense Force vehicle into high gear. No hesitation. The need to help, to do good, was ingrained in him, as it had been in Shara Bey and Kes Dameron. Despite being flawed, complicated people—they always tried to do their best. To help others—to choose the path of justice over selfishness.

Could Poe Dameron say the same of himself?

"This is a setup," Poe said, his voice flat and distant, still processing the realization. "It's a death trap."

Zorii looked down at her feet, then up at Poe, shaking her head. She walked over to the terminal and tapped a few keys before turning to face Poe again.

"I'm surprised it took you this long," Zorii said. "Did

you really think my mother was gathering every rival she could to break bread and sing songs together?"

"It's murder," Poe said.

Zorii laughed, a humorless, dry sound.

"If I recall, Poe, you were desperate to murder Sotin not long ago," Zorii said. "How is this different?"

"It's a trap—these people are coming in expecting an alliance," Poe said. "Instead, they'll get a knife in the back."

"You have to be smarter than your enemies to survive," she said with a shrug. "You have to know when to make tough decisions. Haven't you learned anything?"

Poe took a hesitant step back, hands up.

"I know they're criminals, Zorii," he said. "They're all bad, unprincipled people. But it's not a fair fight."

"Fair?" Zorii said, taken aback. "What's fair, Poe? This life is about scraping and clawing for whatever you can, for any advantage. Do you think the Spice Runners got this far by being fair—by doing the right thing?"

"I think you both might need some time alone," EV-6B6 said, stepping back into the hall. "Sometimes a little privacy helps when couples—"

"I'm not doing it," Poe said, meeting Zorii's eyes. "I won't kill people in cold blood."

"Poe, it's done. It's over," she said, a chilling smile on her face. "They're as good as dead."

"No," Poe said, almost as much to himself as to Zorii. "I can't . . . I won't let you."

The punch came at Poe fast, her fist connecting with his face and sending him spinning. He clutched at one of the cots and stopped himself from falling to the floor. She stood over him, pulling back for another punch. Before she could, though, Poe sent a foot into her shin, knocking her back a few paces—giving him a moment to recover.

"I don't want to fight you," he said. He could feel blood dripping down his chin, a cut on the inside of his mouth. "I don't want to hurt you."

Zorii was done with words. She leapt toward Poe, a swift kick to his head knocking him down to the floor this time. She followed with a flurry of punches to his midsection, keeping him down. Poe caught a glimpse of her expression—her eyes red with anger, her mouth open as if mid-scream. Somehow, his refusal to participate had been the final straw. He'd finally broken her. Finally crossed the line she'd hoped he never would. Despite their arguments, despite her frustrations, she'd probably harbored a hope that Poe would come around, would fully embrace the life she was so willing to be a part of. But he hadn't. And now he stood against her.

Poe understood, to some degree. This was Zorii's moment. All the training, the expectations, the pressure—they had all built to this. She had to show her loyalty—to the cause, to her own mother. She had to deliver for Zeva Bliss. If she failed in this task, it would create a fatal crack in the Spice Runners—a failure Zorii could never abide being responsible for. Whatever friendship they had when they walked into the dank halls of the monastery was long gone. Poe Dameron was her enemy now, and Zorii Bliss didn't show her enemies mercy.

She paused for a second, her breathing slowing. She was atop Poe, her hand gripping his tunic and her fist ready to strike again. Poe waited a moment—he wasn't sure why. Maybe he was hoping she'd come around, realize the error in the plan. Help him up so they could try to derail her mother's insane, bloodthirsty trap. But she seemed frozen—staring down at Poe, his face bruised and battered. How had it come to this, he wondered?

The moment passed, and Poe pushed her off of him in a fast, brutal motion, knocking her onto her back, a low groan escaping her mouth. Poe got to his feet. He thought about helping her up—to try to salvage something between them—but he was interrupted by a low rumbling sound. The monastery began to shake—slowly at first, then more violently.

"What . . . ?" Poe asked. "What's going on?"

Out of the corner of his vision, he caught Zorii pulling herself up onto one of the empty cots. She rubbed her chin. Their eyes met, and she spoke two words that chilled Poe to his very core.

"It's starting."

CHAPTER 37

Poe darted toward the door, hoping to outrun Zorii—but before he could make it into the hall, her arms wrapped around his ankles, yanking him to the ground. His head slammed into the stone floor, blinding him for a minute. Next thing he knew, she was standing over him, her blaster drawn. The building still shuddered, but the small quakes were more consistent now, adding a droning, vibrational effect to the entire affair.

"You either help us or you're against us," she said. Her face was scraped and bruised, blood caked on her chin. "I don't want to have to kill you, Poe, but I will. Don't doubt me."

He didn't. If there was anything about Zorii Poe believed, it was how deeply connected to the Spice Runners she felt. How much the life had consumed her. She wasn't just a thief—she was a Spice Runner of Kijimi, and nothing he did could change that. She would never divert from this path. He'd been foolish to even consider that.

He let his head fall back on the cold ground. Her breathing calmed a bit, but her grip on the blaster didn't. Was this the end, Poe thought? To be killed by the woman he once considered his closest friend? The one reason he felt he couldn't leave the Spice Runners of Kijimi? He closed his eyes for a moment and said a silent prayer. He wasn't sure to what, but he did it anyway. The shaking stopped—at least on the outside. Poe's head felt like it was experiencing its own kind of aftershock.

"There appear to be a few armed officers heading this way . . . and they seem quite upset. . . ."

Eevee. Poe opened his eyes. Zorii turned to EV-6B6's voice and stood up. She walked toward the doorway and peered around the corner, EV-6B6 standing behind her.

"What?" Zorii said. "I don't see any—"

The electrical charge leapt from EV-6B6's fingertips into Zorii, causing her to spasm and scream in anguish. Her body began to jerk and twist from the shock as her blaster rattled to the floor. Poe stood up.

"Eevee, stop it," he said. The droid complied, and Zorii slumped to the ground, unconscious. "What the hell was that?"

"No need to thank me," EV-6B6 said as she moved out into the hallway. "I managed to connect with the terminal there and have gained limited access to Zeva Bliss's plan—which Zorii has already activated."

Poe gave Zorii one last look before following EV-6B6.

She was breathing. Slowly, but breathing. He pocketed her blaster and followed the droid.

"So, what's her plan then, Eevee?" Poe said, wincing as he picked up speed. "What's Zeva Bliss doing?"

"From what I understand, Zeva Bliss has gathered her closest allies and enemies to discuss partnership but will instead execute them," EV-6B6 said, as if she was discussing fuel levels on a starship.

"I know that," Poe said, trying to keep up with the speedy droid. "But where? When?"

EV-6B6 pointed toward the end of the hall. Poe froze as he saw a dozen or so of Zeva Bliss's personal armored guards ushering a handful of gruff, unhappy people in the opposite direction.

"Right now," EV-6B6 said. "Right there."

"You'll never get away with this," BoShek said, without much conviction in his voice. One of the Spice Runner guards poked at him with a blaster. "Watch it. You'll regret doing that."

"Sure I will," the hooded guard said. "Now get moving."

Zeva Bliss watched as her security detail pushed and prodded her new prisoners from the monastery to a long field outside—a coliseum-like structure that had once been home to religious and mystical ceremonies, back when Kijimi was more spiritual than criminal. Now it would serve as an execution garden, the place where Zeva Bliss would vault ahead of her competitors and finally push the Spice Runners of Kijimi into the upper echelon of the galactic criminal underworld. It was a move that had taken years to plan. That had to be executed with precision and forethought. She'd waited patiently in the war room—prattled on and on about her hopes and dreams to this cabal of fools—for the signal from Zorii that everything was in place. Then the explosions began. The smuggler ships and transports that had ferried the likes of Tarand Crowe and Astrid Fenris to Kijimi were being destroyed by massive laser cannons hidden in the monastery's stone structure, just as a giant doorway to the stage was opening.

She watched as the seats surrounding the performance area were filled by her own people. Her Spice Runners. The scoundrels, bounty hunters, two-bit thieves, and murderers she'd cobbled together over the past few years to form a greater whole. All those who had sworn their allegiance to not only the Spice Runners of Kijimi but to her—to Zeva Bliss. They would bask in the glory with her. They would experience her crowning achievement alongside her. Her moment of victory.

"No word from Zorii," one of the guards said, his voice low so as to avoid being overheard. "Should we send out some troops to find her?"

Zeva did not look at the messenger, feigning disinterest.

"No, no, I'm sure she's fine," she said. "But we must find that Poe Dameron. Something tells me he doesn't have . . . the stomach for the mission I've sent my daughter on."

The guard nodded and stepped away.

Zeva Bliss did not tell her underlings her innermost ideas or, perish the thought, how she was *feeling*. But the knowledge that her daughter—her diligent, precise, and calculating daughter—had not checked in did worry her. It was unlike Zorii to go silent at such a critical moment. A time when Zeva Bliss would want her standing beside her to celebrate the demise of their deadliest foes.

She would chastise Zorii later, Zeva Bliss thought as she drew her long sword from its scabbard and stepped into the center position. A wild roar emanated from the crowd—hoots, hollers, screams of victory. Zeva Bliss had not expected the rush to overcome her, but she felt every part of her pulsing with energy. She raised the sword up to the sky and was met by another boisterous wave of cheers. She let the whooping die down before she spoke, her voice loud and forceful.

"The time for patience . . . is . . . over!" Zeva said, her voice booming through the space. "After we're done, no one in the galaxy will be ignorant—no one will claim to not know who we are. No one will dare challenge us. Now the Spice Runners of Kijimi will take their proper place—by destroying our enemies and writing our names across the galaxy in their blood!"

The crowd responded with more cheers, these tinged with a manic, desperate violence that had been absent just a few moments before.

Poe Dameron's heart sank as he peered at Zeva Bliss from the doorway to the coliseum, EV-6B6 at his side. He watched as the smugglers and bounty hunters who'd come to Kijimi expecting a deal to be made were ushered toward the center of the wide, dirt-caked field, blasters trained on them. How could Poe hope to make a difference here?

"They appear to be moving all of the visitors outside," EV-6B6 said.

"I can see that," Poe said, keeping his voice low. "But the question is why."

"Well, if I was the leader of the Spice Runners of Kijimi, and I had all my competitors in one room," EV-6B6 said, her voice retaining its usual positive tenor, "it would make sense to not only murder them but do it as a public spectacle to instill fear and terror among your own—"

"Okay, okay, I get it, Eevee," Poe whispered to the droid. "We have to do something."

"The odds are certainly against us, but I think we should try," EV-6B6 said without missing a beat.

Then the shuddering started again.

But it was different, less focused—and more familiar. Poe could tell the noise and vibrations were a surprise to the Spice Runners, too—as they scrambled to figure out what was going on. Zeva Bliss's men looked around, trying to keep part of their attention on their prisoners while also trying to figure out why it felt like the planet itself was shaking off its mooring.

Then Poe saw the ship, and he felt a wave of relief.

The New Republic shuttle was large and clunky, but it landed a few meters from the bulk of Zeva Bliss's troops as if that was standard operating procedure. The Spice Runners were still trying to regroup and figure out a plan of attack when the ship's rear hatch opened and the boarding ramp hit the ground.

Sela Trune stepped down, her blaster trained on Zeva Bliss.

"Surprise," Trune said with a smile.

"Sela Trune, is it? I have to admit, I thought you'd be older," Zeva Bliss said as she calmly stepped toward the new arrival, sword dangling at her side. "Nonetheless . . . welcome to Kijimi."

Bliss tried her best to appear unflappable, but even at that distance, Poe could see the Spice Runners' leader was rattled. This was not part of the plan. This was an unexpected twist. And it was happening in front of her entire membership.

Trune didn't respond. She stepped on the dusty ground and kept her blaster locked on Zeva Bliss.

"It takes quite a bit of nerve to come barreling into my home, Officer," Zeva Bliss said, circling Trune, a new confidence in her movements. *What does she know?* Poe wondered. Why was she suddenly acting like she'd taken Trune by surprise? "Especially all alone."

Alone. Was it possible the New Republic Security Bureau officer had made her way to Kijimi without backup? He knew Trune was passionate—just based on their brief encounter on Ledesmar's starship. But was there more to her desire to capture the leader of the Spice Runners? Something . . . personal?

"This is my fight, Bliss," Trune said. "I wouldn't want to share my victory with anyone else."

She pulled a small datapad from her side pocket and tapped a few keys without looking away from Bliss or lowering her blaster. The ship behind her came to life. Three laser cannons popped up from the ship's hull and sprayed the crowd of Spice Runners behind Zeva Bliss with fire, sending them scrambling for cover—and creating a wide rift between Bliss and her gang. They were alone now.

"Trune, your timing is impeccable," Bliss said, stepping toward the officer. "I figured you'd given up. But I should have known better."

Bliss darted forward, raising her sword and swinging the blade down hard. Trune barely dodged the attack, rolling across the ground and getting a few shots off. One grazed Bliss's armor, leaving a mark, but Bliss barely noticed it. She raised the sword again.

CHAPTER 38

Trune sent another volley of blasts in Bliss's direction, one of them knocking the other woman back. She chastised herself for underestimating Bliss's armor. She'd come to Kijimi hot and angry—frustrated by her superiors' lack of initiative and desire to shut down the Spice Runners. By now, the New Republic Security Bureau had noticed her absence—had logged the missing ship. If she made it out of this alive, she'd have plenty to explain to her bosses. But she'd had no choice.

She blasted Bliss's sword out of her hands. The Spice Runners' leader cursed loudly as she scrambled to her feet. Trune moved closer—too close. She didn't expect Bliss's kick to come so fast. Next thing she knew, her own weapon was skittering across the dirt, out of reach.

They were circling each other—each fighter poised to strike, each spring-loaded and ready to careen toward the other. The brawl itself had been brief, but Trune could already see the wear and tear on Bliss. This was supposed to be her big moment in front of her entire organization.

Instead, she'd been blindsided and embarrassed. She had to end this quickly to save as much face as she could.

"You've made a terrible mistake," Bliss said, shaking her head. "You can't beat me. Even if my people can't reach you."

"No, Zeva, you've made the mistake," Trune said. She'd wanted to savor this moment, to wait until she was sure she'd won, but her own impatience got the best of her. "It's you who betrayed the very words you stand for."

Bliss hesitated, her posture softening, and Trune took the opportunity to strike, sending a punch right into Bliss's visor. She heard a pleasant crack as the blow knocked Bliss to the ground. She thought she heard a unified, audible gasp from the collected Spice Runners watching the brawl, unable to cross the makeshift ditch her ship's cannons had created without becoming easy targets. Trune didn't let herself think about her audience much, though. Instead, she pounced. Trune felt her knuckles cracking and scratching on the hard metal of Bliss's headgear, each punch hurting her almost as much as it probably hurt Bliss. Trune slowed as she felt Bliss's grip weaken, the Spice Runner leader's movement lethargic and groggy.

Trune gripped Bliss by the collar, lifting her head so they were face to face. Trune could see Bliss's eyes through the shattered and cracked helmet. Could smell the blood coating her face. Bliss's heavy, labored breathing was coming in uneven bursts.

"Finish me," Bliss said, her words coming out like a wheeze. "It's what you want, isn't it? To avenge your dead family . . . ? To have my blood on your fingertips?"

Trune gritted her teeth. Bliss wasn't wrong. But she would do it on her own terms. The New Republic's terms.

"I've already finished you," Trune said, a dark smile forming on her face. She could see surprise creep into Bliss's eyes. "You just don't know it yet."

Bliss stiffened in Trune's grip, as if the truth had been injected into her bloodstream. *Does she know?* Trune wondered.

"I couldn't believe it—that you'd even consider it possible. That Tomasso, your loyal, unbending deputy would betray your trust," Trune said, whispering now, wanting only Bliss to hear her killing blow. "It was so easy . . . so easy to plant the seeds of doubt. To make you consider . . . then believe . . . that the one person who'd always stood by you was actually looking to take your place."

"No, no . . . the proof, the facts . . ." Bliss sputtered. "Who? How?"

"Marinda Gan was all too willing to sell every secret she could muster for a chance at freedom," Trune said, building up steam as she got closer to the truth that would crush Zeva Bliss. "It was just a matter of using her secrets against Tomasso . . . and you."

A short, moaning sob escaped Zeva Bliss's mouth, the muffled noise jarring, disconcerting. She was human after all, Trune thought. She shook off the momentary distraction and pressed on.

"Facts can be fabricated, Zeva Bliss," Trune said, savoring each word, watching as each one stabbed the other woman's heart. "Truths bent and twisted to fit the story . . . the story I wanted you to believe. When, in truth, it was an entirely different betrayal that gave me what I needed to find you . . . and crush you."

Trune had been too caught up in the story—too caught up in her moment of victory over Bliss, the woman who'd ordered the attack that stole her family—to notice Bliss's hands moving furtively. She didn't see the small blade in her hand. Saw her arm jerk upward too late. The blade wasn't long, but the jagged knife entered her midsection with a focused fury. Trune felt the blade twist inside her, sending a burning, unfathomable pain through her entire body.

Bliss caught the look of anguished surprise on Trune's face, the officer's moment of victory withered away.

"For shame, Trune," Bliss said, pushing the blade so hard into Sela Trune's midsection that the New Republic officer was lifted up. "What a silly mistake. To think you'd bested me with words? It is the blade that wins the war, my dear. And I always carry a spare."

Bliss shoved Trune aside as she stood. The knife remained embedded as she desperately tried to pull it out, her groans and whimpers growing more frantic and pained. Zeva walked toward her fallen sword and picked it up, taking her time as she returned to Trune.

"It is time you learned the same lesson your family learned years ago, Sela Trune of Yungbrii," Bliss said, a bloody smile visible through her battered helmet. "You never cross the Spice Runners of Kijimi."

The blaster shot connected with Bliss's shoulder, knocking her to her knees. She stood up slowly and turned around.

Who dares?

Bliss looked over at the young man, his eyes wide with fear, his hand gripping the blaster with a tightness and focus that screamed nerves and anxiety. She stepped toward him, sword raised high.

"Have you also come to Kijimi to die, Poe Dameron?"

CHAPTER 39

While New Republic Security Bureau officer Sela Trune began to duel Zeva Bliss, Poe Dameron found himself at an unexpected fork in the road.

"Dameron, come on—we have to find a way over that canyon to help our leader," said one of the hooded guards, pointing toward Zeva Bliss, who was now locked in combat with Trune. "We have to take that New Republic suit down before her friends join in."

They don't know what I did, Poe thought. The only Spice Runner who knew about Poe's decision not to take part in Zeva Bliss's murderous plan was Zorii, who was—hopefully—still sleeping fitfully inside the monastery. And EV-6B6, of course. She knew, too.

Poe nodded absentmindedly at the guard and grabbed EV-6B6 by the arm, dragging her toward the entrance to the monastery. Out of the corner of his eye Poe could see the handful of armed Spice Runners ushering their prisoners away from the Bliss/Trune battle and toward the field's far wall. The crowd seemed awed into silence, watching Zeva and Trune duke it out. The brawl was probably more entertainment than they'd bargained for, Poe mused.

"Are you taking me somewhere, Master Poe?" EV-6B6 said as she squirmed. Poe realized he was still gripping the droid tightly and released her.

"They still think we're on their side, Eevee," Poe said, jerking a thumb at the Spice Runners. "So we have to use that to our advantage."

"It's good that they still believe we're Spice Runners," EV-6B6 mused. "But we're severely outnumbered, don't you think? Not to get pessimistic, but . . ."

Poe gripped the droid by the shoulders, shaking her slightly.

"No, I refuse to think that way, okay? We're going to get out of here, Eevee," Poe said. "Just follow my lead, all right?"

EV-6B6 pulled away from Poe's grip, which he took as a sign of agreement. Poe walked toward a Spice Runner guard, standing watch outside the monastery entrance Poe had walked through a few minutes before.

"We need more weapons, we're running low—think you can swing by the armory and stock up?" Poe said. "Things are nuts out here and we can't really afford to be two men down."

The guard turned and sped away after a few mumbled

words of agreement. Poe fought back the urge to smile at EV-6B6. Another guard—the same one who'd ordered Poe to join them, perhaps, Poe couldn't tell—came upon them.

"What're you two doing here?" he said. "You want to help?"

Poe started to respond but got cut off.

"Good, good. We're trying to figure out how to get closer to the fight," the guard continued. "That damn ditch isn't gonna be easy to get across. Second one of us tries, that New Republic cop can take us out. But I think we can wait it out. Eventually Trune is going to slip up and we'll be able to step in. But we need to get into position now. It's taken forever for these amateurs to piece together a plan, but I think we've got it. Thing is, we need someone to watch the prisoners while we move in. Do you think you and your droid can handle that?"

Poe nodded enthusiastically.

"Meet us by the far wall," the guard said. "You'll take over watching the prisoners so we can give Zeva Bliss some backup."

"Yeah, I just need to give the droid a once-over and then I'll bring her around," Poe said. "Catch you in a few."

The guard seemed a bit confused but shrugged and walked toward the mass of Spice Runners and prisoners moving through the field. As he wandered off, their armory envoy arrived, lugging a large case.

"Got as much as I could," he said. "This'll do some serious damage."

"Excellent, this is perfect. I'll be sure to put in a good word with Zeva Bliss herself," Poe said, leaning forward and trying to make eye contact with the guard. "This is the kind of work that should never go unnoticed."

The guard tried to contain his excitement.

"Oh, well, great—thank you," he said. "That would mean a lot, I mean—"

Poe slapped the guard on the shoulder tentatively.

"Now, get back to your post," Poe said. "We can't risk any other incidents, you know?"

"Right, right," the guard said, taking his previous position by the entrance.

Poe and EV-6B6 began to drag the large case over the dirty field and toward the prisoners. Poe recognized a few of the smugglers being held at gunpoint—Sotin, Crowe, Barso, and Fenris, for starters—but many were new to him. The plan was risky, but he couldn't think of any other way out. He couldn't beat back the entire Spice Runners of Kijimi organization by himself. And who better for a thief like Poe to trust than other thieves?

"Don't answer that," he muttered to himself.

"Did you say something, Master Dameron?" EV-6B6 asked.

Poe ignored the droid as the handful of guards monitoring the prisoners swiveled toward the sound of the dragging case.

"What's this, Dameron?" the lead guard said, his features masked by a dark hood.

"Rations," Poe said. "Figured our prisoners might want a final meal."

"Meal?" the guard said. "Are you mad? We're about to execute them all."

"You talk a good game. Especially for someone training a gun on an unarmed man, Spice Runner," Crowe said to the guard. The smuggler licked his lips, almost as if he knew what Poe had in mind. "Toss me a gun and we'll see who gets executed."

"Just following orders," Poe said to the lead guard with a shrug. "From Bliss herself before she got caught up in this."

Poe turned to see how the battle was going. The combatants were two dozen or so meters from Poe and the prisoners. From what he could tell, Trune was atop Bliss, their faces close. It wasn't looking good for their leader, which was good for Poe.

"Fine, fine," the lead guard said. He pointed his blaster

rifle at the case and spoke to his nearest underlings. "Get this over to the prisoners."

The guards complied, opening the case. But they didn't find sealed ration packets inside. The cache of blasters and rifles would be the last thing they saw for quite some time.

"Enjoy your last meal, folks," Poe said, disabling the two nearest guards with a quick volley of blaster fire. "I hear this dinner does wonders for life expectancy."

Unfortunately, the remaining guards weren't as easy to incapacitate, positioning themselves between the cache of weapons and their prisoners. Poe's heart sank. He'd revealed himself as a traitor, only to see the plan torn down. Poe could see the desperation in the prisoners' eyes as the remaining guards tried to split their attention between them and Poe. He thought he heard EV-6B6 moving slowly behind him, toward the guards.

"It appears Zeva Bliss has been killed," EV-6B6 said, her tone uncharacteristically sad. Poe turned to look toward the battle, as did a few of the guards. Before Poe could ask a question, he heard a scuffle and the familiar sound of blaster fire. He looked back to find the lead guard writhing on the ground—Tarand Crowe standing over him, a blaster pointed at his head.

Crowe didn't bother with a snappy catchphrase, instead sending a few shots into the guard's head before he moved on to disable another incoming Spice Runner. The odds were getting even.

Some of the prisoners—Caryn, Fenris, Adlerber—just ran, heading toward their ships and hoping to get off-planet. But others, like Crowe and Barso, relished the fight too much. Poe almost allowed himself a laugh. He *had* pulled it off.

As he started to pivot, he saw a familiar shape speed past him. Without a second thought, Poe reached out and grabbed Sotin by his collar, surprising the slender criminal and tugging him back with a jerk.

"Thought that was you," Poe said, unable to hide the smile on his face. "Funny how we keep running into each other."

"Oh, ah, Poe Dameron," Sotin hissed, unable to make eye contact. "Thank you—for, your help. You—"

Poe swung his elbow into Sotin's face, sending the smuggler spinning backward. His head hit the ground with a loud *thwack*. That would have to be enough, Poe thought. There was no time for grudges. At least not to the degree Poe wanted.

"Eevee, I think we just might make it out of this," Poe said as he fired a blast at an incoming guard, knocking her backward. "I can't believe it. Can you? I really owe you one. I can't believe a droid saved my—"

Silence. Poe turned to his right—to the last spot he'd seen the droid. Quiet wasn't really EV-6B6's strong suit, Poe knew—and he understood why she'd gone quiet now. Instead of EV-6B6, Poe found a burning, shattered husk, the droid's head blown clear off and her internal circuitry laid bare for all to see, thick smoke rising from the dismembered shell.

"No, wait, Eevee—what . . . ?" Poe said, reaching for the droid but stopping himself, accepting that the damage was done. Even Babu Frik's magic touch couldn't save his friend.

Footsteps. Amid the firefight, Poe heard footsteps. He looked up to see one of the guards, blaster pointed at him. He was close. Close enough to have done some serious damage to EV-6B6. Poe felt his grip tighten around his own blaster, felt his face flush red with anger.

"Think you can just betray us, young pup?" the guard said, his scarred blue face scrunching in anger. The Chagrian's sharp horns and fleshy head tentacles seemed poised to strike. "One doesn't just leave the Spice Runners of Kijimi."

Before Poe could think to fire, the Chagrian's hand had gripped his throat and lifted him up into the air, his other hand clamped over Poe's wrist, making it impossible for Poe to shoot his blaster. He could smell the burnt wiring and circuitry that had once been EV-6B6 below.

"What—who are you?" Poe asked between gulped breaths.

"My name is Gezlar," the Chagrian said, tightening his grip on Poe, his dark smile widening. "But that's of little use to you now. I knew there was something off about you the moment you arrived. You looked too clean. Too pretty and pure. You didn't have the blood of a Spice Runner in you. And I was right."

Poe scratched at the Chagrian's viselike grip, his one free hand's nails digging into the light blue flesh—but it didn't seem to affect Gezlar. If anything, it made him angrier. Poe's vision blurred, then darkened around the edges. This was it, he thought. He'd gotten so close.

Then Gezlar hesitated as a loud, pained scream interrupted the melee. The large Chagrian looked away from Poe and toward the center of the field, which had been cordoned off by the blasts from Trune's ship. Poe followed Gezlar's gaze and his heart sank.

Even from this distance, Poe could see Zeva Bliss hoisting up the shattered body of Sela Trune and tossing it aside like an overloaded bag of trash. Trune landed hard and didn't move again. Gezlar stared, hypnotized by the violence.

Gezlar's grip on Poe's hand loosened slightly, allowing

Poe's fingers to tighten around his blaster. As the Chagrian started to turn back to finish what he'd started, he was met with a shot to the head. The massive hand wrapped around Poe's neck dropped, and the blue behemoth collapsed to the ground.

Poe coughed loudly, rubbing his neck, which felt rough and scratched but otherwise fine. He gave EV-6B6's husk one last look and made his way toward Trune. Toward the right thing.

Zeva Bliss was walking back to Trune's prone form as Poe sped toward them, finding a small patch of dirt that hadn't been destroyed by Trune's ship, which allowed him to cross into their private ring without too much difficulty. Zeva's back was to him, and Poe had little time to think about strategy. Probably because there wasn't any to formulate. They were in the final stage, and it was all about luck and instinct. He fired two shots at Zeva Bliss.

One missed. The other made contact, sending Bliss to her knees.

The leader of the Spice Runners of Kijimi got to her feet and turned around slowly, and Poe got a look at her broken and battered helmet before she spoke, her mouth forming a bloodied, maniacal smile.

"Have you also come to Kijimi to die, Poe Dameron?"

She woke up angry—and in pain.

Zorii Bliss came to, her head foggy. Her skin was tingling in a strange way. Her mouth felt dry and her balance was off as she got to her feet, quickly at first but then with more deliberation. Whatever that droid had done to her, it had been bad.

The room was quiet and empty, aside from the small terminal at the far end. She didn't hear anything happening outside the space but was certain something was going on. How long had she been out?

Most important, where was Poe Dameron?

Poe.

Zorii shook her head. No. She wouldn't let her emotions interfere. Poe had betrayed them. Betrayed her. She had known this moment was coming fast, she just hadn't wanted to accept it. Hadn't wanted to consider that someone she'd come to care for didn't have the same mettle she did. But the reality was right in front of her face: Poe Dameron was not a Spice Runner of Kijimi. His continued existence put their entire operation at risk.

She groaned as she tried to pick up speed, leaving the room behind and scanning the vacant hallways. She thought she saw some motion at the far end, toward the exit. She heard sounds, too. Cheers?

Poe.

She didn't want to think about him. She wanted to think of the idea of him—a traitor. An idealistic weakling unable to make the hard decisions that were part and parcel of being a Spice Runner. But her mind—probably the aftereffects of some mild concussion, she reasoned—didn't make that easy. The images kept popping up as she made her way down the hall. That kiss on the Moraysian cruiser. The embrace in Babu's workshop, and how natural it felt, even after what seemed like an eternity of iciness. The hyperspace jump and Poe's bemused grin. How he'd daydream about them running off somewhere together before she'd shot him down. He cared for her, even when they weren't close or talking or even in the same room. She knew that.

Then why did he betray her?

"Stop it," she muttered to herself. "Stop it, dammit."

"Zorii Bliss?"

Zorii spun around. It was a guard. He seemed out of place—confused.

"Yes?" she said. "What's going on? Where are the prisoners?"

"They're, well, that's the prob—"

"What's happening?" she yelled, grabbing the guard's arms. He tried to back away but she held on. "Where is Zeva? Where is my mother?"

The guard shook free of her grasp, rubbing one of his arms as if Zorii's hands had burned him on contact.

"That's the thing," he said. "She's outside. . . . She's in combat. The prisoners have escaped. They're running loose out there—but your mother is trapped. She's battling this woman, she looks to be a New Republic officer. Young, short hair—"

Trune.

"How? How did the prisoners escape?" Zorii asked, making her way toward the exit. Toward her mother. The guard was following along, keeping pace—but also keeping his distance. "How is this happening?"

"It was, well, it was your friend Dameron," the guard said, shaking his head in disgust. "And that insipid droid. They brought over some rations, but they were weapons—"

Zorii didn't let the guard finish. She turned and marched out of the monastery. There was no time, she thought. She had to do something.

What she walked into was pure chaos. It took her a moment to make sense of it. Guards firing indiscriminately. Pirates and smugglers stampeding toward freedom. Screams of surprise and agony. She stepped over what looked like a melted droid. There were no sides. There was no reason. Calling it a melee would be generous. She picked up a fallen blaster and holstered it as she made her way to the center of the wide stretch of land. Then it came into focus. The New Republic ship. A ditch that seemed to circle a few combatants. One was her mother. Zorii could tell even from that distance. Another was on the ground, beaten, perhaps dead. Trune? Zorii wasn't sure. But then a third—making a cautious approach.

Zorii ran toward the scene, but she was too far away to intercede. Then the interloper came into focus.

She saw Poe Dameron fire on Zeva Bliss, knocking her mother to her knees—blindsiding her.

The leader of the Spice Runners of Kijimi recovered, standing and turning to face her attacker. Zorii couldn't hear what Zeva Bliss said to Poe. But she had an idea. Zeva didn't like being shot at.

Zorii Bliss ran.

Poe sent two more blasts at Bliss, no longer interested in a snappy response. There was no room for laughter anymore, he thought. Visions flashed through his mind—his mother's abandoned A-wing. His father crying to himself in his darkened house. Vigilch impaled. Tomasso bleeding out on an unfamiliar world. EV-6B6 blasted to pieces. He'd seen too much, too fast. He realized this now. He felt so foolish.

Bliss stumbled back, surprised by Poe's offensive. Picking up on her momentary distraction, he made a beeline for Trune, who was still on the ground, her chest barely moving. He knelt beside the fallen New Republic Security Bureau officer and took her hand.

"We'll get you help, okay?" Poe said, trying to sound confident but aware her survival was an impossibility. "We'll find a way off this planet."

"What happened, Dameron?" Trune said, her voice sounding like boots on shattered glass. "Come to your senses?"

"Something like that," Poe said. "I'm sorry. Sorry you had to come here and die, just looking for me."

Trune let out a brief, hoarse laugh.

"Get over yourself, kid," she said, wincing at every other word. "It's not about you. It's not all about you. The Spice Runners killed my family. Didn't want them . . . to . . . destroy yours . . . too."

She was gone.

Poe closed Sela Trune's eyes with his fingertips. He could hear Zeva Bliss approaching him from behind. He stood and turned to face her.

"I knew this wasn't for you," Bliss said, raising her sword as she walked toward Poe. "But my daughter tried to convince me. She said you had the heart of a Spice Runner in you. I guess the only way we'll know for sure . . ."

She swung her sword, the tip of the blade slicing at Poe's chest, tearing the fabric of his shirt and leaving a deep cut.

"Is if I cut it out myself," Bliss said.

"You're a murderer, not a thief," Poe said, pointing his blaster at Zeva Bliss, surprised at his own words. "You have no code of honor. The Spice Runners are a fraud."

Bliss let out a long, manic cackle and took another swing at Poe—the blade grazing his blaster.

"What a quaint little fool you are," Bliss said. "To think that there's any kind of honor among thieves."

Poe got another shot off as Bliss recovered from her sword's miss, but it went wide. She pushed—hurtling forward, sword raised—and tossed Poe back with a knee to the chest. The wind was knocked out of him as he landed on his back. He still held his blaster, though, and said a silent prayer as he swung it around for another shot.

Before he could pull the trigger, Bliss whirled the

sword around again, slicing Poe's weapon off at the barrel, the tip of the blaster dropping onto the sandy ground with a soft, hopeless sound. He tried to get up, but Bliss was too fast—she sliced at him, the sword cutting deep into his right shoulder, pain shooting through his entire body and blood flowing out of the wound with an immediacy and intensity that made Poe wonder if she'd killed him. He gripped his wounded arm and stumbled back, trying to sidestep her follow-up swings as she chased him down a small sand hill toward the far wall. The crowd of Spice Runners looking on was alive again, enjoying the latest undercard match, and let out a long whoop of enjoyment as Poe slipped and fell backward, his head slamming into the ground. Blood and dirt and sand caked his body. His head spun. He could barely make out the shape of Zeva Bliss as she walked toward him, the tip of her sword caressing his chin. This was what it felt like to tiptoe toward death, Poe thought.

Zeva Bliss pulled back, though, and for a second, Poe toyed with the idea that the Spice Runners' leader might grant him mercy—his brain speed-living a life in a Kijimi prison, visited by a chastising Zorii and perhaps his father. But that low-grade nightmare was put to rest as Zeva Bliss swung her sword down on Poe's midsection, barely missing his stomach. Poe had shifted to his right just in time to avoid being sliced open—instead earning a deep, painful gash on his ribcage. The pain was like fire, spreading across his body and joining his already electrified arm to form a chorus of anguish that threatened to send Poe into a deep, dark state that he might never climb out of.

Her sword was up again. The end at his throat, the tip poking at his jugular. There'd been a time when Poe Dameron feared nothing more than death, nothing more than a life unlived. But those days had faded, he thought. His only regret now wasn't the choices he'd made—leaving Yavin 4, following Zorii, joining the Spice Runners—but not having the chance to make more choices. To return home. To join the cause his parents had helped define. To fight for something other than his own selfish thrill seeking.

"Any final words, Poe Dameron?"

CHAPTER 40

Poe took a deep breath. It had gotten hard to swallow. His side and arm ached. His hands were sticky with his own blood.

"I rarely offer my enemies such an opportunity," Zeva Bliss said, sword still on Poe as she took a few steps to her right. "But I feel you deserve it, Poe Dameron. For your brief, mostly honorable service to the Spice Runners of Kijimi."

Poe opened his mouth to respond but was silenced by a loud, animalistic sound.

The scream was primal, high-pitched, but focused, intense—like the sound a fighter makes when connecting a deadly blow, not one of fear or hesitation.

The figure launched toward Zeva Bliss, knocking her over and into the sandy dirt. She rolled over quickly—returning to a fighting stance within seconds. It took Poe that long to realize who'd interceded.

Zorii.

She didn't turn to look at him, her full attention on her mother. Both had blades drawn—though Zeva seemed more adept at wielding hers. They circled each other, not making any moves just yet.

"You've made a grievous error, my child," Zeva Bliss said, genuine concern in her voice. "Think carefully before you raise your hand against me. Against everything you stand for."

Zorii didn't respond. Zeva attacked, swinging high and hard. Zorii parried capably, but it was clear she was overmatched. It was a delay tactic at best. But while Zeva Bliss was the epitome of training and well-executed maneuvers, Zorii had the element of surprise on her side. She sent a kick that connected with Zeva's banged-up helmet, knocking her off-kilter and the helmet at a strange angle, impeding her vision. Zorii turned slightly and tossed Poe a blaster. He caught it and trained it on Zeva.

"Help me, Poe," Zorii said, out of breath. "I know this has gone sideways. I know this isn't how you want things to be. But we can fix it. We can have what you want and what I want, okay? This is our chance. You were right. This was wrong. It wasn't honorable. But there's still time to salvage this. To salvage us. Help me now and we can reshape the Spice Runners to be something else—something new. We can do it together, Poe. If we can defeat my mother, there's no stopping us—"

Zorii lurched forward, the kick from Zeva Bliss

catching her by surprise. To her credit, she bounced back fast, turning to face her mother, sword raised and teeth bared. Poe lifted the blaster again.

Zorii had outlined everything Poe had wanted—months before. Maybe even further back. The idea of running their own crew, of traipsing around the galaxy on their own terms had seemed like a dream come true to Poe then. But he'd seen what the Spice Runners were. Even knowing he'd be able to help Zorii guide them—change the game—they couldn't alter what the organization was, on a base level. Thieves. Criminals. Scoundrels who didn't scoff at dealing with slavers and murderers and the worst the galaxy had to offer. Was that the life Poe wanted? Was that the life Shara Bey and Kes Dameron had envisioned for their only son? Was that what they'd fought for—so many times?

Shara Bey's voice resonated in Poe's mind—soft yet strong. "You should always make your own choices, Poe. We'll never take that from you. But we will teach you enough so you'll know how to choose the right path when the time comes."

"No," Poe said, letting the blaster drop to the ground. "No. I won't do it."

Zorii looked back at Poe, over her shoulder—her eyes wild with a rage he had never seen on her face before. A look of pure anger and betrayal. Whatever she felt for Poe, whatever warmth and affection she'd pushed to the surface to steel herself to make this offer to him, was dead. Gone forever. Replaced by a white-hot anger that could never be doused.

"Then run!" she screamed, her face bloodied and bruised, her mother looming behind her. "Run for your life, Poe—and don't ever come back."

He ran.

CHAPTER 41

Poe sipped the brown, foamy beverage slowly. "Iced mocoa" was what the bartender had called it when he served him. Not bad, he thought.

The cantina was loud and boisterous—it was late enough in the evening that most of the patrons were too drunk to notice the cloaked man sitting at the bar, his face in shadows, sipping a drink usually reserved for first light. But Poe Dameron needed the jolt the brew provided. It was going to be a long night out of Kijimi.

It had been a week since he'd run away from Zorii. His legs ached. His bandaged arm and midsection still throbbed, days later. But he was alive. Barely. He'd managed to find Tarand Crowe amid the chaos—halfway through the monastery, blaster fire raging around them, guards running every direction. Some were headed to the yard, to watch their leader face off against her own daughter. Others were trying to regain some level of control over the prisoners who'd been somehow armed and were making their way back to their ships. Crowe gave Poe cover until they could make their way to Crowe's ship. The smuggler gave Poe a name and a key. Then they parted with a brief handshake.

"You did right by me," Crowe said. "I won't forget that."

"We're even," Poe said with a pained smile.

"You okay on your own?" Crowe asked. "Took a beating back there, huh?"

Crowe seemed more annoyed than concerned. Poe figured he'd reached the limit of the scoundrel's kindness.

"I'll manage," Poe said with a wheeze before turning and darting off into the Kijimi night. Though Zorii had commanded him to run, he couldn't be sure the Spice Runners wouldn't want to find him—and make him suffer for his betrayal.

Crowe's contact lived deep in the underbelly of Kijimi City, and while he was a thief, he wasn't a Spice Runner. Von Tante was a reed-thin wisp of a man—with a shock of white hair and salt-and-pepper stubble and not much else. His eyes were dull but not dead, and it had taken Poe a second to even notice the man as he'd entered his quarters with the key Crowe had slipped him. He'd lost a lot of blood. If Crowe's friend wasn't around, Poe was certain he'd die in the empty quarters.

Tante stepped out of the shadows, eyebrow raised and

blaster pointed at Poe. Despite the intrusion, he didn't seem surprised—almost amused, actually.

"You got a key, which means someone I know thinks we should talk," Tante said, tilting his head slightly to get a better look at Poe. He didn't seem to like what he saw. "Had a rough night, kid?"

Poe's legs buckled, and he struggled to stay upright. Tante stepped toward him and led him to a beat-up chair in the corner of the sparsely furnished room.

"Take a seat, I'll get you something to drink," Tante said. Poe heard clanging and clattering coming from nearby. "On the run, huh? That happens a lot here on Kijimi. Hard to stay in one place when the rules keep changing."

Poe didn't respond, trying to focus on staying conscious. He wasn't succeeding. His mind was drifting off. Then he felt a light slap on his cheek, and a metal cup was thrust in front of him. It smelled of herbs and mud.

"Here, take this," Tante said. "Gonna taste like dirt, but it'll help you. Medic's on the way, too. Called in a favor. She'll get you patched up. Who sent you my way?"

"Crowe," Poe said, the word coming out like a gag, the foul taste of the beverage overtaking him. "What—what is this?"

"Better I not tell you," Tante said. "Crowe, huh? I like him. Glad he's still around. Strange he came to Kijimi, though. He's no Spice Runner."

"Neither am I," Poe said.

Tante—with the help of a medic Poe barely remembered, so delirious was he from blood loss and his injuries—let Poe heal over three or four days. But by the fourth morning, he made it clear to Poe it was time to go.

"This isn't a lodging house, kid," Tante said flatly. "You're hot. Someone's after you. I know that much. Word travels fast on Kijimi. You've done something bad. So bad the Spice Runners are out, full force, looking for you. Best I can offer is a warm bed for a few days, then a path off-planet. I did the first part already."

Poe thanked the man, who had no reason to help him but did anyway.

A late-evening visit to Babu Frik had been risky, but necessary, Poe felt. The droidsmith had been surprised to see Poe—more surprised to see the shape he was in. Though he felt better than he had when he stumbled out of the monastery into the shadowy streets of Kijimi City, he was still a sight to be seen.

"Quick-quick, this put Babu in bad place," Babu said, motioning for Poe to step closer.

"I know you're one of them," Poe told Babu, hands raised. "And I understand if you can't help me. But you saved my droid, and I wanted to let you know she died. She's gone. They gutted her. She didn't deserve that."

"You look bad, too, yeah," Babu said, shaking his head slowly. "Babu Frik cannot help. Big trouble for Babu."

"I understand," Poe said. "But I have nowhere else to go."

Poe waited for a response, a sign from Babu that the droidsmith understood and sympathized with him, but his expression remained blank.

"I've got some intel—there's a ship docked in the city that's leaving tomorrow," Poe continued. "I need to find a way onto that ship. But I can't make it through the streets—much less wander the docks—without hiding who I am. My face is everywhere. The Spice Runners want me dead. I need—"

The droidsmith made a low growl, silencing him.

"I not help you," Babu said. Poe's heart sank. He'd be captured for certain. "But you thief, no? Maybe you find thing you need here. How Babu know until later, something missing?"

Poe nodded slowly as Babu turned around and

rummaged through a small box of what looked like junk to Poe. Then Babu Frik slid a small disk onto the table that separated them. He scooted off his seat and scampered out of the workshop.

Poe stepped closer and picked up the device. Then he smiled.

The holographic disguise matrix hadn't been perfect—but it had done the job, and Poe was thankful. Babu's device had given him enough cover to walk the streets of Kijimi City unnoticed. Well, when it was working. The device was, basically, a personal hologram projector. It allowed Poe to look and sound like someone else. Which was handy while in Kijimi on the run from the Spice Runners . . . of Kijimi. The devices had a sordid history—used often by bounty hunters and other unsavory figures trying to evade detection. Poe figured he fell into that category, at least in the eyes of some. It was obviously stolen tech and not in the best shape. So Poe relied on a dark cloak and kept to himself as he made his way to the cantina—where he'd meet a man named Zade Kalliday and his starship, the *Midnight Blade*.

But Kalliday was late, which made Poe nervous but also

gave him time to eat something. His stomach growled. It had been days since he'd had a proper meal, and he couldn't think of a better place to have his last on Kijimi. The bartender slid him a plate with a shawda club sandwich on it that Poe soon devoured, his appetite getting the best of him. He fought the urge to lick his fingers as he finished.

His thoughts wandered back to the monastery—Zeva Bliss's sword at his throat, sand and blood mixed together, his vision blurring. Zorii. She'd saved his life, offered him a chance to lead the Spice Runners together. A chance to fulfill the dream he'd had since they first started working together on the *Ragged Claw*. An offer Poe rejected. He'd left her to face off against her mother alone while he ran away to fight for something he hadn't figured out yet.

Poe wondered how she felt. But he knew the answer. Betrayed. Angry. Hurt. He couldn't fix that. He'd never be able to, he thought. He left the Spice Runners for something else, for a cause Zorii found comical and foolish. He'd never get the chance to explain his side to her. He'd be murdered on sight if he tried. His time as a Spice Runner was over. But it hadn't been all bad, he thought as he patted his mouth with the coarse rag that served as a napkin. She'd learned to fly, and he'd learned how to be a better scoundrel—how to dance in the gray areas of life.

Perhaps, over time, she'd come to appreciate that, too. But he wasn't banking on it.

Poe stared upward, a wan, nostalgic smile on his face. He wasn't sure if it was the familiar voice that had drawn his eye, but he knew her immediately—before she uttered another word. Senator Leia Organa. The news footage was from the Senate, and Organa was responding to another colleague's comments in the Senate chamber. Poe was catching them mid-debate, but he didn't need a map to figure out what they were arguing about. Poe locked on to the regal hero's face and was immediately hypnotized by her passionate words.

She spoke plainly, without bravado or overly emotive gestures. It was as if she was speaking directly to Poe Dameron, and she drilled down into him in a way no one else had been able to. In moments, the collected scrapes and cuts and scar tissue of the past few years—the darkness he'd experienced and seen with the Spice Runners, Zorii, Tomasso, Sela Trune, EV-6B6—everything crumbled, replaced by something else. Something new but also very, very old. The words were resonant but not unknown to Poe. In a way, he heard his father and mother speaking to him through the senator's lips. Poe had abandoned those ideals and beliefs in an act of desperation—because he had wanted to explore the galaxy on his own terms, to get off

Yavin 4. But that had been flawed. That had been wrong. Not having a choice wasn't always a limitation. Sometimes it was something bigger. Like destiny.

"You cannot defeat evil once and consider yourself victorious," Organa said, her inflection clear, confident, but also wary. "It is our duty as the New Republic to challenge evil when we see it, no matter how scarred or hurt we are from past conflicts. We either stand for what we believe in forever without limit or qualification, with strength and bravery, or we shall fall to the same elements that crushed the Republic decades ago."

Poe stood with a jolt, electrified by Organa's words. She was a legend to Poe. A name whispered in stories he'd heard as a child. But also a person—an old, trusted friend to his parents during their shared time in the Rebellion. He felt a sudden, deep, and impossible-to-rationalize connection to her. A need to reach her, help her, that would've been laughable had he tried to explain it in words. But he felt it all the same. He knew what he had to do next. He knew where he had to go. Finally.

He felt a tap on his shoulder. Poe turned to his right and saw a man with an expectant look.

"Hey, you waiting on someone?" the man said. "Name's Zade Kalliday. Tante said you were looking for a lift. If the price is right, I'm your man."

Poe smiled.

"That's me," he said, shaking Kalliday's hand. "Thanks for the seat."

"Hey, nothing's free, my man," Kalliday said. "But I'll get you there. You know where you're headed?"

"I do now."